I0542053

Roxy Kitty Publishing

Splendificent 2 © 2020 by Dacy Alex

Cover design © 2020 Oliviaprodesign and Mazz Draws

Splendificent 2

By
Dacy Alex

Prologue

Dear Father,

There was a great evil done to the earthen realm when Astrid was selected over me by you to sit on the throne of power. A great evil was done to me by you as well. I will not leave these evils unavenged. I have had my share of misery and woe since my rebellion against you met an end and my brother was torn from me by that untamable wench, my sister Tristabelle. With great deservings, my king, you and the rest of my family have earned all the misery I can bring to you.

Since I have been exiled from Golden Land, I have endured countless offenses and infinite pain. Yet it is the Earth realm that weeps. It begs for my protection. It knows that darkness arrives and we will be disgraced and defeated by its anger. As bandit betrays honest man, vampire enslaves woman, wolf devours child, and a cruel darkness closes in, you have denied the earth realm its savior. You would let me perish without picking up The Chosen Spear in the earth realm's aid? Without me you will die on your knees, unable to cast a stone in the Earth's defense. The dangers of the outer realms come with hands of fire, Father. Astrid is nothing more than a rodent. The feeblest one possible to sit on the throne. Fire kills rodents but it shall never melt The Golden.

Prince Gorick Elvrina "The Golden"

Chapter One: Big Sis Anika?!

Dawn Nyfall locked her eyes onto the volleyball players gathered on the gymnasium floor and took a deep breath.

"Yes, my daughter Giselle is extraordinary. But she's not your type of extraordinary like the others in the condo are," Dawn Nyfall wearily explained to Anika Lindgren. Dawn looked for some understanding from the woman who sat beside her. This woman with dyed silver hair resting above bold silver eyes, who paid more attention to the volleyball players in front of her.

Giselle Nyfall sagged awkwardly in her seat at the Sky Reach Field House on the Washington Square New York City campus of Hemera University. She guessed maybe she could melt into the floor to spare herself her mom's drubbing. She'd seen weirder than a human puddle since she arrived in New York a week ago. If one of her roommates could drink blood and teleport to Hell, surely Giselle could dissolve into a puddle and escape her mom's overbearing degradation before the volleyball game started.

The ladies of Hemera Skylites and Buffalo Institute of Technology and Cosmetology Hamsters (aka The BITCHS) were about to batter the volleyball while Giselle's ego took its own thwacking.

Slumping lower and lower, the freshman felt much like an emotionally battered slug.

Dawn went on, brushing a lock of copper hair away from her dark grey eyes, "Giselle is smart, she's sweet, she's kind, she's klutzy, she breaks expensive things, but not intentionally. She can't help herself. She trips over nothing at all,she burns things and places. Again not intentionally. That's just who she is. She's extraordinary but she's not a princess. Not like that one you have roomed her with. That one is different. They're all different. Too different."

If only her mom knew!

"Giselle is wonderful and so talented," Dawn went on. "But she is not ready for this. Her father and I thought she was ready for independence. But she is not ready to leave my care." Dawn hurried to add, "And frankly, there are too many fire hazards in that condo!"

The weasley faced Stuart Logan leaned into Giselle, bumping her head with his homemade Drew The Hemera Cloud mascot helmet. He was Drew's biggest fan. "You burn shit?" he said under his breath. "I've been meaning to fuck with that hobby." This was her support as she endured Dawn's one woman firing squad.

"That's not a hobby! That's arson! And no, I don't burn shit," Giselle lied. There had been the prom floats. A whole aisle in Bed, Bath and Beyond. The Nyfall family barn that hailed back to the early

1800s when the clan immigrated from Sweden. But those had been accidents!

"That princess..." Anika said with one of her trademark smirks. She was always smirking, Giselle found, "... called Giselle... ever so delightful!"

Dawn turned over the shoulder of her white floral print top to her only child. Averting her eyes, Giselle focused on Dusty Blackwood, her volatile housemate and pint-sized beauty who perfectly filled out her blue and white volleyball uniform at the end of the bench. But Giselle had to turn away from Dusty lest her mom chastise her later for "letting your perversions leak."

Dawn and Giselle never thought they looked much alike. Dawn had a rounded face, Giselle's was heart-shaped. Both had big eyes, though Giselle's were blue and innocent, and Dawn's grey eyes were always searching. Dawn had longer, fuller lips, whereas Giselle had heart-shaped ones.

The real divide between mother and daughter came from the hair. Dawn possessed "the best red can get." On the other hand, Giselle's blonde hair was so bright it would be better classified as white, marking her as Dawn would say, "a clumsy khaleesi."

Their similarity lay in their stacked figures, which made parent-teacher conference meetings a must-drop-in for Giselle's old principal. Dawn was a touch thinner than Giselle, but the freshman sported the thicker butt. A butt which once sat on a chair of thumbtacks her cousin laid out to prank her.

"I'm certain she needs mommy but she can do a great deal worse than Big Sis Anika," Anika offered.

"Big Sis Anika?" Dawn sounded like she had vomit rising to her throat. If only Dawn knew Anika kind of sort of fondled mommy's girl and mommy's naughty girl more than kind of sort of liked it.

"Aunt Anika just sounds so old," Anika widened the smirk on her square-shaped face, grey-white eyes shining at Dawn. She held that gaze as she adjusted the updo of her silver hair.

For Giselle the events of the past couple days leading up to the fall semester had been a tornado built with fire, fury, and orgasms. Giselle arrived at Hemera from Beverly Hills, California, the recipient of a computer glitch that left her without housing. Head of Student Services, Anika Lindgren, had the brilliant idea to stash her with Anika's hand-selected extraordinary young women in an Upper East Side Manhattan penthouse.

Almost immediately upon arrival, Giselle was thrust into a supernatural morass where she uncovered a sex curse, got kidnapped, filmed a supernatural orgy, and found the real reason her housemates were extraordinary. Just days ago she had found herself the victim of bizarre hallucinations leading up to one where she defeated a Prince of Hell at the school's carnival and then fainted. Except then Princess Tristabelle informed her she very much was the slayer of demons.

Giselle's mother had canceled a meeting with members of Congress in D.C. to come to see her when Dusty let her know that Giselle had fainted. Dawn sang delighted words when Giselle first told her of her upgraded living situation. Dawn's tune turned into a dirge when she met the extraordinary young women. What Dawn found was a gambling addict, a pint-sized malcontent, a gold-digging influencer, but at least a sparkling princess. What Dawn didn't know is that these were a vampire-succubus hybrid, a pixie deemed too violent by the Fairy Kingdom to be promoted to a fairy, a shape-shifting fox spirit, and a magical sword-toting pure elf.

Dawn continued in a measured voice, "Where is the R.A.? You've left five eighteen-year-olds unsupervised in an Upper East Side penthouse."

Anika put her hand to her slim chest in offense, "No one will dare besmirch the virtue of my Extraordinary Young Women."

Too lat for those babese, thought Giselle.

"I thank you for all that you're trying to do for Giselle. But she will be coming home."

Given that Giselle's dad, Stephen, was a tech guru inventor and Dawn was on the board of several major nonprofits in California, it wouldn't be difficult for moves to be made to get Giselle into a California school even with the semesters being close to starting.

"How the others will miss the mousy little dear. You may have to fight them for her." That line should have been a joke except for Anika gently nudging it into threat territory. "New York is a great experience," Anika commented. "You can meet such —how should I say —varied people. Dawn, you might even meet someone you consider extraordinary."

"Hey," Giselle's voice was shaky as her hands. "The game is about to start."

The stars of this late August afternoon, the Hemera players gathered on their half of the court. Blue and white uniforms were nearly molded to their co-ed bodies that were ultra-tight, ultra-leggy and ultra-toned.

In gold and silver, the BITCHs' opposing players, however, looked like they might stretch the NCAA's definition of female.

Drew, the school's six-foot-two fluffy cloud mascot, set the tone for the first athletic competition of the school year. The tone perhaps one of horror as Drew was truly a terrifying bestial creature of an enormous white head, blue body, white toga, beady eyes, devilish slanted eyebrows, and a nonsensical tail that looked intentionally phallic. But to Stuart he was a hero.

Drew roved the stands with no shame in his game, twerking in a disgusted elderly math professor's face. An act sure to land the mascot another in a long line of sexual harassment complaints.

"Walk your walk, Drew!" Stuart bellowed.

"The small one," Dawn started. "Dusty. You said her dad is a professional wrestler."

"Brady Blackwood," Anika answered. "The All American."

The All American prick, Giselle thought.

"He and his brother, Baron, are a legendary tag team known as the Music City Gunslingers. Little Dusty surely takes after them," Anika answered.

That she did. Dusty often quoted her father and uncle when leveling threats or guarantees for violence for the litany of offenses she perceived to be against her. Giselle recently got promised a "Brady Hammer" onto a steel chair if she ate the last piece of strawberry shortcake. She ate it anyway.

Anika went on to say, "Dear Dusty was the number one ranked volleyball player in the country. It was a challenge getting her to come to Hemera. Her mother found it agreeable. But Dusty plays the rebel better than you play the piano."

"Giselle told you I played?"

"An educated guess," Anika's grey eyes lingered on Dawn's long fingers.

There was another difference between Giselle and Dawn. Dawn had musical ability; Giselle had failed every song on Guitar Hero in elementary school.

Anika murmured, "As for Dusty, in the end, I didn't get the little thing at all. She just swore fealty to a very convincing princess."

Giselle had never heard that story. Giselle had no idea how Anika scouted, approached and recruited these four. Given their lineages, they seemed to be supernatural aristocracy. But Anika just seemed to be a witch working a regular job living in a condo her ex-husband paid for. Why did they assemble under her rule? What was Anika even assembling them for?

Giselle just decided to keep a careful watch on Dusty who stood as maybe five-foot-one inches of unsportsmanlike conduct. Dusty's arms were folded beneath her ginormous jugs as she sat relegated on the end bench, stewing in ire over her lack of a start.

"She keeps getting kicked out of practice for her attitude. She's lucky she's still on the team," Giselle whispered to Stuart.

Stuart offered, "If I had a chest that big, you'd never see me get upset. I'd just be feeling myself up staring in the mirror all day. But I been doing that all day anyway thanks to these sick gains."

Gains meaning gains of skinny fat. Not gains of muscle.

Giselle juggled her huge blues on little Dusty as the crowd gave a loud groan.

"Did something happen?" Dawn questioned.

"A terrible call," Anika responded too lazily for Giselle's liking. How could Anika not realize what was soon to darken Hemera's proud day?

Giselle started to sweat. She started to get indigestion. She knew the poor official was about to feel the wrath of a menace.

Yet the menace Giselle feared stayed pouting on the bench.

Instead, it was Hemera's Coach Bud Clay— he of the pitiable comb-over and rotund gut— pleading The Skylites case to a mustached official. Sadly, that was just too much effort for ol' Bud to make before exhaustion consumed him and he slunk back to his seat, where he cracked open a cold one to refill his tank.

This poor judgment might have been left to die with the crowd's disapproval and Bud's lack of questioning, but not with Dusty Blackwood playing for Hemera. The menace woke.

"You gotta be kidding me!" Dusty screamed, blonde ringlets shaking with the ferocity of Medusa's snakes. Giselle just now noticed Dusty didn't keep her hair like the other players. Dusty kept it like she was going on The Voice.

"Young lady, sit down," the official barked the exact wrong thing to bark.

"Why don't you bring yer little pedophile mustache down 'ere and make me?"

"Ooooooh," the crowd bleated, many leaning back and laughing.

"That's an Extraordinary Young Woman?" Dawn spat to Anika, while reaching her arm out to protect Giselle—from what Giselle did not know.

"Now are you gonna reverse that call or not?" Dusty asked. "Cause if you ain't gonna reverse that call, if yer gonna let that stand—"

"Young lady—" the official started.

"I ain't no lady."

"Sit down!" the official barked.

"I'll be sittin down in a squad car after I get through with you."

Dawn turned huge pools of grey horror towards Anika, expecting to get them mirrored back. Instead, she got the cool breeze of Anika's grey eyes and self-assured smirk.

Giselle started to question whether Anika could be bothered by anything. Phones across the arena were recording this run-up to a smackdown and Anika gave less than a shit. Did she lack the brain function that allowed people to be nettled? Was it a witch thing? From what Tristabelle told her, witches brewed potions. Did Anika brew something that gave her nerves as cold as a glacial lake?

Drew decided to make light of Dusty's hissy fit. He rubbed his hands against his ghastly eyes to brand her a whiner.

Tiny Dusty marched over to this foolish being and gave him a giant shove, which, much to the delight of the fans and especially Stuart, sent Dusty's rack on a massive wild bounce worthy of the hottest Japanese anime. This sports bra absent jiggling caused Drew to reach out for a grab even as he fell flat on his back.

Not only did he fail to grab hold of Dusty's jiggling jumbos, as Giselle would term them, but he also found himself in an eternally futile struggle to turn back over. Turtles across the globe felt his agony. But Dusty was no friend of turtles or mascots and began assailing him with her Adidas kicks.

"She's attacking that mascot," Dawn noted with her long fingers covering her mouth.

At least she didn't give him a Brady Hammer.

Stuart whispered to Giselle, "All that jiggling got me Super Soaker Floodinator wet," for which Giselle hurriedly shushed him.

"Stuart, you better control yourself," Giselle snapped.

"I dunno if I can. I'm an animal in these streets."

Tweet! TWEEEEEEEEET! As much as the fans liked the sight of Dusty's bouncing cannons, their ears abhorred the sound of Bud's shrieking whistle as he came between Dusty and her cumulus victim.

"Blackwood, back to the locker room!" Bud ordered.

Giselle assumed that Bud was about to suffer a stone-cold ass-whupping.

The guess proved incorrect as Dusty gave a theatrical bow to the legions recording her breakdown and departed towards the locker room.

"I better go after her," Giselle announced, followed with a sag of shoulders left bare by a square neck rainbow cropped tank top.

"Wait! Where are you going?" Dawn hurried asked.

Leaving her mom with Anika and Stuart was possibly a recipe that would lead to Dawn eating a dish at a psych ward. But The Tiny

Terror Of Nashville needed to be calmed and contained before she got herself further meme'ed and then expelled. Thus Giselle ran off after the fairy kingdom's meanest export.

"Can you believe that?" Dawn asked, throwing up her hands. "She ignored me and left."

Dawn couldn't tell if Anika was smirking because she enjoyed Dawn's misery or because she always smirked.

Whereas most would immediately distance themselves from any association with little Dusty, Giselle hurried down the stands, past the dumbfounded players, and through a barren hallway. She glided past posters of motivation and accolades of past Hemera stars, past the notice about the freshman camping trip, past the flyer for a rap concert by the Irish rapper SeaSeaSea, and to the women's locker room.

Giselle remembered hearing a story about an ad exec Hemera alum donating a stack of cash to revolutionize the Sky Reach locker room. It was not money wasted. In this locker room the logo of Hemera glowed upon the ceiling; there was a giant video board playing ESPN. Each locker was constructed of stainless steel with a 43-inch monitor and USB ports all standing in front of walls lined with LED lighting. To Giselle it felt like she transported to the Starship Enterprise.

On proud display in the center of the room was Stuart's first and second star of the game, Dusty's beach ball sized tits. The sight of these glorious bombs took Giselle back to her steamy engagement with them in front of the Church of Saturday and their skeletal leader.

After getting a rundown of Giselle's lewd and demonic adventures, Anika had handed her the high compliment of, "You handle the supernatural like you were born a werewolf. Or at the very least a particularly sharp goblin."

Giselle felt as though she could start drooling like a hungering werewolf fresh out of the full moon's gate over Dusty's topless self.

Dusty, with hands on hips and head tilted, demanded, "Giselle, if you got something to say, then get it said and get it said quick."

Giselle knew conflict resolution, damn it. She had seen just such a situation play out on a low-quality video on Pornhub. A low-quality video that had played when she didn't know the iPad was linked to the Bluetooth speakers and her mom heard the groans of skinny Czech pornstars.

Nevermind that! Her mom was stuck with Anika. Giselle was a free grown woman.

Dusty was a cute pint-sized beauty with big baby doll eyes, an adorable upturned nose, and a circular mouth that always seemed to show her two front teeth and big chipmunk cheeks. But all Giselle could see right then was her pair of over-sized breasts.

"Girl, you look like you seen a potato chip shaped like Jesus," Dusty noted.

I once ate a chip sort of shaped like Britney Spears.

Dusty turned her doe eyes onto the entryway. "I oughta go back out there. I at least gotta fight someone."

"That's totally not what you should do. That's, like, on the bottom of the list of things you should be doing. Princess Tristabelle! What would she do? As a Sister of Frejya, I think she'd be all over you right now. To calm you down!"

"Ya think so?"

"I've only known her for a couple days, but that totally makes me qualified to make assumptions about her personality and potential actions," Giselle said, not being sarcastic.

It was rather convenient that Dusty's crush was a follower of a goddess that preached spiritual release through fornication. Who knew having a pagan around could prove so useful?

With ass to whup could Dusty really let Giselle fondle her boobs like overgrown stress balls?

Of course she could!

Giselle bent like she was worshiping Dusty. She kneaded and rolled those orbs as if she were trying to unearth some kind of hidden treasure.

As crazed as Dusty got over a bad call, Giselle was just as crazed over her tits. Though what if Dawn caught her? Giselle wouldn't be on a one-way flight back to Beverly Hills, she'd be on a one-way flight to the Sacred Heart Convent!

"Keep it up! Or I'll pound you into the dirt!" Dusty snapped.

"What? Why am I being threatened?"

"Sex is pain! I read the first 75 pages of Fifty Shades of Grey before my mom burned it."

Giselle paused to look Dusty in those doe eyes and told her with all sincerity, "Dusty, you are my spirit animal. Or my spirit slut. Whichever,"

Tall Giselle had to lower herself into a squat just to get her eyes level with these ginormous things. It'd be easier if she could get Dusty to lie down so she wouldn't have to squat, but then Dusty would complain about her making short jokes and that ran a 75% risk of Giselle getting hit. So although in a less than comfortable squat, Giselle had her face on the warpath, gobbling up all that Dusty had to offer. Her tongue was becoming an out-of-control race car, zipping around the circular track of Dusty's globes.

"Yeah, suck these all-natural jugs!"

"Mmmmph?!"

"What are ya trying to say? You think these babies ain't natural?"

They could have been made out of Kryptonite for all Giselle cared. All she wanted to do was submerge herself in the jugs. She fastened her mouth around Dusty's sharp right nipple and yanked and sucked as though she were milking the country babe. Once done lathering the right nipple in spit, Giselle attacked the left one. She engulfed it and sucked it as if she could muster the power of a leviathan.

"Dang, Giselle, yer going after 'em like a baby goes after their mama," Dusty declared.

Giselle's ever questing hands found Dusty's sizable booty. The thick piece of Nashville bred ass was still encased in the teeny tiny volleyball shorts that had to be against some kind of regulation. Deciding to be daring, Giselle let her fingers worm through the tight fabric to find she has unfiltered access to Dusty's ass crack.

"For some reason I always pictured you wearing teddy bear panties," Giselle commented.

"Teddy bear panties?!"

Giselle took her soft, delicate hand and gave Dusty's bottom a not so soft delicate slap. The little blonde leaped from shock and let out an adorable yelp. So adorable Giselle made sure to draw it out again with another hard slap.

"Blackwood! What in the sam hill are you doing?" came the unexpected voice of Coach Bud.

"Ah!" Giselle shrieked. "This is totally not what it looks like! She's got a strained pectoral muscle, and I'm just helping loosen it. That's pretty obvious, right?"

"We're getting clobbered out there, Blackwood! I came back to get you, but... you're gonna have to take a leave of absence from the team."

Dusty was unmoved. Rather she started jostling her hooters and informed Bud, "But then you wouldn't be able to stare at these double D's all day long." Then she turned around and bared her juicy, tanned ass. "And ya wouldn't be able to check out this rump neither. I don't think ya want me off the team. The big fella down there sure don't."

Giselle just noticed Coach Bud was sporting a huge hard-on. That and a lot of armpit sweat.

Dusty stretched herself stomach first on the floor, so that her tits welled up like twin blobs, "What do you think, Giselle? You think he don't want this prime teenage booty?"

"Uh, isn't there a cute assistant coach you could make an exchange for?"

Apparently, Bud's mini-sermon about team duties and attitude was nothing but a front. Because when presented with this sultry eighteen-year-old offering herself up to him, his pants were around his ankles, and his faculty code of conduct contract went to the wind.

Coach Bud mounted Dusty, providing Giselle the unusual sight of a rotund middle-aged man layering himself upon a busty teenager. He proceeded to pound her with a relentless hunger. It was as if he had been aching to do this all along. Giselle swore she saw a gif similar to this of a man just throwing his body up and down on a prone blonde hottie.

"Gimme all ya got, Coach! Skylites reach for the sky!" Dusty ordered.

Giselle was sure Coach Bud would be reaching for his heart during the heart attack he was bound to have given how much energy he was exerting. Poor Coach Bud couldn't or wouldn't let up, the tightness of her snatch, the hotness of her body, demanded that he furiously smash into her. To Giselle this seemed like what might happen if Juggernaut from The X-Men got a hold of Minnie Mouse.

Dusty, however, didn't mind being battered by such girth, both erectile and otherwise...

The country gal barked, "Gimmie 110 percent of that cock, Coach!"

The coach picked up the intensity. It was an act that seemed an impossibility. In a blur of motion, he crashed downwards, then rose back up only to crash down again with even more force. His thick member expanded her sex to its limits. The prone babe was stuffed to her very walls. His weight seemed to force her into the ground even more, further smushing her huge flotation devices.

"You bought yer A-game today, Coach!" Dusty yelled.

"Why are you speaking in clichés?" Giselle asked.

"These ain't clichés! These are original Dusty thoughts!"

"No, they're definitely not," Giselle answered.

It was easy for Coach Bud to bring his A game when he was fucking the MVP of team hot. As Coach's missile continued to land against her cervix, Dusty's stacked little body rocked with orgasm. The babe lost control of her brain, as it was instead piloted by the continuation of climaxes that assailed her.

Yet she could still rattle off clichés, "Yes, Coach, make your nasty bitch take one for the team!"

With Dusty locked into some kind of orgasmic programming, Coach Bud redoubled his efforts to pound her silly. That heart attack

Giselle predicted had to be soon to arrive as he increased his hammering of the little babe to maximum effort.

"Aiiiiieeeeeeeeeeee! Ghost!" came a scream from a woman in the throes of fear. It was loud and sharp enough to yank Giselle away from the throes of passion.

"Hmmm, you gotta get out there, Giselle," Dusty decided.

"Usually people go in the opposite direction of danger," Giselle remarked.

"Them folks ain't Dusty Blackwood, but I'm occupied so I want you to go check things out."

Giselle felt a sting of fear that Dusty obviously didn't feel for her.

But then why should Dusty fear anything, Giselle questioned. As a pixie she could manipulate the four elements to her will. Fleur told Giselle Dusty had an exceptional talent for the task. Giselle had first-hand sight of this as she had watched Dusty turn a glass of water into something more dangerous than an M4 Carbine gun against a pair of raven-headed monstrous demons.

Giselle's talents were drawing and designing levels in Super Mario Maker.

Even so, she followed orders and carefully trod out of the locker room.

There stood dread. There stood darkness.

There stood "The Stalker" Prince Trygyrr Elvrina.

The prince of Golden Land wore an outfit Giselle couldn't imagine anyone outside of Final Fantasy would attire themselves in. A grey cloak swooped over his shoulders, its inner edge embroidered with an abstract purple pattern. All his fingers bore gold rings. He wore a black tunic with the dancing lady of Clan Elvrina present on a necklace.

Empathy stirred in Giselle for the girl who thought him a ghost. Pure Elves don't just appear in the human world. One like Trygyrr exuded a certain aura of danger even with his strong, handsome jaw, his soft features of big eyes, hairless face, and pouty lips, and the streams of black hair that covered his elf ears.

Giselle reached out to touch him. As she expected, her hand passed right through him. She had reached for the man who had surprised her in the great supernatural crypt, The Historium, the man who had toyed with her. She got only a dissipating pool of light.

"How the hell are you doing this?" Dusty demanded.

"An Astral Projection, friend. Blood magic."

Blood magic. Giselle had heard the term in the Dragon Age video games. There it was known as the most sinister of all magics.

"Blood magic?" Giselle repeated softly. "That's bad."

"I do bad things..."

Trygyrr ran a hand across Giselle's cheek. It felt like nothing and still felt revolting.

"May I have a moment alone with you?" He asked, voice like a kitten mewing.

"Fine," Giselle spat, "what do you want?"

He murmured in delicate tones, "Be not alarmed. Let us share in the pleasure of each other's spirit and essence."

"Prince Trygyrr, do you realize no one likes you?"

"People hate what they cannot overcome."

"And that's you?"

"That is death."

"Are you here to kill me? Because my mom gave me a rape whistle! And I'm mature and I can use it!"

Giselle hoped Trygyrr wouldn't notice her blue eyes hovering past him. They focused on the corner of the hallway where she expected her mom to come round at any moment.

"Giselle, my friend, I understand you have been troubled. Beset by demons. Plagued by unexplained visions. How troubling that must be for you."

Gislle's eyes fell back onto the elven prince, "Your sister snitched!"

"Tristabelle did not betray you. I see, I hear, I learn."

"Are you spying on me?"

"Are you mad that The Stalker stalks?"

"What do you want from me? I'm just a regular girl with mommy issues who wet the bed until she was ten...eleven. It was eleven. But that doesn't mean I'm not mature."

"Where the supernatural world bleeds too aggressively into the human world is where I strike."

"You don't think an Astral projection in the middle of a hallway at 12:23 in the afternoon is the supernatural world bleeding too aggressively into the human world?"

Trygyrr smiled, which objectively was an attractive smile but was to Giselle quite hideous.

"Why did you chose to attend Hemera University?"

"I always wanted to go to school in New York City."

"There are many schools in New York City. Yet you are at Hemera. Was this the only school to allow you through their halls?"

Giselle thought for a second, "It was the only school I applied to. Ugh, Prince Trygyrr, I can't imagine growing up with you. 'Hey, Trygyrr, let's toss the old ball around.'" Giselle started a poor Trygyrr imitation, "There are many balls within these halls; was this the only ball to allow itself into your hands? What of the blue ball? What mysteries does it yet hold over yonder?"

"Elves do not throw the old ball around."

"Just say whatever you wanna say already."

"New York City is an omphalos for the supernatural."

"Like I know what an omphalos is."

Trygyrr shrugged and went on, "An epicenter, Giselle. It is said, but far from confirmed, that Hemera lies over the Silver River. The Silver River runs below the Ley Line in New York City. So it is said. The Silver River leads to Tartarus."

"Where the Titans are!"

Trygyrr nodded and smiled, "It is said that a great demon was sealed within the stones that make up the buildings of Hemera."

"Sounds like someone's architecture project met their synthetic marijuana addiction."

"I would suggest you explore Hemera. Find what it is that attracted you. Free of the influences of my sister and your friends."

"But not free of your influence."

Prince Trygyrr bowed towards Giselle. Even though it was Trygyrr it was somewhat exhilarating having a prince bow to her.

"You have my protection, Giselle."

"Well, I don't know if I want your protection."

"You will, Giselle. Now I will let you go and rejoice in our partnership."

Trygyrr faded out in a sweeping wave of shimmering rainbow light.

Giselle was rejoicing in her partnership with Trygyrr the way Giselle's disobedient Yorkie rejoiced at his partnership with his punishment crate.

Buuuuuutt maybe there was wisdom served as a side to Trygyrr's entree of creepy smiles and cryptic words. Maybe wisdom was the main course. Perhaps exploration would satisfy her curious appetite for supernatural knowledge.

Giselle fired off a reassuring text to Dusty, whom she assumed was still spilling clichés in response to Coach Bud's jackhammering.

With Dusty out of the way, Giselle strapped on her imaginary purple backpack, greeted her imaginary anthropomorphic monkey and became *Dora The Explorer* Hemera edition.

She emerged from Sky Reach into Washington Square Park, half expecting to step into Tartarus itself. Of course she did not, which led her to wonder if Trygyrr was merely teasing her.

Bustling, Giselle thought, was a cliche term but it was the perfect term to use to describe the park that housed part of Hemera's campus. Little kids zoomed by on scooters. A juggler dazzled with her expert handling of pins. A few Hemera students tossed a football back and forth right behind a piano player treating the park to renditions of Lady Gaga songs.

Giselle shot a text to her pal, "Dusty, is your mom really The Tooth Fairy or was Fleur fucking with me again?"

It was five minutes before Dusty replied, *"She ain't always been The Tooth Fairy. She was a dancer, a Nymph, in Fairy Revolution Wrestling. But the FRW owner pulled some strings with the Fairy Council and she became the Tooth Fairy when the old one retired."*

"OMG" Giselle replied, " That's so awesome! Your mom is bigger than Jesus!"

"No she ain't."

"Jesus saves, but the Tooth Fairy pays. You have to be so proud of her!"

"Me 'n her don't always get along. She wants me to be prim and proper like my sister, Eleanor."

Giselle remembered that Eleanor was a member of the Fairy Best Investigators, the Fairy Kingdom's version of the FBI.

"You're prim and proper like I'm coordinated and popular."

"But I'm rough 'n tumble like my dad. And I'm always gonna be rough 'n tumble. Ya can't just demand a new Dusty like I'm Chinese food. Dusty and Shrimp Fried Rice don't mix."

"Giselle and Shrimp Fried Rice don't mix either so text message high-five."

Now where could Giselle start unearthing the mystery Trygyrr had buried at her feet?

The spiritual building! Giselle had seen a guy with a beard in front of the building handing out fliers about free yoga classes, and dad, Stephen, had always said never trust guys with beards handing out free anything.

What Giselle found was a meditation and calmness seminar and a support puppy playpen. But unless those dogs were the products of hell hounds, which Fleur insisted were real, Giselle had come up empty. Though she thought a calmness seminar an odd feature for a school that boasted a hockey team that led the NCAA in penalties in minutes for a decade running and whose team consisted mostly of felons.

Giselle stepped back into Washington Square Park and let loose such a loud sigh that the bearded yoga guy patted her on the shoulder.

Giselle thought Prince Tryggyr's note that the Silver River led to Tartarus an odd one. That was a prison for Greek Titans, whereas the Elvrinas were believers in a unique subset of Norse religion. Not just believers, they were part of it as protectors of the earth realm.

Giselle was getting herself lost in theological theory. She had to find something supernatural to shove in that oh so cryptic speaking face of Trygyrr Elvrina. She'd make him eat a supernatural and shit sandwich.

The library had to contain a bevy of supernatural weirdness. The original Ghostbusters film couldn't be anything but a good clue.

The building was something of a monument, a marble testament to classical beauty. It was flanked by a pair of knights known as Tower and Strength.

"Golems!" Giselle declared to Tower. "You can't fool me, crafty golems. You're mine to control! You're like a level one blob compared to me!"

As this was New York no one paid much attention to the crazy lady yelling at the statue.

Once inside the library, Giselle found the largest marble structure she could ever imagine. She could not fathom the tuition payments and donations that went into crafting this statement of superiority.

"The least crowded floor," Giselle told herself, "that's the floor that's gonna have the spooky stuff."

After looking at the directory, Giselle guessed the least used would be the roads and transportation records floor.

The floor, as Giselle guessed, was empty and lacked the majesty of the rest of the building. There was no attendant and no students were among the rows of computers and file cabinets. It was so plain compared to everything else Giselle had seen that it put a tinge of fear in her. About the only thing interesting Giselle saw was a gold and black striped-pattern door.

Then her phone buzzed, and she leapt in shock.

It was just Dawn. The Dawn, who kept calling, and whose fury at being ignored was mounting every time she hit the wall that was voicemail.

Finally Giselle answered, "Mom?"

"What do you think you're doing?"

"Uh, can't talk now. I got swept up in a school safety committee sweep!"

Giselle looked to her right and hurriedly said, "Someone spilled cranberry juice! The puddle is sure to cause someone to slip and die. Not to mention it's an attraction for disease-carrying bugs so we gotta rope this thing off. Bye!"

Before Giselle could get scolded, she clicked off her phone.

But she was right. It was a good idea to take note of that cranberry juice! But then Giselle started thinking about her Nintendo Switch and maybe getting pink and green joy cons. The next thing she knew, she was slipping on a puddle of cranberry juice and landing smack against the wall.

That second Giselle's head smacked against the wall was the second the lights went out.

Suddenly a trail of glowing green embers streaked down the wall.

Giselle's big blue eyes came out of blurriness to see the embers leading her to a door she hadn't noticed.

"Alright, Giselle, all you have to do is walk through that door and not die in a fiery explosion. Which probably won't happen because this is a magical girl anime, not a mecha anime."

With a bit of trepidation in her step, Giselle marched to the mysterious door. But when she placed her hand on the handle, the door illuminated in rows of colored blocks and the handle froze in place.

"A puzzle game? Psh, this is amateur shit."

Blue went to yellow, red went to green, blue went to red, while orange went to blue, and so on and so on until the colored blocks disappeared in front of Giselle's eyes.

"That was easy mode."

The handle loosened, and Giselle yanked the door open only to be blinded by a sweeping of light and blasted by a gust of hairstyle wrecking wind.

"That mysterious light can't possibly ever become a problem," she decided and wasn't being in any way sarcastic.

But what was a problem— what was a huge problem—was the man who emerged from the door with the ears and tail of a horse and an erection worthy of Giselle's favorite pornos. While this might be an invite to an interesting hentai scenario on screen, in real life, it proved a problem as the beast roared and took a swing at Giselle.

The only reason Giselle avoided having her jaw broken was that she tripped over her shoes backpedaling in fear.

"I'm in deep pickles!"

There was another roar, and this time the beast tried to stomp on Giselle's face. She was quick enough to roll out of the way and found her way into the closet.

The beast was in pursuit of Giselle; it emitted a guttural grunt and led with its lengthy erection. There was only one thing Giselle could think to do, and that was to smash his erection between the door and the doorway. That earned a crunch so loud that Giselle had to cringe. It also received a yell of fury from the creature that was certain to break the library's rule to keep a silent and respectful space.

The thing pushed its way through the door, forcing Giselle to remember a prom night mishap for her next attack. Her delicate fingers curled around the upper half of the erection and she squeezed not-sodelicately with every last bit of strength in her body. The creature forced out a final roar of misery before it faded into a cloud of grey dust.

"Whew! Giselle earned 500 experience points. Two hundred experience points until level up," Giselle declared.

Her mom didn't know what she was talking about. No ordinary young woman could have fought off that monster. No ordinary young woman would have even stood their ground. That was real maturity, Giselle decided.

After adjusting her hair back to something not resembling a tumbleweed, Giselle stepped through the doorway to find a miniature pillar. The pillar held nothing atop it besides a glimmering source of blue light. It looked well-worn, but possed legible Greek writing that Giselle couldn't make out.

"I think you'll be coming with me," Giselle determined.

Before she could grab it, her phone buzzed with a text message.

It was from Dusty: "*911! Emergency meeting tonight with Princess Magalinda!*"

But Giselle fired back, "Need to get to Madam Wanda's! Got something big!"

Chapter Two: Meet The Parents

Where the hell had that daughter of Dawn's gone?

This was so like Giselle, Dawn thought, as she excused herself past a smelly man handing out fliers on free yoga classes.

Dawn's grey eyes swept Washington Square Park to find many blondes, but no blonde who was her daughter. Those grey eyes fell upon her phone where last Giselle spoke of the student safety committee or other such nonsense.

Giselle? Safety? Ha! This was a girl who when once asked to show her seventh grade class schedule, got her foot caught in her backpack and tripped down a flight of stairs, barreling into her vice-principal and breaking his leg. Safety? Giselle? Ha!

Dawn pushed her way into the Student Center, which seemed to serve as part café, part study area, part counseling center, and part meditation space.

How much meditation space did one school need?

As Dawn was about to order Siri to dial Giselle yet again, her grey eyes caught a most curious sight.

There, behind a half-eaten brownie, sat Giselle's unlikely roommate and fellow "extraordinary young woman" Princess Tristabelle Elvrina of Golden Land.

Dawn had had to catch herself from saying "holy shit" the moment Giselle had introduced her to Princess Tristabelle. Giselle had told her she was rooming with royalty, but Giselle had failed to prepare Dawn for the fact that Princess Tristabelle might have been the most beautiful woman alive.

Tristabelle's purple almond eyes were burrowing into the stubble-lined diamond-shaped face of a man with exceptionally long black hair.

Whatever they were talking about made Tristabelle's red cupid bow lips form a sharp frown above her square chin.

It wouldn't be polite to interrupt royalty, but perhaps the princess knew where Giselle might have scampered.

It seemed quite odd to Dawn that a real-life princess might keep tabs on Giselle. The only princess Giselle had any sort of familiarity with was that Princess Peach character she was fond of dressing up as.

Dawn approached the princess, remembering Giselle stating, "The Elvrinas are more Tyrells than Lannisters but they're still pretty tough."

How could Giselle think of describing royalty as "pretty tough?"

Dawn was stunned, utterly stunned, by what the princess wore. She sported a jungle print asymmetrical dress that didn't seem to give a crap about covering her pendulous breasts. She also was adorned with a pair of upside-down triangle hoop earrings. The earrings were nothing special but something about them drew Dawn's eyes to Tristabelle's ears.

"Lady Dawn!" Princess Tristabelle exclaimed as Dawn approached her. She jumped out her seat causing those hefty funbangs to wobble. Dawn thought of Giselle going crazy over them. "You should not—"

"Lady Dawn?" The man asked, pale eyes dancing, "... a member of Golden Land's elite?"

"Me? Oh no? No, not at all. I was raised in Missouri," Dawn replied, blushing.

"You have the air of aristocracy," he purred, leading Dawn to blush.

True, the Nyfalls were a wealthy family, making their fortune off her husband's tech innovations, but in Dawn's mind that hardly put her in "Lady" territory.

"Lady Dawn Nyfall is the mother of my roommate, Giselle. Lady Dawn, this is Lazarus, Fleur's father," Tristabelle spoke with hesitation in her voice.

"I apologize," Lazarus stated, head bowed.

"For what?" Dawn questioned, head tilted.

"I've grown very used to apologizing for my daughter over the years."

"That is hardly fair," Princess Tristabelle rebuked Laz. "Fleur is a fine friend. When a meat emulsion proprietor cheated Dusty out of a proper amount of mustard, Fleur threatened to bloody his nose for his insult."

Lazarus laughed and nodded to Dawn as if to say "see what I mean?"

Dawn had found Fleur to be the oddest of the "extraordinary young women," thanks to Fleur's first words to Dawn being, "How'd you pop out this fuck-up Giselle? You drink a lot when pregnant?"

Dawn couldn't leave Giselle in the company of these women. Two of them were so obviously prone to violence that any rational parent would be concerned leaving their fragile daughter at their side. Furthermore, Giselle couldn't keep her perversion in check. She was sure to pounce on this busty princess and do something Giselle referred to as motherboating.

But instead, Dawn only said, "Fleur is a unique soul."

"We have so much to be proud of," Lazarus stated, "With daughters walking the halls of Hemera. Think about our daughters leading the next generation of the world's elite."

The princess noted while looking at Lazarus, "Lady Dawn, did you know every window on Hemera's campus is one hundred percent UV repellent?"

That seemed like one of those stupid facts Giselle liked to rail off, such as every year Hemera baked the largest red devil cake in the state of New York City.

"They were donated by myself," Lazarus informed them. "Too much sun is secretly a terrifying thing."

"You sound like a vampire out of one of my daughter's favorite TV shows."

Lazarus offered a toothsome smile.

"My daughter," Lazarus began, "I have to be honest with you, can be risky business. She's been in a lot of fights and arguments in her short life. And the whippings she's delivered to men have been shameful. The insult she can deliver? Shameful."

"My husband and I believe in being the example for what we want Giselle to be."

That was true. Giselle was an exceptionally lovable daughter, caring and kind. But how Giselle became so perverted and so irresponsible boggled Dawn's mind. Dawn would never just take off from her mother and hastily avoid attempts to communicate.

"Then I am shameful more than anyone," Lazarus declared. "Shame on me for raising her that way. But I hope she can find some joy with your Giselle, and that Giselle can find some joy with her."

"That's sweet," Dawn replied, "but my husband and I aren't sure this is the right environment for Giselle. She's such a fragile child. If she's going to break, its better to break near mom."

"I know what it is to be alone and scared facing a new world," Lazarus commented.

"I don't know if it's that's bad for Giselle," Dawn replied. "I think she's too oblivious to think that way sometimes."

"Giselle has been a model of bravery since her arrival," Princess Tristabelle stated. "Why, I was told how bravery runs deep in the Nyfall lineage. Giselle's grandfather, for instance, is a devout holocaust denier. What courage it must have taken to deny Hitler the right to the holocaust still to this day even with the fuhrer having passed."

"I think Giselle should have better explained what a Holocaust denier is," Dawn suggested before sighing.

Lazarus gave another big smile, "Lady Dawn, you and Giselle need to sit with Fleur and me for dinner before you leave. It wouldn't sit well on me if I couldn't take you both out before you leave."

There was something in that smile, something warm and rich and yet a little dangerous that had Dawn blushing.

Lazarus passed Dawn his business card with one final smile before heading off to the lower level of the building.

"Perhaps," Tristabelle muttered, "I should escort you back to the condo, Lady Dawn."

"No, don't mind me. I'll make my way back on my own. I just need to get a hold of that brave daughter of mine."

Then something about Princess Tristabelle halted Dawn. Something she had only just taken notice of.

"Your Highness, where is your protection?"

The princess's eyes appraised Dawn as if she were crazy, "Protection from whom, Lady Dawn?"

"Protection from all the bad people in the world.."

"Ohohohoho!" Princess Tristabelle chortled. "I shall tell you what I told your daughter. It is the bad people in the world who need protection from me!"

***

Madame Wanda's Psychic Emporium was buried deep in the Red Hook section of Brooklyn, well away from the privileged Upper East Side condo in which Giselle and Dusty pretended they were on Gossip Girl.

The gloomy place looked and smelled like it was not buried in Brooklyn but buried under Brooklyn. Light scarcely reached through the dirty window, and if it could, it would turn tail and run from the animal skulls that lined the shelves and the jars of eyeballs that lingered about. New since Giselle's last visit was a row of owl figurines on the front counter, covered in what could be dried blood and eerily missing their eyes.

On the other hand, Madame Wanda herself, a full-breasted dark-skinned beauty in a golden robe, only looked like she was playing the part of creepy skull-hoarding psychic. She looked too put together to be the type to collect ravens' heads and eyeballs.

Giselle knew that she was anything but an actress out for a quick buck. This woman was legit. A woman who has instilled the fear of god and less holy things in Stuart and helped Giselle's Hot Squad, as she termed them, save the men of their condo from the sex curse.

"You know what thing is or not?" Dusty barked, while she wrote her name in the dust of a shelf housing ornate daggers.

Little Dusty, now the coach's favorite, had been allowed to skip out on the post-game meeting. In her midriff exposing rainbow striped shirt that also was sorely lacking in ability to cover her twin titans she'd be anyone's favorite.

"Do I?" Wanda asked herself, overlooking the pillar Giselle swiped from Hemera. "It is a terrible thing. I risk much just being near it."

The mood remained shadowy and overcast, aided by the ill-at-ease look Madame Wanda shifted from the pillar on the round table cloaked in purple cloth towards Giselle.

"You should not have brought this here."

"Our first choice was Antique Roadshow," Giselle retorted.

Madame Wanda groaned at the joke. She then noted with gloom, "I had never thought to see something like this in America. Have you heard of Crius? The Greek Titan?"

Both girls shook their heads.

"He was one of the four pillars to hold the heavens and earth apart."

Dusty asked, "Is that thing supposed to be him?"

"Negative," Giselle answered. "Crius is stuffed away in Tartarus."

"Correct," Wanda replied. "All the Titans are imprisoned in Tartarus and have been for many a turn. But this object channels Crius. This is a Dark Object. It is something capable of great destruction and malevolence."

"What's this about tartar sauce?" Dusty asked, scratching the back of her neck. "I'm getting kinda hungry."

"Tartarus," Madam Wanda corrected. "In the Greek cosmology, it is a great pit beneath the earth. It is a gloomy storm-wracked prison of the Greek Titans, imprisoned there by the Olympians."

"All that is a bunch of made up junk anyway," Dusty countered, hands on hips. "Yer telling me, there's my queen's Allfather, all her Norse gods, a Norse hell, then there's Fleur's Christian hell and Jesus and god. Then there's probably a bunch of Hindu and Muslim stuff somewhere out there in the cosmos too. So somebody tell me how all this crap can exist at once?"

"The collective conscience of humanity is responsible for all the phenom of the many realms. It is theorized that the reason the supernatural exists is that the collective conscience of humanity created it," Madam Wanda spoke in a soft tone.

"In that case, the collective conscience better be responsible for us winning an NCAA championship and me being on Sportscenter," Dusty snorted.

Madame Wanda pushed the pillar towards the center of the table with enough delicacy that Giselle could tell she respected the might of the craftsmanship.

"Why was the damn thing locked up in a closet at Hemera?" Dusty wondered.

"Prince Trygyrr," Giselle answered, "says you can get to Tartarus from beneath Hemera."

"Or maybe he's full of it," Dusty snorted.

Giselle spent her life running through the academic and social rigors of a top Los Angeles private school to prepare herself for Hemera, make the dean's list, get a good internship, and a great job. What she found in New York were sex curses, kidnappers, and demonic constructions. Her old friends, or at least the ones her klutziness didn't cost her, would be pledging to sororities, and she was dealing with stalking elves, sex curses and Dark Objects.. How could anyone focus on a U.S. history up to the Civil War class when there were Titans snoring below.

"I greatly revile and fear the creature who left this at Hemera," Madam Wanda said with a shudder, "You must dispose of it at once."

"Done deal, Madame W!" Giselle chucked it into the dark orange garbage bin.

"The fuck is you thinking, bitch?" Madame Wanda erupted. "I know your stupid white ass ain't dumping that shit in here! I'm gone off that Crown Royal and them Black and Milds. I know you ain't fucking with me like that."

Giselle threw her hands up in dismay as Dusty snicked. "You said dispose of it at once!" Giselle whined. "That's a disposal bin. It literally says disposal bin!"

"Toss that shit in the fucking water or a dumpster! Damn! You musta got me twisted!"

"Ireallyreallyreallydidn'tmeantoupsetyou... whydon'tIcomebacklater..." Giselle didn't need to hear any more of Madame Wanda breaking character. It was like hearing Scar say he never wanted to give Mufasa that work.

"Go on and dump that thing," Dusty instructed. "Madam Wanda's gonna tell my fortune about how I'm gonna wind up the co-queen of Golden Land with Princess Tristabelle and have a honey moon in Valhalla. Ain'tcha?"

Giselle was then out the door and quickly on the hunt for a dumpster or maybe even a sewer or perhaps anywhere but Madame Wanda's disposal bin to ditch this dangerous object.

When she turned around the corner she found brick buildings blotted with boarded windows on their façade. Road barriers thick with graffiti leaned against the buildings. Prominent was an artwork of a woman whose body was a wheel, with her face masked by a blindfold. An actual white cat stood below the woman's misty legs, licking its paws.

"Stay back, kitty, I have the demonic infinity stones."

Giselle need not search long for someplace to dump the box as when she turned from the feline and the wheeled woman, a man who stood no taller than 4'11" held his hand out and offered a less than welcoming smile. Positioned behind him were far taller, but somehow less intimidating men all dressed in black.

"Fuck my life," Giselle muttered.

Chapter Three: SKM

"I'm in the fuck my life hall of fame," Giselle bemoaned, her pained words earning a smile from an Asian goon with Japanese text tattooed across his forehead and down his cheek.

The short leader's backup brawlers were dressed in various loose-fitting black clothes while the boss was decked in black pants and a top that clung to his muscular frame. He seemed sleeker, meaner than his companions even though he was smaller. The only thing he shared in common with his associates was the initials "SKM" tattooed in sharp script on his neck.

"I am a mature young woman," Giselle started, "And a mature young woman deserves a little bit of introduction before you stab her to death."

"Our employer has been trying to track Dark Objects across New York City," the small man stated. "It was nice of you to dig one up. We'll show our appreciation by giving you a quick death."

"Okay, cool stuff! Byeya!" Giselle yelled, determined to avoid losing her grip on the pillar and her grip on her life.

Giselle put her JV cross country skills to work and rushed away from the goons. She hit a sharp turn into the alley behind Madame Wanda's building. A garage door across from Wanda's was tagged with word "Meggido," which Giselle, from an ancient history elective in tenth grade knew to mean Armageddon.

It may well have been Armageddon for Giselle as her turn carried her into a group of four more "SKM" goons who wore the easy-to-move-in clothing of their brethren. In short order, their all-black clad leader and his crew arrived to box Giselle in. In Giselle's mind the leader sort of looked like a ninja that spent all his money at Lululemon.

"This happened to Bella in Twilight," Giselle remembered, "and she got out of it. How?"

"Edward saved her," offered a towering pale man whose face was tattooed to make him look like a dog.

"Shit," Giselle muttered. "But good memory. I love Twilight. Books and movies. Not so much the last movie. But all the others? Wow!"

"I thought the last movie was good," the pale man stated. "It was paced well."

"Give us the goddamn box. Now!" the Lululemon loving ninja bellowed.

"Something's wrong, Claude," a henchman with braided hair put forth in a shaky voice.

Something was indeed wrong. Mister braided hair's nose was shattered to the point it was no longer recognizable as a nose, thanks to a running elbow from one Fleur Flanagan.

"Holy crap!" Giselle spat out, as one man nearly provided his pants with a holy crap as he watched Fleur send a spinning kick with her opaque Nikes to dislocate one of his partners' jaw.

Claude, the leader, acted in a flash of ninja-like terror, whipping a throwing star of all things into Fleur's shoulder.

"Fleur!" Giselle shouted in worry, not noticing that white cat darting below her feet.

"Jeez, what a pain," Fleur lamented at her shoulder, then brought that exact pain to another goon by depositing the throwing star just an inch away from his kibbles and bits. He fell to the ground, shrieking his agony with his eyes fluttering open and shut.

"What the hell are you?" Claude snapped at Fleur.

"I'm just a bitch looking to fuck some shit up. There should be some goofy fox girl coming to fuck you up too but she got caught up doing a selfie with a Maltese."

"Double holy crap! Triple holy crap! Quadruple holy crap! Infinite holy crap!" Giselle and her limited vocabulary shouted as the pale man lunged for her. Thanks to simple klutziness alone, Giselle avoided his grapple by tripping over the kitty and falling flat on her denim shorts.

The pale man didn't appreciate any interference from the cat and bashed it with a thudding kick.

"Bad move, bad person," Giselle barked. Against any semblance of good judgment, Giselle grabbed a stone and threw it at the pale man for harming the feline.

It proved to be a bad move for Giselle as the bad person made a bad lunge for her yet again. Unfortunately for him and his dental health, Fleur slid in to remove several of his teeth with a sliding boot.

"Well, aren't you an annoying prick? Don't think about touching Giselle's big jiggly white ass!"

Another thug let out a roar of a crazed beast and delivered a left cross to Fleur's face, staggering her backwards.

Through a bloody mouth, Fleur bellowed, "In the immortal words of former Celtic Kevin Garnett, 'hell nah! Trash ass bitch!'" and then rifled an opaque Nike into his stomach that hurled him backward.

He came back at Fleur, bashing her in the stomach with a knee. Fleur crumpled to the ground next to Giselle.

However, Fleur turned her position to her advantage as she tangled up her foe's ankles in her legs and brought him to a nose-breaking meeting with the pavement.

"Mega holy crap!" Giselle screamed while clutching the white kitty. It wasn't clear who was protecting whom in that embrace.

Another goon grabbed Fleur from behind, attempting to choke her out. Sadly for him, Fleur ruined his plan and probably the rest of his life by harshly flipping him forward to the ground. Before he could register what just happened, Fleur was using her right Nike to push his face into the hard alley ground. After that, very little was recognizable of the man's facial features.

Claude remained calm under pressure as he whipped out a sai from beneath his shirt and used the three-pronged weapon to skewer Fleur in the stomach.

Fleur's face registered agony with her features twisting into a frown, and her eyes slamming shut. Yet her misery was but a fleeting thing as she came back to life, yanking Claude across her shoulders then tossing him head-first into the ground at her side. A satisfying crunch rung out. Claude went limp— just another victim of the babe with the big happy grin.

"I'm gonna need you to come at me all at once," Fleur decided. "This one-at-a-time, piecemeal approach isn't working with my need-it-now Gen Z mentality."

The SKM crew broke and broke hard. They ran like the very hounds of hell were nipping at their heels. But it was just little ol'

Fleur, with the full face made adorable by puppy fat. Though even looking at the pale blue eyes, the trademark red ribbon on brown hair, Giselle still couldn't recognize this version of Fleur.

"That stupid redhead is disgustingly unreliable," Fleur complained. "And she shed all over my favorite blanket."

"Oh. My. Gaaaaaawwwwdddddd!" Giselle howled, her big blue eyes glossy with wonder. "You're like Batman, not the Christian Bale Batman or Ben Affleck Batman, but definitely the Arkham Games one. It's like the press triangle button appeared and you said eff that, I'm pressing triangle AND square, and L1 and B, and the Playstation doesn't even have a B button! You're a vampire Batman! Wowie!"

Giselle's video game rambling may have actually been appropriate as Fleur looked over her bested enemies as if she were in an online game searching for "phat loot."

"SKM goon, SKM goon, SKM goon," Fleur mumbled until that big happy smile reappeared on her face. "Hey, this short one is an SKM ninja."

Giselle and her new feline pal peered at Claude, while both keeping a tentative distance.

"I don't know what an SKM ninja is," Giselle lamented. "Are you a ninja also? Are you an ABC, DEF, CNBC ninja?"

Fleur went on to say, "Pft, I'm not part of some gang of paint by numbers tattooed losers."

Giselle found Fleur to be babydoll cute. She had gigantic innocent pale blue eyes, a stream of chocolate-colored hair usually pinned by a ribbon, a face full of baby fat and full red lips. What wasn't babydoll like was her figure, which was chiseled and honed to rock hard perfection.

"Anyway, thanks for saving me. You followed me?"

"Dusty told me what was up. You've got a real annoying habit of getting in the worst possible situations so we decided to come after you. It'd be a pain in the ass if you got kidnapped again or murdered with your mom around. What'd Wanda say about what you found?"

Giselle explained Prince Trygyrr showing up, the nature of the pillar as well as Tartarus and the link to Hemera. All of which earned a scowl from Fleur.

"So what can we do?" Giselle questioned.

"Not take advice from creepy elves. He reminds me of the supernatural equivalent of the guy who masturbates in the 2010 Corolla when the kids are on recess and says he didn't know the kids would be on recess when he started jerking off."

"I'm not sure how you came to that conclusion. But what do we do about this pillar?"

"This lame shit might be connected to the cursed guys at our condo, which could be connected to my dad. Or it could be extra bullshit we have to deal with. I wish I was dead."

"You're so cute when you've decided something's hopeless."

"Cute?" Fleur rolled her pale blue eyes. "Ugh. You wanna die."

Giselle noticed something very peculiar about Fleur's appearance. Not the bloodstains on her green and white striped shirt, not the fact that she had no wounds from being stabbed by a sai and a throwing star. No something else was off about Fleur.

"Fleur, why do you suddenly look like Rouge from X-Men?"

"Huh?"

"You've got a white streak in your hair."

"Are you serious? Already?" Fleur's hand went directly to tug at the sudden streak of bright white that had exploded from her otherwise Godiva chocolate straight hair.

"Is this normal for you? Getting a Vidal Sassoon color job?"

"I need to remedy this shit quick. I could bite you," Fleur mused, "but you're a real whiner. But then again that big white ass looks like a big ball of cookie dough."

"Sugar cookie cookie dough!"

That must be Fleur's favorite flavor because without a word the brunette buried her doll face between Giselle's sumptuous cheeks. The demon-vampire hybrid started growling like a wild boar as she ran her face up and down and bottoms that were so tight they could have been painted onto to Giselle's generous helping of derriere.

"Eeep!" Giselle shouted as her legs began to buckle. "You can't eat ass in an alley!

Fleur pulled back with the comment of, "Shut up for a second. That's not enough. I'm better at sucking dick anyway. I'm gonna drain this guy limp.

"Drain him limp?" Giselle questioned to herself, then turned to her white feline buddy, "Mister Kitty, our friend Fleur is a vampire."

"You're explaining things and not going all eeep or whatever. Maybe, Tristabelle was right. You are too stupid to be scared of this shit."

"Tristabelle didn't say that!"

Fleur's full lips pursed in thought, "Maybe it was Sofi."

"You're the only one who talks like that. Just drink his blood so we can go."

Fleur dropped to the ground and started unbuckling Claude's weapon belt. That got a quarter of an eeep from Giselle. When Fleur pulled down his pants and underwear that got half an eeep. When Fleur

waved her hand over his limp penis to turn it into a full-blown erection
that got a full eeep.

Tasting the swollen and angry member, Fleur turned her pale
blue eyes on Giselle for approval that wasn't exactly forthcoming.

"Ah! You can't blow a guy in an alley!"

"Says who?"

"Civilization! Alleys are a no-blow zone."

"I'm a trailblazer in my field."

"What field is that?"

"The field of shameless whoredom."

Much to Giselle's consternation, Fleur did not adhere to the
no-blow treaties established many years ago. Instead, Fleur's tongue
went on a pleasant journey along the outside of his bulging erection. It
was a Sunday drive of blowjobs, as Fleur drunk in inch after inch.

"You get your dick sucked by a hot white chick, but you gotta
get your ass kicked by her too," Fleur commented. "Is it worth it?"

"I don't like the idea that white chick blowjobs are so valuable
you'd suffer a beating for them."

"This white chick's blowjobs are."

"All right, can I just nudge you into a doorway? Not even fully
inside, just a doorway?"

"Nah."

Fleur did stop blowing Claude, which lets Giselle breathe a bit easier.

Giselle was promptly made to breathe a lot harder, as Fleur's strong and mighty hands begin a mighty and robust stroking of the man meat. Fleur could be very well choking the life out of someone with her grip, yet Claude dripped like a leaking faucet. A leaking faucet that Fleur took a mouthful of. The sucking started to drain the brilliance of white from the "rouge streak" in her hair. As the white returns closer and closer to the trademark brown of the Boston babe, Giselle has had enough...

"All right, Fleur, you meet me, you dislike me on sight. I find out you're half-demon, half-vampire. We have an orgy to save the guys in the condo. A couple days later you're beating ass to save my life you start talking about ninjas and goons. Your hair turns into Anna Paquin. You say you're gonna bite me, but then you start giving a blowjob to a dude you just beat up in an alley, and you act like I'm the crazy one! Are all demons like you?"

As if to defy Giselle, Fleur swallowed and sucked even harder on the ninja's beefstick. The brunette honey made the tightest ring she could on the dick and yanked on the delicious flesh. In a matter of moments, Fleur descended to the very root of his flesh pole, moaning and grunting as she did so.

Fleur's pale blue eyes fluttered, the horny babe wearing an expression of total lust. The feeling of the stiff joytstick filling her mouth, trembling and ready to explode had her burning with passion. Her fingers were like a lit match to gasoline as they explored her hungering hole.

"Fleur, you are an animal."

If Giselle thought that was going to be the end of Fleur's display, and she did, she thought wrong. For Fleur swatted Claude on the hips, getting him to pump his hips upward, his hard rod journeying deep inside her welcoming throat while her roommate ran her hands through her bright blonde hair and her heart-shaped lips descended into further frowns.

"I'll show you a trick, cheer ya up," Fleur announced..

"Nope, no tricks. No tricks."

"Too bad. Welcome to the After School Slut Club."

"Mature young women don't watch blowjob tricks in the alley while their mom is wondering where they are."

Fleur, of course, didn't listen to Giselle's whining. After all this was the most awesome "trick" in her oral arsenal. Showcasing her fitness prowess, Fleur extended her minuscule height into a push-up position. If the other guys weren't knocked out, their loins would spring to life as Fleur proceeded to do not only push-ups but blow Claude at the same time.

"Okay, that is a pretty cool trick, no lie," Giselle admitted.

"What can I say? This tramp's got talent."

Up Fleur went, bringing with her a wad of spit, and then down she came for a mouthful. With eyes alight with intensity, Fleur moved up and down, her wide lips yanking hard on the dick with such intensity that she was announcing she owned any damn man she wanted not just this one.

As she raked her teeth across his shaft, Fleur expanded her jaw muscles to the point it would be throbbing were she human. The president of The After School Slut Club looked the part as she swallowed his beefstick, inhaling it fully into her gullet. Giselle had no choice but to be impressed and was keen on getting an application to The After School Slut Club

"This is an incredible way to tone your chest and stretch your jaw muscles," Giselle decided. "Your ideas are intriguing to me and I wish to subscribe to your newsletter."

Fleur was so hungry to woof down cock that her blowjob-push-ups went into fast forward, a lightning round of sucking that defied the laws of physics.

"Ewww!" came a voice storming with horror. Blowjob stopping horror.

Giselle's eyes jumped up to find Sofi, who wasn't shocked at the sight of the blowjob, but rather staring at her phone.

Sofi's long, full pink lips expressed, "How dare that bitch post up in the same outfit I just showed off on Snap. I'm gonna kill her!"

"Hey, Sofi," Giselle greeted the voluptuous beauty with the curly red hair.

Sofi's long upturned eyes finally caught sight of what Fleur was doing, "College girls giving oral sex in the alley," Sofi mused. "I saw a report on that on VICE. Or maybe that was a video on my dad's laptop. It's so crazy how all that porn magically appeared on there without him ever knowing or doing anything."

"Nah, it's just a meeting of The After School Slut Club." Fleur announced.

"Hey, good idea!" Sofi stated. "Let's take back the word slut one rich dick at a time. Now hold on, I have to tweet about sex scenes in Hollywood films being misogynistic ."

Who could hate women when they looked at Sofi? She wore ripped up jean shorts that said "can't stop, won't stop," showcasing her huge honey buns, and a mega underboob exposing black cut out crop top, She also wore a bracelet with a star charm, but Giselle doubted anyone was going to be looking at her wrist with an ass like that.

"Ugh, you don't have an authentic bone in your body," Fleur groaned.

"But I got a New York Knick's bone in my body so kiss these tities," Sofi said and tried to force her torpedo tits, as Fleur termed them, in Fleur's face. But Fleur was in a fuck the Knicks mode; she squirmed away from almost by buried under a mound of brown flesh.

"I had to suck something or else I'd desiccate," Fleur explained. " And I got his blood flowing so this guy is ready to be interrogated. Let's get him into Madame Wanda's."

The next bizarre sight that greeted Giselle's vision was Fleur performing her best Geico Caveman imitation and just dragging Claude onto the ground towards the shop. Two taxis passed the Hot Squad and spared not a glance towards Fleur Flintstone's unusual means of hostage transportation. On the girls went with Giselle carrying the white kitten.

The girls arrived into the shop where Dusty and Wanda sipped on ginger tea.

"I really don't appreciate ya'll interrupting my psychic reading," Dusty complained. "I was in the middle of finding out how me and Queen Tristabelle are gonna have a threesome with Princess Kate on top of a griffon."

"There are griffons?" Giselle asked, shocked.

"Hey, asshole, what gives? What's the deal with that pillar?" Fleur questioned Claude. "Giselle, you say my stupid dad came up to you at the carnival?" Fleur asked.

Adoration, love, admiration... these were all things Giselle felt for her father, Stephen, a shrewd if not awkward tech guru. She remembered him teaching her how to code, how to build a gaming PC, how to construct a website, and reading technical journals in a failed attempt to steer her towards are more profit-earning major.

Hatred, disgust, loathing... these were all the things Fleur felt for her father, Lazarus of Bethany, history's first vampire, and also a saint.

Fleur had described the origin of vampirism as an STD passed from a prostitute to Lazarus eons ago. Lazarus was killed in a fight with the STD in him then rose again at night. Thanks to the GOAT use of public relations, the world thought he'd been resurrected by Jesus and made him a canonized saint. Satan had contacted him about creating a demon-vampire hybrid. Thanks to the money offered, Lazarus took the deal and bred with a succubus. The product was Fleur, a day-walking vampire-succubus whom Lazarus had grown sick of paying child support on. So tainted were his feelings towards his daughter that a lust for murder had replaced his paternal bond.

Giselle's dad wouldn't even ground her.

"Uh-huh," Giselle replied as Fleur frowned. "He said 'Tell her you talked to the man who makes her feel bad in the morning. Tell her you talked to the man who's going to take money out of her purse. Tell her you talked to the living saint. Tell her you talked to Lazarus of Bethany. "

Fleur let out a little laugh even as she pounded her fist into her palm, "Hearing his bullshit just pisses me off. Did he have long, beautiful hair? Like the wind is giving his head a blowjob?"

"You guys have some weird ways of describing your parents!" Giselle pointed out. "But it was most def blowjob hair," she added, whipping her golden locks around, "like pornstar blowjob hair."

"So what's up, face tats? " Sofi prodded. "Who are you working for? Or are you a rapper? I've had sex with a few rappers, but you gotta at least be on a few Apple Music playlists before I sleep you."

"Being on Today's Country playlist'll do it for me," Dusty claimed. "Even if yer just in the backup band."

"Whores and music snobs," Fleur quipped.

There was a choked gasp from Claude. Then another. Then a third. Then a fourth. There were no words.

Madame Wanda's coal black eyes shifted from her cup of tea onto Claude. "He has a spell placed on him to prevent him from answering any questions."

The SKM tattoo on his neck flared with white light. A white light that got brighter and brighter until it was an explosion of light in the dim shop. It created a blinding flash of brilliance. But when it faded Claude's life was darkened by death.

The girls passed unsure, frowning looks to each other. Sofi, being brave enough to poke the dead man, got only the empty stare of a man without life.

"Creepy," the redhead whispered, her wide green eyes shut.

Wanda, shuddering, spoke into her cup of tea, "He was an SKM ninja. SKM was once a feared supernatural organization based out of Japan, but reaching across the globe."

"But," Fleur added in, "when their leader disappeared, the group became mercenaries and errand boys with katanas. Too bad about their leader, heard the pussy was juicy."

"Fleur, how much does your dad hate you?" Giselle queried, snuggling against her kitty. "Are we talking Link/Ganon level?"

"I don't know who those dumbasses are but we seriously hate each other. He's sick of paying child support on me, and me and my mom want our fucking money. I'm sorry you all had to get involved, but at least I got you an orgy with some rich dudes."

"Very feminist and sex-positive of you," Sofi announced then started tweeting something about female movie characters being oversexualized, then posted a thong pic for her Patreon subscribers.

"A Dark Object by itself," Madam Wanda started, "is just an object. To work it one needs to be a witch with a propensity for risk. Or a demon sorcerer."

"Demon sorcerers are the lowest sorcerers in the sorcerer caste system," Fleur noted to Giselle.

"Caste system?"

"It goes like this. Healing sorcerers are at the top. There's few of them and they can heal wounds, calm people, or sooth trauma. Light magic sorcerers come next. They can shoot holy rays that can defeat the living dead or the undead like vampires. Fire and ice magic sorcerers can manipulate water and fire kinda like Dusty. Earth and Wind magic ones can do the same with their elements. Dark magic ones are the second lowest. They manipulate the dark energy in the world and cause disease, malaise, rapid aging, tooth decay, depression, et cetera. At the bottom are demon sorcerers. They are your cleaning crew of the supernatural world. They can summon demons, but they can banish them as well and are usually called in to deal with demonic incursions. They are specialists so you might get one that deals with Christian demons, Muslim demons, Greek demons, you get the point."

"But it sounds like demon sorcerers are useful."

"They take a lot of abuse and have a lot of grudges," Fleur stated with a lazy shrug. "So you get a lot of desperate ambitious assholes. Lemme put it this way; do you wanna fight over the last McNugget with a man who hasn't eaten in a week?"

"Look, we gotta get back to the condo because Princess Magalinda is supposed to tell us something over the magic mirror," Dusty reminded them. "Me and my queen have our new student orientations tomorrow so we can talk to Big Sis Anika about all this mess then."

Madame Wanda gripped her cup of tea tightly while biting her lip. It was a look of a woman who heard something she had no wish to hear.

"Productivity!" Giselle declared. "We are so on top of things and we got a pet cat. Wave to everybody Tyr."

Giselle made the cat wave to the others which seemed to annoy it.

"Why do you get to name the dang cat?" Dusty moaned. "I wanted to name it," Dusty finished her complaint by pouting like a five-year-old.

Fleur snickered as she quite enjoyed Dusty's pouting. But behind her was the slow rise of Claude. The rise of a man who has the grip of the reaper trying to hold him down. The rise of a man who had one foot in the underworld.

He looked to Giselle and spoke in a flat tone, "I am at your service, mother of the night." Then he died again.

That was when Giselle toppled to the ground in a distressed faint, Tyr barely able to jump on the table before his owner crashed into the floor.

Chapter Four: Magalinda

Five brownies.

Princess Tristabelle had all but inhaled five brownies in a row when the other girls recanted the tale of Prince Trygyrr, SKM, Fleur's alley blow job, and the Dark Object.

Upon hearing the tale of the blowjob Tristabelle had said, "Fleur, you performed fellatio in, as the Americans would say, hella crackhead style yo, without consecrating the ground in Frejya's name? Truly abhorrent!"

When told about Prince Trygyrr's visit to Giselle, Princess Tristabelle stated, "His abuse of his duties knows no bounds. And to use an astral projection! He is an obdurate villain at times. Though I may misjudge his aim in protecting Giselle. You are a curious thing."

"Giselle, you're about to be a whole princess. You are sugar daddy goals," Sofi announced. "I need to get a prince zaddy. "

Dusty sat a red velvet cupcake on the monochrome kitchen island in front of the stress eating princess. Tristabelle gobbled it up in a very unladylike manner. This forced Dusty to rifle through the monochromatic cabinets for more snacks.

"Not enough carbs, too little calories, not enough sugar," Dusty complained at all the snacks. "Ugh, who wants to eat healthy anyway?"

"What about your sister?" Fleur asked. "When's she supposed to hit us up? We can't keep Dawn out of here forever."

Dawn had been ushered out of the apartment on errand duty, based on a royal request from the sweet tooth of Princess Tristabelle to make Dawn's school bake sale best-selling triple chocolate cheesecake. There was simply no way to refuse the begging of a real princess.

"Come then," Princess Tristabelle ordered as Tyr skated across her feet. "We shall use the magic mirror in my room to contact her our—"

DING!!!!

The doorbell.

The girls were used to the doorbell ringing from their many male admirers or these male admirer's angry wives. Thus they had learned to ignore it. Dawn had only just left into the New York night, so it was unlikely to be her.

Even so Giselle walked to the hallway. She journeyed underneath the waterfall-like diamond chandelier and peered at the security camera.

"It's Prince Krisdane!" she exclaimed, feeling a heady rush of excitement at the appearance of the gorgeous elven prince, his ears glamoured to be invisible.

Giselle felt a surge of adrenaline at the sight of him. His brown hair was in an artful tumble of curls, his purple eyes were hooded below long eyelashes, his pouty lips pursed into a whistle. Then they began speaking.

"There's some girl in a pink witch hat," Giselle said, feeling a stab of jealously. But that jealously was quickly replaced by wonder. If elves rarely left Golden Land, how come Prince Krisdane stood just floors below her.

"Magalinda and Krisdane? Unacceptable!" came the booming voice of Princess Tristabelle's royal authority. "How could they come to America? Elves do not just willy nilly travel to different lands. Father said so himself. A lack of order leads to wickedness, and the next thing you are under a bridge, on a dirty mattress, wondering where your pants are and if that growth is dangerous."

"That was an awfully specific example," Giselle commented. "If they came to America it must be important. And come on, they're your siblings, and Magalinda is wearing a witch hat. You can't leave her out there wearing a witch hat."

"Very well," Princess Tristabelle muttered.

Giselle had never felt such glee in letting someone inside her place in her life. Not even that clown for her third birthday party who later was found guilty of murdering three Skid Row prostitutes. Krisdane was back! The gallant Prince Charming of Golden Land was back. Her joy was so great she forgot that Princess Magalinda had a grave issue to discuss with the girls.

The front door to the condo opened to bring in Prince Krisdane whose head was already lowered in apology towards his arm-folding younger sister, Princess Tristabelle.

The other elf—her ears glamored too—was far less demurring.

"My adoring sister!" Princess Magalinda exclaimed, arms held wide.

Princess Magalinda, in Giselle's mind, was an anime character made real. She sported heavily-curled brownish-blonde hair beneath a pink witch's hat and a slinky pink gown with a lust worthy boob window in the front and pink high heels.

Maggie was certainly worthy of being part of the line of drop-dead gorgeous Elvrina royals. She had an oval face, huge crystal blue almond eyes whose insides slanted more than Tristabelle's, the bronze skin to match her sister, a button nose, and a circular mouth with thin lips that Giselle could just tell often broke into a sneaky smile.

Noticing Giselle's stunned expression, Maggie stated, "Wherever she goes, The Fluffy Bunny, Maggie Elvrina has them dropping their jaws. That's me by the way, The Fluffy Bunny!"

"We got that," Fleur said, arriving next to Giselle.

"Oh my god! She's so cute!" Sofi declared, long upturned eyes soaking in Magalinda.

The Princess responded with a very theatrical twirl that swirled the pink gown she was wearing.

Dusty was the last to arrive, entering with the question, "But how'd ya get to America so quick?"

"Weeeelllll," Maggie began, holding her hand to her forehead, "my careful manipulation of magic portals got us here. Sure, we may have encountered a terrible and angry monster named Prius in Jamaica, witnessed a beheading in Syria, and interrupted a performance of Romeo and Juliet in Texas but I got us here!"

Princess Tristabelle shot a glower at Krisdane as she spoke, "Surely father must have given his warm blessings to send you to me."

Krisdane sheepishly shook his head.

Princess Tristabelle stomped toward the living room, passing underneath the Shakespearean quote that was stenciled in cursive on the ceiling, "Hell is empty and all the devils are here."

"Order and respect have been overthrown," Princess Tristabelle whined. "Law has vanished so that elf may make a cameo in Samir's beheading."

"That's hella racist," Sofi complained. "You don't know if it was an Arab dude being killed."

Krisdane caught up to Tristabelle, "As this situation concerns a matter of the state and a matter of the family we had no choice but to subvert father's rules. No one wished to tell you. Just us."

"Why don't we go into the living room and you guys can explain," Giselle suggested.

Giselle led everyone into the picturesque living room, remembering how impressed her mom was with the décor. It was something off of HGTV with rich cream-colored furniture, a movie screen positioned between two marble pillars. What stood out most to Dawn was the crystal installation of a voluptuous woman whom Giselle had explained to be Maya, the Hindu personification of illusion.

Fleur barked as she flopped on the comfiest chair in the room, "Why'd you show up in America instead of on the magic mirror?"

"I could have made the perilous journey through space and time on my own," Maggie boasted as she stood atop the Ottoman like she was standing atop a conquered mountain. "But some girl named Giselle brought Krissy here!" Then she theatrically held her hand to her heart and gave a mighty lousy impression of Krisdane, "I must travel with you, Magalinda! Not even you in all your resplendence can protect her from this terrible, terrible threat. You, Magalinda the Fluffy Bunny, discovered with your brilliant witchcraft that outshines in comparison even Golden Land's High Witch—Yes, you, Maggie will graduate at the top of your class at Lady Chevalthorn University of Witchcraft! They'll change the name to Magalinda Elvrina's University of Witchcraft! They will build you a statue made of gold! What a wonderful talent—"

"What danger, Maggie?" Tristabelle spoke through gritted teeth.

Krisdane wore a polo of thin gold and white stripes with the familiar dancing lady of the Elvrina clan on that pocket. From that pocket he pulled out a neatly folded piece of paper and passed it to Tristabelle.

Tristabelle snatched it with her purple eyes rolling at her sister's dramatic setup.

Krisdane edged closer to Giselle, which gave her a tremble like Cupid shot an arrow into her most intimate regions. Sofi went "awww" at the sight, leading Giselle to dub her the best BFF in the history of BFFs.

"Read the letter, Tristabelle," Krisdane told her, voice urgent.

Tristabelle read silently, but Sofi hovered over her shoulder to read key pieces aloud, "Dear father. There was a great evil done to the earthen realm when Astrid was selected over I by you to sit the throne of power."

Tristabelle's fingers dug into the paper. They were more like fangs ripping into a dreaded foe.

Sofi kept reading, "I have had my share of misery and woe since my rebellion against you met an end, and my brother was torn from me by that untamable wench, my sister Tristabelle. With great deservings, my king, you and the rest of my family have earned all the misery I can bring to you."

Those normally perfect features of Tristabelle twisted and turned into a frightening scowl.

Sofi read, "Without me you will die on your knees, not even able to cast a stone in the earth's defense.The dangers of the outer realms come with hands of fire, father. Astrid is nothing more than a rodent. The feeblest one possible to sit the throne. Fire kills rodents, but it shall never melt The Golden. Expect me," Sofi finished with her eyebrows raised, "Gorick Elvrina, The Golden." Sofi then let out a long groan. "Ugh, reading sucks.

"For real, for real," Fleur agreed. "Throw that shit on Spotify," The English major argued.

"That letter," Krisdane began, "was delivered by a hooded messenger a mere two days prior. The hooded messenger laid it into father's open hand then breathed his last breath."

"That fellow died and got his soul banished," Dusty decided. "To the darkness of Bolivia!"

"Bolivia is a rash dog's get, stupid," Fleur corrected her.

A memory came rushing back to Giselle's mind. In the Historium Trygyrr had said something about an enemy of the state roaming through something called the Corrupt Forest. The old scene played out perfectly for Giselle, how Trygyrr told Tristabelle that the king questioned her loyalties in the matter.

"Gorick is the third-born child of our family. " Krisdane informed everyone. His right hand was clinched, his eyes closed. It was painful for him to speak.

Maggie lowered her voice into what she must consider a scary tone and added, "But when the oldest Bernhard, decided to become a Berzerker, he gave up all rights to the throne. After all a Berzerker is a terrible, frightening and spooky abomination!

"He's an elf and that can transform into a bear? " Giselle asked, the words making her stagger a bit. She had tangled with video game berzerkers and even watched Youtube videos about the history of such a being. And now there was at least one roaming the earth.

"You're a sharp one," Maggie claimed to Giselle with a wink, "I think I'll keep ya."

An elf that can transform into a bear is totally cheating! Giselle complained.

Maggie continued, "Astrid became next in line for the crown. But that wasn't fitting for the powerful, the strong, the beloved Gorick The Golden. He had to be king. He had to be the king now, now, now, NOW!

"When Bernhard left," Krisdane started, "it was as though there was molten lava forming inside Gorick's heart. It bubbled and swelled until it exploded with an attack on Hildegard Castle. Our home."

Tristabelle looked up to the sky as she spoke wearily, "The earth had seen no better leader than Gorick The Golden. He was the first Elvrina since the seventh century to hold The Chosen Spear, a gift from The Allfather to the Elvrina whose leadership is beyond compare. He defeated the Rend Mare of Harmony Woods."

Krisdane added, "Brought down the rampaging golem that killed Lord Liselotte and his son. Stabbed Calamity Jonas through the heart after he unseated father from his horse and was like to kill him. Chased Emperor Grim of the Corrupt Elves from the borderlands deep into the Corrupt Forest."

I wonder what makes a Corrupt Elf and a Pure Elf. Isit just a change of DNA. Do elves have DNA? Wonder what their Ancestry.com results look like.

"And Gorick is just a dang handsome sort of guy," Maggie finished with hands on hips and head nodding.

"I suppose," Tristabelle stated, still looking to the sky, "we were all great fools not to see the fate Gorick was to give us. I was there that day he chased Emperor Grim back into the Corrupt Forest. I blackened the eyes of those who told me to give up on my brother's return. And he did return! It was a fantastic day for me. How proud I was of him! But the man who returned to me was far different than the man I loved. His mind was sullied by thoughts of encroaching darkness from the outer worlds."

"Far more dangerous than that which myself, Astrid and others fight to keep back," Krisdane shared.

"Suddenly Astrid was unfit to be queen so my brother said," Tristabelle stated, "Unfit to keep the darkness at bay. I could hear him in shouting matches with father. Though Gorick did the shouting as my father would never rise to that sort of emotional theatre."

"Then when it was time for the Winter Solstice festival to begin in Gladsheim," Maggie began, her voice taking on a dramatically ominous tone, "and Rodgir, Trygyrr, Krissy. and myself were long departed. Gorick The Golden led his supporters in an assault on Hildegard Castle! And whoa, whoa, was it a toughie for my family without Rodgir and Krissy around. But Tristabelle saved the day and saved Astrid from the Chosen Spear. But we lost our—

"Enough!" Tristabelle snapped. She turned to stare out of the panoramic windows that oversaw the beauty of New York City, "What matters is that father chose to exile him rather than execute him."

"Couldn't this be, like, the elf equivalent of a drunk text?" Sofi wondered. "Just talking shit to talk shit?"

"You DM the president, you're gonna fuck up his kid and see how that ends up for you," Fleur joked.

Dusty settled next to Tristabelle, leaning against the window, "It still don't make sense why ya had to come to America behind everybody's back though."

Maggie began pointing to herself, prodding her supple chest, "Everyone's favorite witch, myself, was home for The Golden Goddess Festival in Alfheim just when this letter came. I swiped it off of our father's desk and did a little locator spell and found Gorick right here in the United States!"

"Ain't those things barely accurate?" Dusty questioned.

"Weeeeellllllll," Maggie trialed, "they're normally twenty percent accurate but for a legendary and awesome witch like me, they're twenty-two point sixty percent! But I can get a better reading when I'm closer to him. So hello, America, meet Maggie!"

"Then, you'll find him and arrest him?" Giselle questioned, leaning forward in her seat.

"Arrest?" Princess Tristabelle didn't bother to turn around. "Giselle, I oftentimes find you humorous." She said no more than that.

"Wait," Giselle began, "you're going to do an extrajudicial execution of your own brother? What happened to following the king's order?"

Tristabelle said nothing. Didn't even pay Giselle so much as a glance.

"I am certain it will not come to death," Krisdane claimed. "Mother could not stand to lose another child."

"Another?" Giselle asked, but said nothing more when met with a cold glare from Tristabelle.

"Ugh," Fleur groaned. "This piece of shit brother of yours might be in America but then he might be in Siberia. The thing with the cursed dudes at the condo, SKM, Dark Objects, is a Lazarus of Bethany move to get at me without getting at me at the same time."

Giselle thought back to what Anika said about Golden Land, *"You should know that the world you live in is a leaf in the path of an unseen tornado. But in between that leaf and that tornado stands the unmovable wall of Golden Land..."*

So what would happen to the leaf if the unmovable wall of Golden Land crumbled?

DIIIIIIIING!

"Mom!" Giselle shouted. "I totally forgot about her. How could I forget about her? Mature young women don't forget about their moms!"

DIIIIIIIIIIING!

"Oh, right, I should totally answer that!" Giselle shouted.

Giselle hurried to the hallway, nearly slipping and almost crashing into the Basquiat.

Having not destroyed any priceless, art she looked at the security cam and saw her mom. With Mister Blowjob Hair, Lazarus of Bethany. This sent a sharp wave of fear into her stomach.

"Fleur! Fleur! My mom is with your dad!"

Fleur was there in less than three seconds thanks to her vampire speed. Shoving Giselle aside, she slammed her finger on the intercom.

"What do you want, you slimy shit?" she barked.

"Since you won't," Lazarus began, "have one of your roommates invite me in."

"Like hell!" Fleur barked, kicking the wall and putting a dent in it.

Oh right. Vampires need to be invited in. Giselle thought to herself.

"Exodus 20:12," Mister Blowjob Hair spoke, "honor your father and your mother so you may live long in the land the lord your god is giving you."

"Don't quote the Bible to me, fuck face. You know I hate the Bible."

"Children are a heritage from the lord, offspring a reward from him," he replied in sweetened tones.

Fleur had her fists pressed against the wall so hard she was cracking it, "Quote the Bible one more time, and I'm gonna slice the shit outta you!"

Giselle hurriedly cut in front of Fleur to take over, "Mom, you can come up. Mister Flanagan, you should leave, please."

He spoke one more Bible verse, "Hebrews 12:11. No discipline seems pleasant at the time but painful. Later on, however, it produces a harvest of righteousness and peace for those who have been trained by it."

Fleur stormed off in a rage, using vampire speed to roar down the hallway in a flash. That was just as well for Giselle, who thought she'd be facing a Fleur versus Dawn confrontation.

Instead, Dawn arrived carrying grocery bags, her mouth pushed to the side in confusion.

The redhead took a moment to think before speaking, "Wow. Giselle, is Fleur okay?"

"Fleur totally got hit with the berserk spell!"

"Giselle, please speak normally."

"She's a little angry. But her dad really makes her super mad. And anyway you can't be with him. There's something really wrong him."

Dawn waved her hand at Giselle's concerns, "We shouldn't judge people of differing belief systems. Did you know he's a regular donor to the GOP? And I've never heard of him."

"His daughter isn't acting like a rabid wolverine for fun."

Dawn placed her hand on Giselle's shoulder, "A lot of kids rebel against their parents."

"I wish I could reload the save and direct you down the route where you don't meet him."

Dawn let out a frustrated sigh and picked up the bags, "I'm going to bake now, and then you and I are going to have a long discussion about responsibility and your place in New York."

"Wait, wait, wait," Giselle's heart-shaped lips formed a big smile, "Do you wanna meet a prince?"

***

Anika had worked interior decorating magic to put the girls' rooms into order. Each bedroom was remodeled to be more than a resting place. It was transformed into an expression of the girls' heritage and personality.

The headboard of Princess Tristabelle's bed had been handcrafted by gnomes with engravings of elven warriors to fit the princess' militaristic side. Her magic mirror was surrounded by intricate ornate carvings of who humans knew as fairytale characters but Princess Tristabelle knew as her elven ancestors.

The princess had the biggest closet of all the girls (even bigger than Sofi's). Tristabelle's had an island in the center with storage compartments for accessories, marble flooring, and a hundred-year-old chandelier.

Ahead of new student orientation, the princess put on a silk scarf tied dress with a starry night pattern. With Giselle's mom around,

her elven ears were glamoured to look human by a pair of big hoop
earrings.

Princess Tristabelle had put her siblings into a hotel room at
The Pierre. Without them present, it freed her from their interference
and commentary on what she had to do.

The only one she included in her current plans was Dusty,
who barged her way into her room at 5:50 a.m. with the comment "rise
and shine, my queen, we got ass to kick!"

Dusty had thrown her support behind Princess Tristabelle's
sudden war with brother Gorick. It had her clad in daisy dukes and
white tank top, sitting on her queen's bed with the royal standing in
front of her magic mirror.

"You do not need to involve yourself in this, Dusty,"
Tristabelle stated. "Put simply, Gorick is the most dangerous man in the
earthen realm. He is no mere scoundrel! Why, I remember when I was
squiring for him, a baby frost giant found its way to a village in the
crown lands. Gorick shortly had it leaking from spear holes in every
part of its body. I assure you he has only grown fiercer since then."

"You used to squire for him?"

"Why, yes. In his mind a girl's worth was measured by how
quickly she learned to sew and knit. He did not like Astrid fighting, and
he surely did not want his youngest sister drawing her blade at his

command. He only accepted me as a squire to run me off to more docile pursuits. But he found me to be such a dogged warrior, it was if I had the manner of one raised by werewolves. He began to respect me. Then he began to love me. Then he betrayed me. I appreciate your devotion, Dusty, but do not—"

Dusty leapt off the bed in a hurry; her 4'11" frame somehow looming much larger. She spoke, "You and I ain't my pa and Uncle Baron. But me and you are still a tag team. And when you mess with one woman, you mess with the other woman. That means Gorick's messing with two women and these two women, me and you, are gonna do what my pa and Uncle Baron did to the Global Party Exchange, and that's beat that bastard within an inch of his worthless life."

Princess Tristabelle didn't say anything. She didn't have to. That was the type of loyalty that only needed a firm nod in acknowledgment.

"Magic Mirror, oh Magic Mirror, Constantina Elvrina, oh pretty pretty please," Princess Tristabelle spoke tightly.

A haze of purple mist replaced Princess Tristabelle's reflection. It was so thick and vibrant one could think it could be reached out to and touched. But within ten seconds, it faded away to reveal the back of a head with hair braided into a flower.

"Sister," Princes Tristabelle spoke.

The blonde-haired woman turned her wheelchair around to face her mirror. At the sight of her sister, Princess Constantina's long delicate lips broke into a pleasant smile.

"Sister?" the woman spoke through long lips.

There was no esteem in the world, Princess Tristabelle felt, that was higher than that which she held for Constantina. Her sister was the lone pure elf in history to be confined to a wheelchair. Yet her bravery and high spirits were something even the hardest hearted could admire. It had been on a treasure hunt with their brother Rodgir where Constantina's fate was sealed. Though she aided Rodgir in escaping the Tokoloshe gremlins in South Africa, she was struck by a curse from their master that denied her the use of her legs.

It boiled Tirstabelle's blood to think about Rodgir's recklessness and the life it cursed Constantina with.

Constantina had wider eyes than Tristabelle, bejeweled eyebrows, a square jaw, and an older yet more sympathetic look than her little sister. Giselle had said she looked like a glam model.

"Constantina," Tristabelle began, "I am loathe to trouble you with my squabbles constantly…"

"You would not be the Tristabelle I loved if you were not locked into some mortal struggle with some sort of monster or churl."

The almond set eyes of Tristabelle slammed shut as she fell into a confusing wave of thought. She hadn't determined how to best lie to Constantina, just that she needed to lie. About Krisdane, about Magalinda, about knowing about Gorick, about everything. If Constantina had any idea what her younger siblings were embroiled in, she'd rush to tell their mother. Constantina could tolerate a certain taste of adventure in her younger siblings but interloping to America and battling Gorick were tastes not made to touch the younger Elvrina's lips.

"We got ourselves a real bad son of a bitch causing us a hell of a lot of problems," Dusty spoke out of turn.

"And you are?" Princess Constanina asked, clearly taken aback by Dusty's manner of speech.

"I'm Dusty Blackwood, the Tooth Fairy's daughter and daughter of Brady Blackwood. Like I was saying, we got ourselves a real bad son of a bitch. A real tough one too!"

"What species is he or she or it?" Constantina asked, directing her made-up eyes to her sister.

It was a pure elf. Not immortal, but the hardest of supernatural species to kill. For once in her life Tristabelle had wished elves were as breakable and destructible as humans. She'd exchange her own invulnerability if it eased the procession of her sword, Mistlewoe, through Gorick's heart. But it would take repeated thrusts from Mistlewoe to summon Gorick's demise. The last time she charged Mistlewoe for just such a task Gorick had made a hasty escape. His blood still stained the carpet in the throne room.

Dusty still spoke, "It's a golem."

"In America?" Princess Constantina was so shocked she leaned forward in her chair.

"Now I could hit most folks with the Brady Hammer and snap their spine in half and kill 'em quick. But 'cause this thing is made out of granite I can't do it. Her sword can't do it neither," Dusty remarked, pointing to Princess Tristabelle. "From what my queen over here tells me, yer some kinda super genius, so what we need you to do is think of a way for us to beat this thing's ass and beat this thing's ass for good. Can you do that?"

"It is very concerning that there is a golem in America," Constantina remarked, folding her arms below her chest.

Dusty replied, "The only one who needs to be concerned is that damn golem because it's August, and no matter what you tell us, it ain't making it to see September."

"Invigorating!" Constantina shouted. "Your words of strength make me feel as though I could walk again. I shall help in any way I can. The best way to rid oneself of a sturdy fiend resistant to attacks is to seal it away inside a magical prison. This, though, is beyond the limits of pure elf and fae. In theory, you would need three powerful Dark Objects to act as conduits in creating a surge of dark magic energy. You must have an adept witch or black magic sorcerer to draw out the energy in them. When that business is set you would lay the objects in a triangle about the victim, activating them together and drawing them into a magical prison. In theory."

They had one Dark Object as found by Giselle and as hunted by a ninja led gang.

"In theory?" Dusty remarked.

Constantina answered, "I cannot say there have been any real academic studies on this. Would the prison be in an existing underworld? Would it be an underworld all its own? In that case, can we create an infinite number of realms! Mind-boggling stuff!"

"How do ya get a Dark Object?" Dusty wondered.

"If you defeat a demon," Constantina noted, "it may drop one. The more powerful the demon the more likely it carries a Dark Object. Black magic sorcerers or demon sorcerers might have them, but I often find them to be very untrustworthy.

"Murder, prison, or our death," Princess Tristabelle told herself, "these are the routes laid before us. Dusty, let us go to our new student orientation today and see what we can find at Hemera."

Chapter Five: Ring My Belle

Fleur had said it was a half-assed Hemera new student orientation that grouped dance majors like Tristabelle, parks and recreation majors like Dusty, and wicker basket technology majors together in the biggest lecture hall of the Charles Shango building. And she had been right. It had been a half-assed new student orientation Dusty and Tristabelle had sat through. Now that it was over the students milled about outside the lecture hall. Dean Lorne Pederson and his less than rousing welcome speech, which mostly consisted of self-congratulating, shots at NYU and Columbia, and thinly-veiled warnings not to embarrass him was thankfully fading from memory.

Numerous students hung out with some nervousness on the white-tiled floor. Some tentatively introduced themselves to one another. They made conversation about their class schedule, annoyed the upperclassmen took all the good class times, leaving the freshman early morning slots. Others looked at posters for various clubs on campus, while some read about the freshman camping trip this Labor Day weekend. Some discussed going to see the Irish rapper Seamus McGrath aka SeaSeaSea's concert at the school.

But forget class bonding events, the dean's speech and the explanation of various school services. The main attraction for quite a few attendees was Princess Tristabelle. Several people came just to see Tristabelle, having either already had their new student orientation, or being upperclassmen, or not even being enrolled at Hemera University.

Their heroine didn't disappoint outfit wise, having changed into something different from her morning's attire. With her ample chest poking through a black lace top decorated with gold flowers and a booty hugging pair of black leggings decorated with thorny white vines, she provided her usual stunning sight.

Those noble fanboys and fangirls, stood in front of a poster of the Dean encouraging students to report underage drinking, were represented by a sophomore named Harold. The thin nineteen-year-old claimed slicked-back black hair, onyx black eyes, and was neatly attired in khaki shorts and a blue and white polka dot shirt with the Hemera H on the pocket.

A nearly snarling Dusty, in cowgirl hat, short white shorts that hugged her curvy hips, and a black sleeveless shirt that read "Fairies Are Real" in rainbow lettering hated him. She hated his gang and hated it when he announced their official name.

"We're the Belle Ringers!"

"My word!" Tristabelle exclaimed with a clap of the hands. "I had woke up today thinking I was vain and proud above my station, but your very presence makes me feel otherwise."

"You are excellent, Your Highness," Harold declared, also clapping his hands.

"You are, Your Highness," The rest of the Belle Ringers backed him up, hands clapping en masse.

These losers were annoying, Dusty thought. It would serve them right to toss them into a magical prison along with Prince Gorick. If they were back in the fairy kingdom, Dusty would smack Harold upside the head with a steel chair and teach him his lesson.

A girl with a lip ring named Kimberly Kayley added, "Your performance at the world figure skating championships was breathtaking. ESPN had a stat that said of all blonde princesses to skate on the third Friday of the month, your player power ranking is the highest at 8.7777933."

"I was supposed to say that, Kimberly," Harold whined, shoulders sagging.

What a jabroni, Dusty thought. Even his voice was annoying. She should throw him through a table draped in thumbtacks like her dad did Alvin Moneystacks at Fairy Revolution Wrestling's Dirty Deeds 2015.

Pure elves may have been almost impervious, but Princess Tristabelle couldn't resist the charm of a good compliment.

Dusty snapped, "I ain't need no stupid made-up stat to tell me how awesome she is."

"Shush, Dusty. We will be kind and caring to our fellow students."

Dusty stuck out her lips in a pout. You did not serve Dusty Blackwood cooked kind and caring.

The Belle Ringers took a collective sigh at the very magnanimity, the very charity, the very selflessness of the beloved princess.

Finding all this to be wildly entertaining was the approaching director of student services, Anika Lindgren. Princess Tristabelle gave deference to Anika with a lowered head, even though Anika met her with a curtsy.

Dusty, on the other hand, openly ogled Anika's sleek and toned physique in tight jeans and a lace blouse, unprofessionally unbuttoned as always.

Anika's always smirking lips turned up higher, as her wide grey snowcap eyes took in the scene, "A princess and her court. How adorable," Anika admired.

"We're the Belle Ringers," Harold announced with pride, getting a HARUMPH from Dusty.

"Adorable," Anika flatly claimed. "Would the Belle Ringers like to accompany the jewel of Golden Land and her pixie BFF on a Haunted Hemera tour led by yours truly?"

Princess Tristabelle and Dusty had zero clue they were going on a tour, but if following Anika on her whimsy would get them in a position to ask questions about the string of oddities plaguing them they'd do it. And they did it with big smiles and nods.

"Yes, we would!" Harold delighted.

"Yes, we would!" The rest delighted to a cheer from Harold, who was sort of literally rubbing shoulders with Tristabelle. But just enough that it seemed accidental, which it wasn't.

Dusty's dad hit Dan Black with a bullwhip at FRW Zero Hour 2018 for less than Harold did to Dusty right now.

"Grrrrrrrr!" Dusty hissed at Harold's touchy feelyness, loudly, openly, and more like a werewolf than a pixie.

"Delightful," Anika purred. "Afterwards I treat to Taco Bell. As long as that company's politics are socially acceptable."

Sadly no one seemed to care about Dusty's disgust, and so the tour began with a grumbling pixie shuffling her feet in the caboose of the group.

***

Dusty Blackwood AIN'T AFRAID OF NO GHOSTS! And Anika's stupid stories about the ghostly botany major on a permanent paranormal trip psychotically seeking revenge on her cheating boyfriend, or the ghosts of the failed student presidents still stumping for votes, or the school's hockey team record holder for penalties menacing the visitor's locker room at Sky Reach to avenge Hemera sports losses didn't scare her! Not one stinking bit!

She sure wasn't scared of the Psycho Wave murders that took place on the Hemera campus five years ago, where the victims were bizarrely killed by a culprit that remained at large.

And the only reason she huddled up to Tristabelle was that that stinkin' Harold was huddling up to her too. Certainly not because Tristabelle could summon her magic sword Mistlewoe in case any hockey stick wielding poltergeists attacked.

Princess Tristabelle, Dusty and the Belle Ringers found themselves in a hallway of the Dunston Cheksvin Performing Arts Center. Large posters of past Hemera performances such as Hamlet and Spanish Tragedy hung all around.

Anika spoke, "Janitor Adam Clarkson loved to play a good trick on the faculty of Hemera. And though a few found his droll antics not execution worthy, there were others who found a 39-year-old man's use of a whoopee cushion proof that he had been allowed to soil the genepool for much too long."

The others laughed.

Anika continued with Dusty feeling her words were hammering into her heart. "He was given a message one day that a very lovely visiting scientist had heard about his comedic styling and found it sexy. As men are gullible creatures where their penis stands, he believed this Doctor Gremory wanted to meet him in this very closet."

The Belle Ringers looked to Tristabelle for the proper reaction. Tristabelle feigned fright, so they all do their best to be extra super-duper afraid.

"Why this closet? She would have to hide from the shame of being seen out and about with Fart Joke Clarkson. But Doctor Gremory was no doctor at all. Rather she was a demon summoned by a sorceress who suffered the whoopee cushion gag when she was in a faculty meeting. Gremory took the requested revenge on Adam, stripped him of his soul and used it to create a portal with easy passage between our realm and hell right in this very closet."

"What happened to the janitor then?" a short freshman girl with freckles asked.

Anika answered, "If you listen closely, you can hear Adam crying. Gremory left this fool just enough of his soul to feel despair. Now then, are we off to Taco Bell?"

"Wait!" Harold shouted, loud enough for Dusty to jump in fright.

"What's the big idea yelling so loud?" Dusty complained.

"I've got to see this portal to hell for myself. With your permission, Your Highness."

"Look at this, Princess Tristabelle," Anika's lips formed an entertained smirk. "One of your worshipers would chance a meeting with the devil himself to impress you."

"Is this gonna take long? You promised Taco Bell and I'm hungry! And I want ice cream, too!" Dusty barked.

Anika's always-smirking lips stood in ultra mode smirk as she pulled open the door. All that anyone could see, which isn't much, was the hanging of cobwebs, molded over towels and cleaning supplies. There was not a thing to put their fear of god and his angels in Harold. Thus Harold hopped into the closet in hopes of impressing Tristabelle.

SLAM! went the door.

Pale light crept from the closet, showing an ugly green that spooked the students' faces into turning an ugly white.

"Big Sis Anika? Can ya open the door?" Dusty pleaded, but Anika just smirked at the blood curdling she caused.

A scream raged from behind the door. Harold's scream! Harold's scream of unchecked orgasmic bliss!

"Dearest me!" Tristabelle yelped with her hand to her mouth.

The pale light was washed away by a pink one as Harold's cries of pleasure provided a rumbling and booming soundtrack for the light show.

Soon, though, all the flashing lights worthy of a rave and the screams worthy of a Brazzers video came to a sudden end. Confused by the start of the erotic mania and its end, the students watched Anika open the door to show the resident cobwebs and Harold flashing perfect white teeth in a goofy smile.

"Wow! What a trick! A Belle Ringer praised Anika, as all joined in with applause except a perplexed Tristabelle and Dusty.

"Yes, quite wonderful. Now how about that Taco Bell? Princess, we can have that meeting afterward. Just you and me."

Anika licked those smirking lips at the pixie and the light elf, then strode off with the amazed students happily trailing her like a flock of awestruck sheep.

***

"Are you afraid of the dark?"

This seemed to be a very pertinent question. So Sofi had looked up from her phone and asked it. That was Sofi Poe, asking the heavy hitting questions. Like when her dad's business partner DM'ed her telling her he wanted to whip it out and do the helicopter. Where did he keep this helicopter? How far would they travel? Lunch? Dinner?

Sofi looked like she didn't deserve to be hidden away in the closet with her curvaceous body spilling out a skinpy snake pattern criss cros top romper

"Heck no, I ain't afraid of the dang dark! I'm Dusty Blackwood, daughter of Brady Blackwood and niece of Baron Blackwood. They're The Music City Gunslingers in Fairy Revolution Wrestling, and I'm just a tough as they is, I sure am."

Sofi's long lips puckered and she twisted on a pair of chunky leopard print sneakers. Her Her purse was stuffed with cash because Dean Pederson had seen her entering the building and given her all his money for being so pretty.

"I done said I need yer help," Dusty moaned, tugging on a blonde ringlet. "I ain't gonna let some stupid Belle Ringer make me look like a chicken."

As Sofi gathered, Anika had taken Dusty, Tristabelle, and church bell enthusiasts on a haunted tour of Hemera. Some weird stuff happened when someone named Hal, Hank, Homer, whatever, went into this same janitor's closet Dusty dragged her to. Taco Bell may have been involved but Sofi stopped paying attention at that point.

Dusty announced, "We're gonna wrangle ourselves a Dark Object from this closet."

Sofi thought it was sad that Princess Tristabelle's plan A was to kill Prince Gorick and plan B was to magically imprison him. Elves needed an Instagram or a Twitter where they could go back and forth and work out their issues in a healthy public sphere like humans.

"If you cling to me and freak, I'm gonna record it and start the Pixie Challenge," Sofi warned.

Dusty's doe eyes spat adrenaline and anger, "Grrrrrrr! You best get ready for the toughest daughter of a bastard you've ever seen, Sofi Poe!"

"I'm so ready," Sofi said with a bored flip of her red hair.

Not only did Sofi have to ready herself, but she also had to open the door. Moreover, she had to push Dusty into the closet herself.

There were some 409, empty bottles, cobwebs, a McDonald's bag, some fraying wooden brooms, a half empty bottle of Windex and some bleach. Nothing looked like danger to Sofi, not even the bleach, a substance an e-stalker said she was going to dump down the redhead's throat if Sofi wouldn't follow her back.

"Ah-ha," Sofi wrinkled her nose, "we need to shut this door to get to the jump scares."

Before Dusty could yell no, Sofi slammed the door. Did she lock this god-fearing pixie into a gateway to the realm of the seven deadly sins? Maybe just the door to a juice bar in Purgatoria?

"Turn on the light!" Dusty whined.

"I can't. I think it's broken."

Sofi didn't actually attempt to tug on the rope hooked to the light bulb, and Dusty was too small to reach it, so there they were, a fox spirit and pixie camping out in the janitor's closet of one of the most expensive schools on the east coast.

Dusty started reaching around the time in the most haphazard investigation history has ever seen. She stopped suddenly when she put her hands on what felt like...

"Flotation devices. We're dealing with a water hag," Dusty decided.

"Oh my gosh, we're dealing with you grabbing my tits! Shit, where's the light?"

Dusty announced, "It don't matter! If I gotta kick some demon butts for my queen Tristabelle, then I'll do it blindfolded if I have to."

She was so into her statement of defiance she didn't notice Sofi had her wide green eyes, bangs pushed away, locked onto a passage written in glowing smoky white letters behind a splintered wooden mop.

"I bless you air," she read. "I implore you, Mermeut, you and your companions. Who rule over the tempest."

The text lit with a hellish orange glow then flashed back to smoky white before it came off the wall and rose into the air. It swayed to and fro, moving with a lazy sort of grace, distorting it's lettering.

"I implore you in the name of he who was at the origin," Sofi went on, barely noticing Dusty clinging to her. "I implore you, Mermeut, by this right hand. That shaped Adam, the first man, in his image. I implore you, Mermeut, by Jesus Christ son of the one god. I conjure you, demon of Satan. I conjure you to do harm in this place, to bring the tempest here."

Dusty had gone stiff aside from her clinching and unclinching fists. Sofi finally looked down at her and could see how rigid she had become, like a woman who had been carved of granite and not flesh and pixie dust.

But far more interesting than Dusty were the words that now began swirling. They twisted and writhed until they weren't words at all—but something far more dangerous, far more threatening then just demonic text. They turned and bulged, clouded and heaved, until they became a five-foot tornado. Yet instead of gathering things in its tempest, it gathered itself into a twisting, virulent mass with skeletal arms and hands,

"It has a head!" Sofi realized, from the light that was shining from its big red eyes. Eyes that beamed nothing but malice on a head with a forked beard and braided ponytail.

It began to spin, but instead of sucking things into itself, it ejected smoky blue words.

"I am Mermeut, demon of the atmosphere," Sofi read. It continued to spew words. "Perish now."

"Ain't no one dumb enough to believe yer gonna kill us," Dusty snapped.

"Oh my gosh, if I knew I was gonna die I'd have deleted all my gay porn from my computer," Sofi whined.

To Dusty's benefit its red eyes beamed more than malice, they beamed a lustrous glow that had the once dark closet awash in crimson. So at least they weren't in the dark anymore.

"Son, you better do a lot less spinning and lot more disappearing," the newly brave and newly lit Dusty Blackwood demanded.

Mermeut surged forward, using its mass to slam into Dusty and Sofi. Sofi clattered against a mop bucket, dropping her phone in the process, while Dusty toppled to the floor near the door.

"Oooh, I'm gonna wack you good!" Sofi announced, springing up with animal like agility.

She pounded Mermeut in the eye with a looping punch. It wobbled him but not enough to stop him from coming back and cracking her in the side of the head with his fist. Sofi fell instantly, her vision clouded by a mist of pain.

Dusty was on her feet with fists balled up. She drove for Mermeut's eyes, but he was too fast and again barreled into her. The pixie's face registered sharp surprise with an eye raise as she was thrown back against the splintered mop.

Sofi slung a bottle of Windex at him, only for it to be swallowed into his body then spat back out at her at an alarming speed. She used her animal-like agility to avoid it. Though as she saw the bottle burst into pieces against the wall she winced as if seeing someone's bones splinter.

Sofi then read its next series of hazy words, "Perish now."

"I done told you once," Dusty warned, angrily snapping the mop over her knee. "Do a lot less spinning and a lot more disappearing."

Yet it continued to launch words at them.

Sofi began, "Child of the-OH!" But she was stopped when Mermeut launched himself into her. He connected with her body with enough force to propel her backward. The attack launched her into the door. Her body plunged through it; poor Sofi landed in the hallway with a thud and a groan of pain. Her long eyes had to watch Mermeut twirl out the janitor's closet and take a trip down the hallway.

"We gotta go after it!" Dusty bellowed as she helped Sofi to her feet with one hand, while the other held the sharp edge of a broken broomstick

Sofi grimaced as she brushed some wooden debris off her shoulder. Then she took off with Dusty after Mermeut.

Mermeut surged around the corner into a lounge area that was thankfully free of students. What it did have was a collection of purple chairs. One of which was sucked into Meremut's body then launched at Sofi's head upon her arrival.

A human would have endured a broken neck from such an attack but the crafty Sofi made an agile roll beneath the incoming chair.

Mermeut gathered another chair and threw it at Dusty. But the pixie leapt onto the chair, used it as a springboard, and launched herself at Mermeut, aiming her broken broomstick right for his eye. The demon tried to spin out of the way but failed to move in time and his right eye was impaled with Dusty's weapon.

It spewed words such as "agony," "pain," "misery," and "woe," as it spun away from Dusty. It then spun mangled, thin misted gibberish as it lunged for Sofi and missed by a good distance. With each bit of movement it shrunk more and more until it was about as threatening as a tumbleweed.

Then it disappeared for good.

"Oh my god!" Sofi exclaimed, which Dusty thought was about her violent victory. Instead, Sofi pointed to a flyer and stated, "They're doing the Lion King. I have to try out for Nala. Aren't you getting total Beyonce vibes from me? I mean, I'm prettier and sing better but still."

Dusty found interest in a glowing jagged black rock that rested in place of Mermeut.

"Look at that, Sofi! We got ourselves a Dark Object. With the one Giselle found and this one, we only got one more to find."

"Boob bump!" Sofi called.

Dusty and Sofi leaped mushing their globes together. It was like four asteroids colliding. Four tits banging together that shook space/time.

***

"Sure I can draw the dark energy out of these objects!" Magalinda boasted. For some reason, she had decided to hold both the pillar of Crius and the black rock of Mermeut into the air while standing on the desk in Anika's office. Standing on one leg at that. Though only Giselle seemed impressed. Anika stared at her nails,

Princess Tristbelle scowled, Sofi checked her phone, and Prince Krisdane motioned for Maggie to get down.

Maggie didn't get down and let herself get photographed by Sofi and her iPhone. A rare treat for a supernatural who used magic mirrors as opposed to a cell phone. Both Maggie and the desk were definite Insta worthy—with Maggie being of an otherworldly level of beauty who followed her sister's lead in wearing as little clothing as indecent exposure laws could allow   and Anika's desk being a black obsidian jewel with runic carvings on the outer edge.

Anika swiped some dust off one of the two stout limestone warriors that flanked her door and said, "Princess Maggie, darling, you do realize the inherent danger of...well...fucking up with dark energy."

"Of course I do!" Maggie announced, switching to the other leg. "Terrible misfortune awaits everyone nearby if I mess up! Trissy and Krissy, remember when that witch in the Black Rose district back home tried to channel dark energy? There was a terrible outbreak of dark monsters that Rodgir and his soldiers had to stop! And if I mess up, this whole building is going to be eaten by some terrible tentacle monster from the deep beyond! Mwhahahahah! But do not worry, I am the head witch of my class at Lady Chevalthorn University."

"I had thought you were in danger of being placed on academic probation," Krisdane commented innocently.

"That's only because I may have accidentally raised the dead one time. Two times. Two and a half times because I don't think that woman was actually dead to begin with."

Anika shook her head as she said, "An elf, who's a witch, who inadvertently raises the dead. I wonder when an orc who sings show tunes might make an appearance."

Sofi noted, "Well I don't think ditching class to come to America is gonna make your school happy."

"Psh!" Princess Maggie bellowed with a hand wave. "This Fluffy Bunny is saving the throne from the world's most dangerous man!"

"Well, no matter what my mom says I am a mature young woman who faces things with bravery too," Giselle noted to everyone's confusion because literally no one had asked about her mom. "So if it means we might risk pressing Alt-F4 on our lives for this then that's fine with me. I am a mature—oh shit, I was supposed to text my mom where I went! Crap!"

Anika rolled her mountain grey eyes at Giselle's folly. Then she turned them rather intensely onto Princess Maggie.

With a too-graceful-to-be-human twirling leap, Maggie came down from the desk next to her quilted satin purse. It had a ring handle that Princess Maggie pried open while humming a tune she probably thought was dramatic. First, she pulled out a silver pentagram that measured no bigger than a hockey puck. She twisted it upside down and laid it on the ground. That was an action that made Anika's usually smirking lips fall into a frown. Then the princess pulled out a knife with a handle made of obsidian crystal clusters.

"This is an athame," Maggie told everyone, twirling the knife with unerring ease. "I'll use it to channel my magical power. Easy peasy lemon squeezy!"

At that Anika leaned in for a closer inspection of the athame. She pulled back with a sharper smirk than usual.

Next Maggie pulled out a vial of water she told everyone was from a lake outside of Gladsheim, aka The Place of Joy, a city in Golden Land. Anika openly snickered, but cut it short when she noticed Giselle glancing at her. Maggie then took nine dry leaves out of her purse which she said were dried goldenseal. Finally, she brought out a fluorite crystal bracelet.

"Krissy, my chalice please!" Maggie bellowed.

Prince Krisdane set the chalice, engraved with the Elvrina's dancing lady, behind the pentagram. Then he turned to Giselle with the words, "You ought to stay behind me, Giselle."

"You know I beat a goat demon thingie. I can handle the toughies," Giselle boasted to him for the fifth time today.

"I could not face your lady mother if your beauty was wiped from this world on account of me."

"Krisdane, I swoon," Giselle commented.

"Don't ya just wanna grab these big ol things, Prince K?!" Dusty declared then grabbed Giselle's big ol things.

Giselle got them groped and groused by the queen of titanic tits herself, Dusty Blackwood. The tiny pixie showed she was the authority on big boob seduction as her firm, painful touch had Giselle moaning and pushing her hips forward.

Krisdane's face was as red as his deep bronze complexion would allow. Maggie found this to be the height of knee-slapping comedy, and that's just what she did as she througly lol'ed.

The cowgirl's big doe eyes sparkled with glee as she molested Giselle's grand orbs.

"These ain't bad," Dusty commented. "Who's yer surgeon?"

"They're real!" Giselle snapped.

"Stop fondling her," Sofi instructed.

A direction easily followed as Sofi got her, as Fleur termed them, torpedo tits groped by Dusty yet again

"Aie!" Sofi bellowed.

"You got nice fat ones," Dusty stated.

A breast fiend, Dusty couldn't help but groan, grunt and pant as she fondled missile-like tits.

"You could launch these things at Iran," Dusty declared

Instead, Dusty launched one into the air. It was flawless in its buoyance and bounce—a textbook example of how boobs should heave.

"You can't....slow down...be looking at Giselle like that," Sofi commented absent-mindedly. "Not so rough! Prince Trygyrr....quit pinching....already made himself her protector." Then Sofi noticed the glower on Krisdane's face, "Don't trip, though, you can still sub to my premium Snapchat for 25 dollars a month. I said no biting!"

"No you ain't!" Dusty snapped back.

"My, my special little sisters are in a mood today." Anika decided. "What naughty teen twats you are." She said with a laugh,

Giselle wanted to pull a Dusty and kick Sofi in the shin. She had been hoping to avoid the Prince Trygyrr subject with Prince Krisdane for as long as she could manage. She wondered what Prince Krisdane thought of his brother's claim or if he understood what exactly it meant. Even Princess Tristabelle couldn't pinpoint the exact meaning of protection when it came to Prince Trygyrr.

"We shall not be communicating in snaps during out chat!" Princess Tristabelle ordered. "The Allfather in his rage has derided Gorick in his betrayal and has set me against him. I shall make Gorick regret his every last action. He will have an eternity to rot, his only food the bitter taste of my vengeance and the Allfather's judgement. "

"Remember, everyone," Sofi began, "ruining someone's life in the name of god is only okay when you're Norse. Like, if you're Muslim or something, just don't do it."

Maggie hummed another tune she thought was dramatic as she poured her vial of water into the chalice. After that, she placed her pentagram in the chalice earning a nod from a still smirking Anika. The dry leaves of Goldenseal were scattered in a circle about the chalice. Then the bracelet clasped onto her wrist. The two Dark Objects were placed inside the Goldenseal circle as Maggie changed her tune to one she considered even more dramatic. Finally, she took her athame across her hand to draw blood to pour into the chalice. At this Anika started to openly laugh but then caught herself and turned it into a cough.

"What now?" Giselle asked.

"Now I say the magic words," Maggie claimed. "Around I circle you, around and within, sealed with gold, drowned in blood, Maggikadraba! Maggikabam, the darkness I send!"

Nothing happened.

But that didn't matter to Maggie. She placed her hands on her hips, held her head into the air, "What a huge success! Maggie, you are a genius! Thank you for the applause, everyone but they're truly not necessary."

"They're so unnecessary they're nonexistent," Anika said, followed by a bit of a snicker.

"Maybe this is why you're on academic probation," Sofi mused, picking up the unaffected stone.

"That's completely unrelated!" Princess Maggie claimed. "Like how Shih Tzus and shitty shoes are unrelated."

"Big Sis Anika, you're a witch," Giselle noted, "can you try?"

"I am strictly a white witch, dear," Anika said quickly.

"Everyone be silent," Princess Tristabelle ordered, having pulled a compact mirror out of her purse. "Especially you, Maggie. I will contact Constantina." Princess Tristabelle turned her attention to her compact mirror, " Magic Mirror, oh Magic Mirror, Constantina Elvrina, oh pretty pretty please," Princess Tristabelle spoke in an annoyed voice.

A haze of purple clouded the magic mirror for five seconds until it disappeared to reveal Constantina sitting attentively.

"It is most delightful to have you contact me!" Constantina exclaimed. "Your problems are so varied and unique. Not the constant gambling losses to strains of gnomes Rodgir presents. Most delightful indeed! Allow me to guess today's problem. You had sex with that golem."

"Preposterous! I have done nothing of the sort. I only did that one time because I saw no other option."

"Oh? Was there no other option at the Midsummer Solstice Festival when you were caught with your ruby red lips around its-"

"Enough prattle! My issue today is that my witch cannot draw out the dark energy in the Dark Objects. Is there nothing that can be done?"

"Will wonders never cease?" Constantina asked, her long lips in a smile. "You did not have sex to solve a problem. Nor can you have sex to solve this problem. But you can perhaps have your witch work her spell while channeling dark beings."

"Demons?" Princess Tristabelle asked.

"A demon, yes. Or a vampire. The older the vampire the more dark and powerful. Of course, you know that already."

"Thank you, sister," Princess Tristabelle said after a sigh. "I shall let you know how this goes. And my having sex with a golem is a strictly trivial matter! Surely I was not the first pure elf to do so."

"You are the first to earn the nickname the Rock Hard Slut. As the humans say, I wish you luck!"

Princess Tristabelle closed her mirror shut and let out another sigh.

Sofi placed her hand on Princess Tristabelle's shoulder and said, "We have a demon and her dad is the original vampire. We just have to get them together without them killing each other."

Giselle's heart-shaped lips flashed a grin before she said, "Leave that to me."

Chapter Six: Revelation 21:3

Effort? To look good? Effort could kiss Fleur's ass. She was a vampire AND a sucubus. She was born a bad bitch, and she would always remain a bad bitch. All she had on, as she looked in her mirror framed by stone serpents, was a touch of lip gloss that left her full lips with an understated shine. And that was all she was going to put on to head to the vampire club, Pandemonium.

It was a pain in the ass being Fleur, she thought as she plumped down her purple covered bed that rested on a stone slab. Anika had customized the rooms according to each girl's personality so Fleur garnered gloomy and gothic.

Sure it was cool being put up in a penthouse in New York, yeah, it was fun to go to college again, but did she have to save people's lives as part of the bargain? She was a demon; she was supposed to take souls not save them. That's why she needed to be among her kind. To revel in blood, to bask in the consumption of humanity. So that's precisely what she was off to do.

But something was off in this condo. The others were being way too nice to her. Sofi gave her lifetime access to Sofi's Onlyfans, which Fleur didn't give a fuck about but Sofi felt was on the level of Jesus curing a leper. Princess Maggie gave Fleur a charm spelled for good luck, which Fleur was sure wouldn't work because Princess Maggie was obviously an incompetent witch. Giselle offered to let Fleur start a new game on something called Persona 5, which meant nothing to Fleur.

And Dawn Nyfall—that woman was becoming an irritant. Fleur had to hole up in her room to drink her blood bags because Dawn hadn't any hint Fleur was anything more than a vulgar girl from Boston. She couldn't even have a beer with Dawn around because all of a sudden, she wasn't a century old vampire-sucubus hybrid but an eighteen-year-old resigned to drinking orange juice. Who the fuck drank orange juice?

She stuck her feet in a pair of chrome-studded combat boots, just in case someone's ass needed kicking. A spiked bracelet was then locked around her left wrist in case she needed to hit someone, as she often did. Utilitarian effects aside, she looked great with all this on along with an olive mini-dress. For once she decided to forgo wearing a hair ribbon, letting her chocolate locks stand on their own beauty.

At least looking good wasn't a pain in the ass.

"Knock, knock," came the ringing voice of Giselle from outside the door, "Can I come in?"

"No."

"Oh ho ho, you can't deny Giselle Nyfall so easily, fiend of the night."

"Wanna bet?"

Fleur lost yet another bet; Giselle slid threw the door, but tripped over Fleur's laundry bag, which, honestly, was peak Giselle. Around her fallen frame the group's new cat, Tyr, skidded in.

"Hey, cat," Fleur remarked lazily.

After making sure there were no more hazards in sight, Giselle pulled herself upright. Fleur took a look at her stacked body in a sleeveless mini-dress with front button accents and tied side and wondered if there was the soul of a really hot girl trapped in the dorky, disheveled body Giselle was supposed to get.

"I'm in the middle of something," Fleur whined.

"Lies!" Giselle correctly stated. "Sooooo," she trailed on, "you're ready for dinner with me and my mom, aaaaaaaaaaanddddddddd…."

If Fleur had blood pressure, it would be rising.

"Aaaaaaaaaannnnnnnnnnddddd….."

If Fleur could feel indigestion, she would be feeling it.

"And?" Fleur barked.

"Aaaaaaaaaaaaaaand your pappy."

These disloyal, ulterior motive having, fake nice motherfucking bitches! How could Fleur have been so oblivious? Of course, they couldn't drop a Lazarus bomb on her outright. Before a bomb, they'd have to kill her with kindness. Bullets of sweetness designed to prey upon her good nature that would leave her with no choice but to welcome the incoming Lazarus bomb.

The problem was…Fleur had no good nature.

"I'm going to kick your sorry ass," Fleur decided with a lazy shrug.

"Wait!" Giselle said, holding her hands up. "Before any kickings of any allegedly sorry asses might occur, hear me out."

"Hurry up and spit it out, weirdo."

"Okay, so the whole dark energy thing with the Dark Objects didn't work. Maggie couldn't do it. Doesn't that suck?"

"It would if I gave a shit about some lame-ass Dark Objects."

"But Princess Constantina says if we can channel dark beings like a demon and an ancient vampire, we can get the whole dark energy thingie to work. Soooooo for this episode of Giselle and The Hot Squad we're getting you, a demon or a half-demon in the same place as an ancient vampirem and Maggie's gonna be off hidden in a serving cart—

"What?"

"I said what I said. She'll be hidden in a serving cart working her magic. Reservations are like now, my mom is waiting, so lets go-go-go."

Fleur reacted with the kind serene calm one would use when they heard the stupidest fucking idea of their lives. Which is to say she did not react with serene calm and instead burst out laughing.

"Please, let me unpack this bullshit properly. You want to rely on the skills of a woman who is a STUDENT witch and a shitty one at that. You also want to get together with me and my old man who want each other dead—"

"He told my mom he'd be there. He was... what word did my mom use...? Elated?"

"Well, good for him. And you're using your mom as a pawn for this pure elf bullshit."

"When you say that, it kind of makes me feel like a bad daughter."

"You are a bad daughter. Humans don't go to dinner with vampires. Humans are the dinner for vampires. If my dau...if I had a daughter and she put my ass on the line like you're putting your mom's on the line because she wanted to live her Vampire Diaries fantasy, she and I would talk, and that talk would be my hand saying slap to her ass."

Giselle's head sagged in shame. There was nothing to say. No evasion and counter of the blow Fleur struck her with. She'd wear the scar of her guilt for a while. But it was too late to back out now.

"But anyway, why should I care about helping out?"

"So we can defeat Prince Gorick!"

Fleur folded her arms and shook her head, "Gorick doesn't sound like a Fleur problem."

"Does your friend and her mother being alone at the same table with your 2,000-year-old vampire father sound like a Fleur problem?"

Fleur shut her pale blue eyes hard enough that if she had been human she'd have given herself a headache. Her full lips moved very slowly as she said, "That is a Fleur problem."

Maybe Fleur did have a good nature.

***

"Can you not just dispense with this charade of control and tell me what I want to know. Have you seen Prince Gorick 'The Golden' Elvrina or haven't you?" Anika snapped. "I know you have."

Her ex-husband leaned back in his leather chair. The poor chair, pressed upon by so much muscle, wheezed as though it were dying.

The bald black man flashed his glaringly bright white teeth at her. A pencil-thin goatee encased them.

"You annoying twit," she snapped and stamped her feet. She felt distinctly childlike.

"You know what you gotta do if you want anything outta me that ain't court-ordered."

She put her hands on her hips and started looking around the back office of his nightclub He sat in this dingy room and had the nerve to boast that he was the proprietor of the most exclusive and dangerous club in all of New York City.

"You know what you gotta do."

Anika had to know because she couldn't rely on Princess Magalinda's shambolic witchcraft to locate "The Golden." She needed the leg up on this deathly family feud which the rest of the world may have to endure the consequences of. She needed to protect her Princess Tristabelle and direct her where Anika best deemed her directed, which was as far away from Prince Gorick as possible.

"You gonna make yourself useful or what?" He barked.

Anika made herself as useful as her ex-husband liked, dropping to her knees. Right as she hit the ground so to did his black slacks. What was left was something best termed gargantuan.

Her steel-grey eyes watched as it approached. It was a titan. Something missile-like in the thickness and pride in which it stood.

Anika's long delicate fingers cupped his balls just the way he liked. She alternated by fondling his low hanging fruits and getting herself naked, leaving only her high heels on.

She swiped her tongue over his slit, trying to force it into him. Just the way he often demanded she do. She knew how to play his game.

He couldn't even be happy with that. He had to begin chuckling and pouring baby oil on her. Her powerful lean figure glistened even in the dim and dreary light. Her eyes sparked annoyance. She was going to have to go home soaked in baby oil. Someone was going to record her sitting on the subway coated in baby oil. She had to think of Princess Tristabelle, who would probably enjoy being doused in oil. That girl had the vocabulary of a Jane Austen character and the mindset of Stormy Daniels.

But she had to make herself useful, so oiled up Anika got a helping of pre-cum oozing from his bulbous head.

Anika made her mouth into a gaping maw to let saliva stroll to his black shaft. The silver-haired babe churned her saliva as lube as her delicate hand stroked away.

"Take that shit," the powerful male said.

Anika hurried to act, relaxing her throat so that she might swallow the biggest member she had ever encountered. Each time her mouth met with it, she wondered if it would choke the life out of her. As always, somehow, someway, she got him inside her to the point he touched her tonsils. She gagged most obscenely, which was his favorite sound in all of existence.

His thick thighs became a jackhammer thrusting his titan through her narrow throat. Anika's grey eyes became shrouded in clear pools of tears, spit poured from her stuffed mouth, and her core burned with lust.

Anika was helplessly gasping for air as he vigorously pumped himself down her throat. More and more spit fell from her mouth. She was creating quite the pool. The force of his thrusting was so intense she could feel her lips swelling as they hit his gigantic sack.

He wrapped his hands around the side of the oiled-up babe, lacing his fingers through her silver locks. Her tender throat grew raw as he pistoned himself into her. Her throat quickly overflowed with mucus. She felt her whole soul had to expand to accommodate his colossal size.

Her muscle-bound ex-husband kept his thick tool firmly stuffed inside Anika's mouth far longer than usual. It made her jaw ache for she knew she was certainly no Fleur when it came to oral sex.

That girl could write a book! Drool still flowed from the corners of her mouth with the big man thrusting himself deep into her throat.

Then Anika was rather unceremoniously and rather roughly dumped on this man's desk. He knocked over some food cartons and a mug to make proper room for her fit and oil-soaked body to be laid out. Then in what felt like a thunderbolt wrapped in skin, she was taken from behind. He had a mirror on the door, allowing her to see the comic absurdity of her lithe figure mounted by his mighty one.

Her eyes bulged through their socket as his awesome member hit bottom. It was well into her womb and the poor woman's eyes went wide as if this weren't the thousandth time she'd been through this.

"Use me!" she screamed.

He thrust into her like a beast let loose upon innocent prey. His hulking hips devastated her slender frame. As he drove deep into her his monster nested in her fertile well.

"Come for me," he told her. His thrusts became deliciously brutal, his hips pummeling her firm ass cheeks as he drove deep into her, the head of his cock pushing and straining at the opening to her fertile cavern on every stroke. She thought of his jewels, heavy with seed to spill.

"Feed me your cock, big guy!" she bellowed.

That burning sensation. The one Anika always got when fucking him. It was radiating from her flesh being stretched apart. It was as intense as the first time with his thrusts jolting the wind out of her.

"Ruin me, daddy!" she breathlessly yelled.

His body reigned dominant over Anika's, pinning her down in conquest. The girth, the length, the force he fucked her with was more than anyone could rightfully stand. Even for this experienced gal, she felt like passing out when it hit her stomach. Still, she yelled...

"Ravage me, big daddy!"

Anika got what she wanted. Her ex accelerated into a brutal pace, smashing her insides, leaving her lightheaded and dizzy.

As always she felt like a lollipop on top of a big wooden stick with every inch of her ex buried inside her. How she hated this man! But how she loved his meat! If only she could remarry his package and leave the rest of him behind. Damn! He was just too hung and too good at this. But he was such an abhorrent asshole.

"I'm going to cum!" she shouted.

Her spirited sex clenched his meat missile, milking its delicious contents, stirring up a batter.

"Take it aaaallll!" he boomed, perhaps loud enough to hear him outside his office.

Spurt after spurt of gooey juice flooded Anika's fertile canals.

"All right, Anika," he said nonchalantly, looming over her. "I saw that pretty boy prince. I hope I never see him again."

Now it was left to Maggie's bumbling witchery to fail to locate him.

Anika smirked.

***

The restaurant Lazarus had chosen was near Washington Square Park and Hemera University. Giselle disliked the idea of dining near Hemera. Through the currents of the Silver River the Titans were dining on misery and woe. She wondered if Saint Lazarus knew the existence of the Silver River and where its water flowed.

Giselle came into the American fare serving restaurant trailing her mom and Fleur. The dining room was bright with bleached white-oak floors, marble tabletops and Italian leather chairs on elegantly slender legs of black steel.

Lazarus sat in the middle of it all, chin steepled over his hands, wearing a V-neck collared polo with graduated brown and beige coloring and dark brown pants. His "blowjob hair" flowed freely over his shoulders while a woman in her fifties at the next table was ignoring her husband to check him out.

"There you are," Lazarus greeted them with a toothsome smile.

"Hi, Laz," Dawn greeted, clearly exasperated. "Maybe you can get these two to talk," she pointed to Giselle, "This one is sulking," and then pointed to Fleur, "This one is pouting."

Lazarus got very close to his daughter, close enough that they could breathe on one another.

"You have a beautiful smile," he told his daughter.

"Good genes."

Lazarus responded, "The genes of kings."

"I was talking about mom."

"Beautiful woman," Lazarus said, leaning in close enough almost to rub noses with his daughter.

"Fucking gorgeous," Fleur barked back.

"You look great in that outfit," Lazarus said, his pale blue eyes boring into hers.

"Same to you, dad," Fleur said, though Giselle heard "you'll look great six feet underground."

"Where did you get that dress?" he asked Fleur.

"Aritzia," Fleur grinned.

"Expensive," he stated through a smile.

"It was your money," Fleur noted batting her big pale blue eyes.

Lazarus studied his daughter for a moment before a smile broke out across his lips. "Well, we're all starving, aren't we?"

Lazarus may have been a worldwide slaughterer of humanity, but he was ever the gentlemen as he held out the chairs for all three ladies.

The waitress, a short-haired brunette, took their drink order. Giselle got water. Dawn and Lazarus ordered some pricey bottle of wine. Fleur said she brought her a flask of whiskey. Everyone thought she was kidding.

"This is something of a surprise," he stated, again resting his chin on his hands. "I thought Giselle was being whisked back to California."

Dawn chuckled. Giselle thought she had such a beautiful laugh.

The redhead, Dawn, looked stunningly sexy in a sort of faux professional way. She wore those vibrant locks in a bun, put on her prescription glasses instead of contacts, threw on an off-white blazer and skirt combo, and a very much boob-revealing top. People were staring.

Dawn turned her searching grey eyes towards her daughter and spoke, "I see that the situation isn't as..well…chaotic as I thought. The other girls are very sharp, and they care a great deal about Giselle."

If Fleur cared about me, she'd stop looking at your breasts!

"So school is starting soon," Dawn went on, "and we'll get with her dad and then make a final decision."

"It would pay to have royal friends," Lazarus began, turning a smile onto the blonde. "Giselle will never forgive you if you keep her from a trip to Golden Land."

Dawn perked up, rising from her chair, "You've been to Golden Land? But I thought they didn't allow visitors."

"Ah," Lazarus moaned softly, "there is only one place like Golden Land."

"That is?" Dawn asked, leaning forward, hands pressed hard into the table.

"The imagination," he replied. "It looks more like a fairytale or fantasy land than a 21st-century European country. Sometimes when I'm there…I don't know if I passed into my dreams or am I still roaming the earth."

Dawn turned to Giselle with a huge smile that read of delighted shock.

"Prince Krisdane told me their government is an absolute monarchy," Dawn stated. "It seems hard to believe. What about checks and balances?"

"Checks and balances? The Elvrinas are the checks and balances of the world. The dynasty is the only government Golden Land has ever known," Lazarus answered.

Dawn shook her head to process what she heard, "That must make them the oldest government in the world!"

Lazarus said, "Behold, the dwelling place of God is with man. He will dwell with them, and they will be his people, and God himself will be with them as their God."

"They're pagan, dad," Fleur grumbled through gritted teeth.

"Pagan?" Dawn asked, astonished. "That is incredible. And she, Princess Tristabelle, left that fantasy kingdom for all our crime and pollution and bullcrap?" Dawn wondered, nodding to herself as she spoke. "Hey, that's a good story. Fairytale princess comes to America for college."

And then decides to imprison brother in a voodoo San Quentin, Giselle thought.

"I think your story might be more interesting," Lazarus commented, again resting his chin on his hand.

"My story?" Dawn blushed so much she had to hide her face partially.

Saint Lazarus, you're lucky we're not in Final Fantasy or I'd summon Knights of the Round and take you out for good, Giselle thought.

Dawn commented, "Giselle's the interesting the one," her voice was warm and kind.

"I think you should give yourself more credit," he replied. His eyes were as encompassing as an ocean. "But there is something special about Giselle. Wouldn't you agree, Fleur?"

The danger this man posed screamed in Giselle's head.

Fleur poked out her already baby fat-filled cheek with her tongue and gave a slow nod.

The waitress returned to take their food order. Giselle ordered first and got lobster. She stopped paying attention at that point until Fleur rather sharply said...

"I want meat."

"Well, we have delicious prime beef," the waitress noted.

"MMm yeah, prime beef. I like that," Fleur said, licking her full lips. "And gimme a rump roast. And you know what else I want? An extra-long tube steak? Mmm yeah."

"Fleur, control yourself," Lazarus chided, drumming his fingers on the table.

"T-Bone me!" she yelled loud enough to draw a look from a suddenly turned on 14-year-old. "Give me prime roast, and tenderize my prime roast. I want bread too. A sandwich. Gimme a hefty salami between my buns!"

Dawn took a long drink from her glass. A very long drink.

The waitress didn't know what to make of this. All she could do is write down all the meat Fleur ordered, repeating the order to herself as she wrote.

Lazarus said something. but it was drowned out by the sound of every lightbulb in the restaurant exploding at once. It was a harsh concert of shattering sounds. It played a note of fear in the hearts of the patrons as confused shouts went up.

Somewhere Giselle thought she heard the sound of a young woman cackling.

A fire rose in a pillar of explosive strength from Giselle's table. It shot to the ceiling, scorching a hole through it as panicked patrons hurried to the exit.

Dawn shoved Giselle behind her, trying to act as a shield to the pillar. Trying to act as a shield to all the bad in the world.

Giselle just sighed. This pillar, most likely created by Princess Magalinda's spells, was the consequence of fighting all the bad in the world.

"Gas problems," Lazarus noted casually.

"Gas problems?" Fleur questioned.

"Gas problems," Lazarus decided in a flat tone.

"Well, I think we should have run to the exit with everyone else," Dawn declared.

"And then run to a pizza place. I know the perfect one for our special girls," Lazarus commented, way too smoothly for Giselle's liking.

Special? I am special. Maybe?

The foursome headed to the door. Before she exited, Giselle gave a thumbs up to a serving cart.

Chapter Seven: No Safe Word Needed

This was going to be difficult.

This was going to be a violation of trust.

But it needed to be done.

Giselle stood in front of Stuart in his messy-even-though-he's-only-been-there-a-couple-days-dorm, and she stood with pride.

Stuart was hammering away on Final Fantasy XIV on his gaming computer with his glowing green mouse and blue glowing keyboard.

"Stuart, I am special," Giselle announced with a Princess Magalinda worthy dramatic voice.

"Big facts," Stuart responded, "Look at those boobs on you! They're mad huge! And "you can make a lot of money off being special. Just don't be like my cousin Joey Numbers. It starts with you stripping for old bitches. You get that easy side money, so you justify it. Then you start fucking those old bitches for extra cash. Cool? Then you're the go-to guy in the old bitch pussy circle. The Steph Curry of fucking old bitches. Then their husbands offer more to watch. Then it turns into threesomes."

"Eeep!" Giselle squealed.

Stuart continued, "Then they offer you a large sum to have gay sex, and you justify it again. Now you're making big money. But at what cost, Giselle? At what cost?"

"At no cost because I'm not a guy, and I'm not a prostitute! Listen to me, Stu."

She wasn't supposed to tell anyone about this, but she was being swallowed by her secret. And if anyone could give her some outside the box thinking it was Stuart.

"I'm kinda wrapped up in something dangerous," she said, clasping her hands.

"Fuck those Rothschilds!" He shouted, slamming his glowing keyboard on his lap. "Now that you know they created the banking system as a means to facilitate child sacrifice, are you ready to strap up and take them on?"

"No! I'm not ready to take on the banking system. Bank of America has provided my family with great customer service. Anyway, I'm wrapped up in something supernaturally dangerous."

He abruptly shut off the computer. He didn't even bother to properly log out of the game, such was his surprise at what Giselle said.

"You're surprised, of course," Giselle said in a soft voice.

"What are the Rothschilds to the true threats that exist in this time? Madam Wanda always told me to watch out for the fangs at my neck."

"That sounds like her. And she's right. I just got attacked by a supernatural ninja gang named SKM."

The feeling of finally letting out her supernatural secret was like a warm bath with a cup of hot chocolate.

Until she was reminded who she was talking to.

" You know why vampires like wearing black?" Stuart asked, "Because they're showing their Masonic colors and unity in their mind control programming over humans."

Well, vampires can glamor people to think certain things so maybe he's right.

"Say someone needed a tip on a hot supernatural treasure," Giselle said in her most innocent voice. "What could someone do to get that tip?"

"They could ask Madam Wanda."

"Nah, she was pretty shook over this type of treasure."

"Or ask on Craigslist."

Giselle shook her head, "Seriously?"

"You post you're looking for something or someone. And then someone knows a guy who knows a guy, and you got what you got."

Which will probably be a trip to Vermont inside some old guy's trunk.

But Giselle was determined to prove herself a useful and mature young lady. She had found one Dark Object. She had gotten Princess Maggie what she needed to channel the dark energy, she was in beast mode with her main character aura. Thus she shot her main character shot with a post that read:

"All Dark Objects wanted. Very serious."

A succinct, mature-sounding post. Not the "lengthy misspelled ramblings" her mother told her her texts were.

When her phone buzzed, she leaped, literally leaped, in shock. Communication after posting on a website asking for said communication was truly a shock. But she played it cool, fluttered her blue beauties and then checked her phone.

"What's it say?" Stuart asked

"It says, and all it says is 'I have a Dark Object.'"

A few seconds later an address was sent to her along with a rapidly-approaching time to meet and a very steep price for the Dark Object.

"They don't know whose trust fund they're dealing with," Giselle said, then made a finger gun and blew out the "smoke" which erased the coolness of her statement altogether.

"You're not actually going to go get that shit? Are you nuts? Yo, I better come with you."

"Awww, Stuart, come here for the hug."

They fell into each other's arms as dear friends are known to do. They embraced for a long while. Or they did until Stuart got hard and Giselle shoved him away.

Giselle told him, "You need to take Sofi's number, and if I'm not back then tell her where I am."

"The influencer with the nice ass? What's she gonna do if someone hurts you?"

Giselle thought long and hard about this. Finally, she offered, "Face sit them."

***

Giselle stood with hands clasped on backpack straps in front of a strange building in the Theatre District named "Castles." It was a building Giselle didn't feel fit New York; it was painted white and covered with red tiles. On the façade hung framed posters of plays Giselle had never heard of.

"I wonder if this person is an actor. I can beat up an actor probably if I have to. The drama kids at school weren't very badass."

This was Giselle's plan; throw money at the Dark Object owner and hope for the best. If that didn't work…well…Giselle played Street Fighter, and she knew how to fight.

Giselle pushed her way through the doors, which gave off the sound of an old man dying. It sent a wave of shivers running through Giselle's body. Still ever the brave one, she brought her Air Jordans forward to cross into the lobby.

There she found a popcorn machine caked in grime and dust, a snack counter also layered in dust, and the sound of music from the '40s playing from a cassette deck.

"Come to the theatre!" a bubbly female voice shouted. It reminded Giselle of Princess Maggie's.

Giselle clenched her fist Chun-Li style and headed into the theatre. There she found an expansive space with a vaulted ceiling covered by the image a beautiful blonde lounging on a half-moon.

"That's Nyx, the Greek Goddess of the Night," the voice noted.

Giselle still didn't see anyone. How could she when the stage's curtains were closed.

"I came about the Dark Object," Giselle stated.

"Of course you did, love! Just come to the stage," the female voice cooed.

Giselle had once played Juliet in Romeo and Juliet. But on opening night she fell off a makeshift balcony and got a concussion. Her understudy was said to have redefined middle school theatre with a captivating and mature performance.

The second Giselle stepped onto the stage she started thinking that it probably would have been prudent to drag along one of her supernatural roommates.

There was a cackling and crowing like a wild hen as the curtain gave way to a stage that boasted a metal platform that was holding up a wheel laden with cuffs and chains.

"Why helllooooo there!"

Giselle stepped forward, confused, and bumped into a tiny waif of a thing.

"Aah!" Giselle shouted.

"You know my name. Or my initials. Ashley Alison Holtz. AAH!" the petite young woman commented. She had big dark eyes and long black hair that flowed in a majestic river to her waist. She wore a schoolgirl outfit and looked to be about Giselle's age.

Giselle might not have been worried if Ashley's schoolgirl blazer hadn't boasted a patch that read "SKM."

"Did you know?" the young lady asked. "That there are several ways to die mountain climbing besides just falling."

"I did know that," Giselle spoke in a calm manner that betrayed her heaving nerves.

"Beware of falling rocks and dehydration! I have a spell for that—dehydration. I'm a witch, and I think you have a Dark Object for me."

Giselle gave a nervous tug of her white-blonde hair and replied, "I'm…"

Don't tell her your real name.

"Jiselle with a J."

Giselle, you genius.

Giselle with a J went on, "Uh, it's the other way around, Ashley. You're supposed to have the Dark Object for me."

"I lied!" Ashley said then flashed a huge cheesy smile. "Our boss is desperate to get a hold of some Dark Objects for some big demon spell. So I figured, if someone wanted one Dark Object they may have more. Do you have Dark Objects?"

"Just my dildos."

"I bet," Ashley cooed, twirling around the stage. "You're lying to me!" Ashley took a big leap and cleared the distance between herself and Giselle. "The last person who lied to me…I slit his throat! And he was a nice guy. I remember when he fixed my air conditioner."

The pain of such a memory opened a floodgate of tears that streaked down Ashley's cheeks to pool at the floor.

"Don't cry!" Giselle pleaded.

Ashley stopped crying as if she had never been crying in the first place.

"Uh, who's your employer? Maybe we know the same people?" Giselle ventured.

"Just some demon sorceress. I'm a witch. I shouldn't take orders from demon sorceresses. But that's what the SKM does. You're hot," Ashley noted. Though she was rubbing her chin like she had to consider it first. "Schwing!" Ashley shouted. " I reached all the way back to 1992 for that reference. Did you know pigs have sex for pleasure? That's why I don't eat pork. We're denying Piglet the right to hook up with every cold cut."

"You're all the way woke, bro,"

"I was banned from Twitter for threatening to kill this influencer when she didn't retweet my Merry Christmas wish to her. Does that make me sexier to you?"

Giselle remembered one of Sofi's posts asking if a woman can talk herself out of the dick. Well, this woman was talking herself out of the pussy.

"You know I need to go and, uh, buy textbooks for school? So, yeah, good luck with your search, chief."

Giselle yelped as if it stung by a bee. Except there was no bee in sight. What happened was that a pair of cuffs fell upon each of her wrists. It took Giselle a moment to process that the cuffs came from the chains attached to the wheeled device on the platform. It took a second moment to realize the chains had moved on their own. It took a third moment to realize the chains moved on the snap of Ashley.

"The snapping isn't necessary. They're telepathically linked to me. But snapping is fun!" Ashley declared.

A further click of Ashley's fingers and Giselle slammed against the wheel. Her breath popped out of her mouth the second she hit.

She began struggling to get down. Yet she could make no gains with the chains holding her tight against the wheel.

"I was planning to kill whoever I lured here after I got the Dark Object. But you have no Dark Object, and to be honest, you're just too hot! I won't eat pigs and I won't kill hot people unless they're my ex-boyfriend. I have a few ideas on how to kill that chump. A girl is sexy when she's dangerous so you have to be extra turned on right now."

"I honestly haven't been this turned on since I found sex mods for the Sims," Giselle lied.

"Isn't it disappointing when people aren't as hot as their Sim? My mom said my dad could only cum when she cried. Isn't that romantic? I'm the same. I can only cum when you cry," Ashely decided, focusing on Giselle's chest.

There was a generous expanse of boobage for Ashley to grab, and she let Giselle's left orb engulf her questing hand.

"It's overflowing," Ashley remarked. "And look at your adorable face! Aiiiiie such a slut! I bet it's the hottest even through a heart attack. Lucky me!"

Ashley kneaded Giselle's ample bosom the way one might knead dough. The raven-haired witch used her body weight to push Giselle's left tit into itself, welling it up into an oversized blob. A yelp escaped Giselle's lips as Ashley let her fingers snap onto her hardened nipples.

"Eeep!" Giselle squealed

"Did that hurt?" Ashley asked.

"A pixie once told me sex is pain."

"Isn't it though?"

Ashley giggled to herself as she hefted Giselle's right breast. The jug was big enough to bonk Giselle in the face, which Ashley found funny, but Giselle certainly did not. Then her left breast was heaved, Ashley holding it firm to feel the full weight.

"There's nothing better than a freshly ripened woman!" Ashley announced

Ashley fingers seized both of Giselle's nipples in a pincer-like grip. It was enough to cause Giselle to whimper in pain. That whimper did nothing to put the shackles on Ashley's molestation. Instead, the witch used Giselle's nipples as levers to bounce both her titans to her immense glee.

"Boingy bits! Boingy bits!" Ashley hollered in delight.

Again, Giselle whimpered as Ashley made a rough go of rolling her tits. To Giselle, she likened Ashley's frenzied groping to an alien who had never known the blessed greatness of giant boobage.

"Sometimes," Ashley began, "At this stage, I tell my lovers I have a penis as a little prank. People say I'm good at killing the mood. I can't figure out why."

Gisele could figure out why. It was because this girl was annoying as hell.

Ashley forced her tongue through Giselle's mouth in a harsh kiss. Fortunately, it had the effect of shutting the SKM member up. Yet, Ashley still moaned into Giselle's mouth, filling her with chilled, delicious breath. Giselle couldn't tell if Ashley was moaning in pleasure or trying to provide more commentary. Moans of pleasure was the better guess as Ashley began grinding her body against Giselle's. Given Ashley's petite size, Giselle felt almost like an Amazon being molested and slobbered into by particularly horny bunny. The waif couldn't control herself as she began grinding her figure into Giselle's stacked one; she seemed to savor the feel of Giselle's golden globes against her smaller ones.

Ashley began sucking Giselle's tongue into her mouth as if she were performing oral on a guy. The witch's wandering hands found Giselle's rear end and pressed against her voluptuous butt. Her ass groped, and her tongue sucked. Giselle's eyes began fluttering. Her moans joined with Ashley, who let loose her sounds of delight around Giselle's tongue.

Giselle could only wonder what more babble could fall out of Ashley's mouth as the SKM witch pulled back from the kiss.

"Do you wanna hear about my dream where I was a walrus who became an astronaut?" Ashley asked, voice full of excitement.

Sex was pain but did it have to be torture too?

Ashley was saying something about how hard astronaut training was without any hands. While cursing Giselle with this inane chatter, Ashley glided across a stiffened nipple with her finger. Then she flicked her finger back and forth over the bud.

"Like a light switch!" Ashley commented.

Ashley rabidly fondled Giselle with a need that rivaled something animalistic. The raven-haired babe's throbbing sex dripped, leaking an astonishing amount, and her body pulsated heat, despite her telling the portion of the walrus dream where an Iranian terrorist tried to hijack the spacecraft.

"Hold, villain!" came a booming yet flowery voice Giselle knew all too well.

It was Krisdane, attired in a black polo with all-over embroidery of roses and cotton military shorts with a navy stripe. At his side stood Sofi, wearing an iridescent lime mini-dress with exaggerated sleeves.

Krisdane announced, "I cannot allow a wild beast like you to torment Giselle a second longer."

"Asshole to the extreme!" Ashley whined. "Back off, pretty boy, I'm with SKM."

"Fantastic," Prince Krisdane replied. "I will not be killing anyone decent."

"I normally don't kill hot people, but you're working on my last nerve. Who are you?" Ashley snapped.

Prince Krisdane didn't answer at first. Instead, he calmly removed his shirt. It left bare a well-defined abdomen that would have

Giselle drooling under better circumstances. More importantly, it whisked away his magical glamour to allow his elf ears to stand on display.

"You're a pure elf!" Ashley shouted, voice rich with nervousness.

"He's actually a prince, honey," Sofi noted. "So unless you want to get on the bad side of the most powerful family on earth, you need to take your messy, offbrand ass and dip on out of here."

Sofi had barely finished speaking before Ashley made herself disappear in a cloud of smoke.

Even as the mist lingered on the stage, Prince Krisdane ran to Giselle to being prying her off Ashley's contraption.

Just then a heady rush came to Giselle. A sort of blissful shot of adrenaline that she figured could only come from being saved by Prince Charming.

"Your friend Slash told me you went to get a Dark Object," Sofi chimed in while checking her phone.

"Stuart. Slash is in Guns N Roses. Anyway, thank you guys! You saved me from whatever that was."

"That was quite foolish of you to pursue a Dark Object on your own," Prince Krisdane commented glumly.

Giselle hated to disappoint him, hated to seem weak in his presence. He had grown up beside warrior princesses. He wanted a woman who ate lightning and crapped thunder.

"But, I mean, I beat a goat man. I just figured the supernatural world would be on easy mode for me."

Prince Krisdane let out a chuckle that was anything but mirthful. He turned away from Giselle and said, "Giselle, I am 22 elf years old and 44 human years old. I have never seen an easy mode in the supernatural world. Sofi, have you seen this easy mode?"

"I wish. It's so annoying having to show up to the dry cleaners with blood on your ballgown. Like, it'd be better if they found child porn in your pocket."

Giselle rubbed her wrists and nodded with heart-shaped lips forming a frown.

"Were you able to obtain a Dark Object?" The prince wondered.

Giselle shook her head and went onto explain the situation with SKM, who Ashley was, the Dark Objects, and SKM's employer.

"Hmph, a witch," Sofi scoffed. "She's lucky she ran. A pure elf and a fox spirit would have bodied her."

"What do you think about the whole let's imprison Prince Gorick in a totally untested and probably pretty dangerous magic prison?" Giselle asked Prince Charming.

Prince Krisdane started to talk, the word "Gorick" spilling out of his mouth. But then he only passed out a heavy sigh. His head shook, and his tumble of gorgeous curls shook with it.

Giselle felt a buzz in her pocket, and dread fell upon her. Being submerged in Ashley's insanity had distracted her from her phone. Now that she was up for air in the safety of Prince Krisdane, she saw her mom had texted her fifteen times. The subject? Whether Giselle would stay in New York. The ignoring of over a dozen texts probably did nothing to win Dawn over to the "Giselle is mature enough to be on her own" cause.

"Hey, look, that chick dropped something," Sofi said, picking up a business card. "Dean Lorne Pederson, Hemera University. And on the back it says, handwritten, see me soon, beautiful."

Giselle smiled to herself. The danger of SKM, the annoyance of Ashley had all led to another lead.

Chapter Eight: Ride Or Die

In. Up. Hop. In. Up. Hop. In. Up. Hop.

"Goodness!" Princess Tristabelle exclaimed to Sofi, whose movement she was imitating, "I have mastered this charming American dance. As I knew I would."

Sofi grumbled over Saint JHN's "Trap" as Princess Tristabelle executed the dance moves for a filming Dusty with envy-inducing ease.

Too envy-inducing for Sofi, who abruptly snatched her phone out of Dusty's hand. This video was supposed to be thrown onto Sofi's TikTok, but it would soon be thrown into the digital garbage due to Sofi being upstaged.

"Whatever is wrong? Princess Tristabelle asked, still dancing flawlessly.

"You're too good," Sofi whined, looking Princess Tristabelle up and down. The princess wore a golden mini-skirt to show off a glorious amount of her bronzed legs and tank top that her holy grails were struggling to stay inside of.

"She's a dance major and a championship figure skater," Dusty noted, "What do you expect her to dance like?"

Sofi placed her hands on her hips. She was adorned in a skimpy bikini bottom that left most of her thick ass bare and a white top that was hoisted up to create an eye-popping amount of underboob.

"Princess T, you're upstaging me. I'm Spongebob, and you're more Larry Lobster in this arrangement."

"Ah yes, bobbing for sponges! A great American game played on Halloween!" Princess Tristabelle commented, not getting the reference

Sofi then turned to Giselle, who was lying on the cream-colored sofa while playing her Switch. "Giselle, you dance too."

"Uh-uh, I only dance in rhythm games," Giselle commented, not looking up from her Switch as Tyr sat on her shoulder.

"Exactly!" Sofi declared. "Why should I make an effort to get better at dancing when I can simply make myself look better by having a shittier partner."

"Sofi, ya goof, you shoulda asked me to dance with ya," Dusty pointed out, passing Sofi's phone back to her. "Can't nobody dance like the fae. My mama was a Nymph in Fairy Revolutoon Wrestling. Us girls put on gowns, and costumes that sparkle like moonlight. The men dress in acorns and bark. And we got a dance for everything. And when we dance, we make flowers sparkle and cause the leaves to change colors."

"Pretty sure you can do all that with IG filters anyway," Sofi replied as she snapped a selfie in front of the living room window that overlooked New York.

Filters schmilters! Dusty swiveled her hips and ground her tiny body to the blaring hip hop. Her gigantic jugs jiggled and bounced, which would be a thrilling sight on its own. But as she writhed and cupped her breasts, the Bonzai tree by the installation of the Hindu goddess Maya began glowing pink.

At that, Giselle could only exclaim, "I thought that plant was artificial!"

"Do you sluts hear that?" came Fleur's Boston accent as the muscular babe entered the room attired in teen tiny booty exposing shorts with a rhinestone cross on the side.

"Hear what?" Sofi asked, after lowering the volume of the music.

"That rattling noise," Fleur snapped with an explosive wave of her hand.

"What rattling noise?" Giselle questioned.

"That!" Fleur exclaimed, crossing to the center of the room. "Don't you hear that shit?"

"Maybe it's the Psycho Wave killer returning to torment Hemera students after five years in hiding," Giselle stated rather ominously. Though her ominous statement was ruined by her squealing at finding a heart power-up in Super Mario Odyessy.

"This is pissing me off. How do you not hear that?" Fleur snapped with another explosive hand wave.

"Because we ain't vampires," Dusty chimed in. "Ya'll got better senses than any supernatural besides a werewolf."

RATTTTTTTTTTTLE!   RATTTTTTTTLLLEEEEE! RATTTTTTTLLLEEE!

Suddenly as if it were gunfire, the noise that was driving Fleur to madness could be heard by all. It became so loud, so oppressive in its volume that Helen Keller could have heard it.

"It sounds like it's in the vent," Giselle pointed out, trembling. Though not trembling and scared enough to stop playing Mario.

A grey mist began spewing forth from the vent. It was a thick and terrible thing, pouring into the living room at an alarming rate. Eventually, the haze settled into the room as though it were ruling over it.

"Aiyo, what the fuck?" Fleur grumbled.

The haze started to take a shape no one had expected it to take. It solidified into a motorcycle with wheels made of ice. From its base grew a rider, a muscular man bound in leather straps that even covered a face made of ice. He had no mouth, but still managed to speak.

"I'm the Ice Rider here to rock and roll! I took a bad turn on a road in Alberta, but the great president of Hell, Ose, gave me new life as a demon! I've been summoned to Earth and my master sent me for the Dark Objects!"

"For the record I'm Dusty Blackwood," Dusty spoke, her big doe eyes glaring at the Ice Rider, "and I'm not about to let some fifty-cent jackass come in and steal from my queen."

"Hell yeah! I like that attitude!" the Ice Rider proclaimed. "My master warned me about you all so hand over the Dark Objects and I won't crush ya!"

"You ain't getting no Dark Objects, you ugly bastard!" Dusty snapped.

"My master told me I couldn't lay a finger on any of you," the Ice Rider spoke with a shake of the head, "but I can lay some big wheels, baby!"

"For fuck's sake," Fleur complained.

The Ice Rider revved his bike as he made an insufferable noise that seemed like laughter. His bike sped towards Dusty, who narrowly avoided it. Instead, the bike shred through the cream-colored chair.

"Awwww yeah, I love violence!" the Ice Rider shouted. "Mayhem, murder, I'm here for it!"

"Great, now we've got a psycho ice demon thing tearing up the furniture when I was about to watch the Red Sox game," Fleur complained.

The muscular brunette leaped onto The Ice Rider's back, a move that had him comment, "Now you look like a regular biker chick."

"I was on the cover of Easy Rider magazine in October 1989," Fleur stated plainly.

"This ain't a pool hall or tattoo parlor, honey, but we can still get it on."

"What in the sweet sparkling fuck did I do to deserve that?" Fleur questioned.

The Ice Rider quickly soured on Fleur as his passenger. Suddenly the brakes were hit, causing Fleur to hurl into the wall.. Even with vampiric durability, Fleur groaned in pain.

"That is misogynistic," Sofi commented.

The devilish criminal whirled upon Sofi, who made a graceful leap to avoid the attack. Instead of lacerating Sofi, the creature tore apart the bonsai tree with his lethal wheels but missed the crystal installation of the goddess Maya. More importantly, he would have torn Giselle in half if it weren't for Princess Tristabelle pulling her out of the way.

"This is fucking awesome!" the Hell Rider announced. "You chicks know how to party!"

Sofi had converted herself to fox form, a red beauty with a flaming tail. She launched a fireball from that tail that the Ice Rider and his bike slid bellow. This caused the fireball to smack Princess Tristabelle square in the face. But the Princess had the cheery reaction and physical effect of being hit in the face with a pleasant spritz of perfume.

"Violence is like my oxygen!" the Ice Rider roared. "I live off this shit!"

He turned his attention to Giselle, who hurriedly dove over the couch. She almost landed on Tyr, whom she then sought to protect underneath her body.

Fleur was on an intercept course with the Ice Rider and collided with him just as he got to the couch. His wheels shore off the armrest while the bike careened towards Dusty.

The diminutive pixie threw out a kick that connected with the Ice Rider right on the jaw and flung him from his bike. The bike careened into the wall, shredding holes through it as it impaled itself into their home.

The Ice Rider rose quickly but was wobbly and disoriented.

Dusty was far from finished. She grabbed the surprised biker as he rose with one of her arms around his upper body. She then lifted him up and slammed him through the coffee table to create a cacophony of shattering glass and the Ice Rider's wails of distress. Pieces of glass erupted upward before settling on the tangled mess of pixie and demon.

"Would you like to know something about us, my dear Ice Rider?" Princess Tristabelle asked, with her cupid's bow lips in a smile. "We too love violence. Simply adore it. And believe me, no one will derive as much pleasure from this as I."

Those wails became chilling screams of horror as Princess Tristabelle proceeded to stomp the Ice Rider's head until it separated into a sprawling collection of jagged ice shards.

The girls didn't even have a moment to celebrate before they heard the sound of Dawn Nyfall arriving into the living room.

"Eeep!" Giselle squealed.

Dawn dropped her grocery bags to the floor, looked around, saw a motorcycle with ice wheels, a destroyed wall, a headless man, a fox with a flaming tail, a short eighteen-year-old covered in glass, destroyed furniture and shouted, "What the fuck happened here?"

Fleur spat blood on the floor and casually answered, "Rats."

Chapter Nine: Nothing Was The Same

The grey accent rug. The grey dusted ceiling, the grey cushioned seats built into the wall, the grey wall-length night sky painting. Her room at the condo was such a monochromatic place to die in, Giselle thought.

She was surely going to die because her mom was about to kill her.

Dawn Nyfall had been pacing in her Alexander Wang sneakers and chewing on the inside of her cheek. These were the two key features of what Giselle called "ginger doom" mode. Except that the doom wrought upon Giselle wouldn't be a lengthy lecture with the weight of guilt, it would be permadeath.

Giselle was sure of it.

Except Dawn paused in the middle of the room, faced her daughter, who was leaning forward on the bed and whispered, "Sofi is a fox spirit?"

Those were the first words Dawn had said since Giselle fed Dawn the barest portion of the supernatural meal Giselle was feasting on.

"Uh, yeah. The Japanese call it a kitsune."

"What does that mean? Spirit? Is she real?"

"She's real! Just don't ask her to give blood or donate any organs because that's uh…not there."

"And Dusty is a pixie from the fairy kingdom??"

"She should be a fairy, but the fairy council said she's too violent."

"Clearly. And this fairy kingdom is in Nashville?"

"It's kind of outside Earth. like in Fire Emblem Fates when you're in Nohr or whatever but you can also go outside of Nohr and go to the Deep Realms."

"Giselle, you know I haven't the slightest idea what any of that is supposed to mean. Is her father really a wrestler?"

"He wrestles for Fairy Revolution Wrestling."

"The fairies have their own wrestling show?"

"They also have their own Big Brother. And her mother is the Tooth Fairy."

"I don't know how to process that information. And Fleur is half-vampire, half-succusomething?"

"Succubus."

"Which is a demon."

"Yup."

"Well, I could have figured her for being that on my own. And that sweet Laz, her father, is Lazarus from the Bible?"

"He tricked people into thinking Jesus raised him from the dead. The real story is that he caught a supernatural STD which made him the first vampire in history."

"Naturally. But there's something else you're not telling me about Fleur."

"Don't freak out—"

"That's a big request."

"She's Satan's granddaughter."

"She's what?!"

"I hear he's a really chill guy and super unproblematic."

Dawn put her hands to her cheeks and dragged them down very slowly as if she were performing a delicate tearing of her skin.

There were a good twenty seconds before Dawn spoke, "And Princess Tristabelle and her brother and sister are elves."

"Pure elves."

"Elves have pointy ears, but those three don't."

"An astute observation!" Giselle declared, waving her finger through the air. "They use magical items to create the illusion that they have human ears."

Dawn clasped her hands together, squeezing them until the knuckles turned white, "And all the Elvrinas are elves. And Golden Land is a supernatural fairytale kingdom. How is all this a secret? Why aren't I getting alerts from the L.A. Times about a magical fairytale kingdom and Satan's granddaughter running wild?"

"There's supernaturals in the governments who keep the humans in the dark."

"So those people who say the President's cabinet is made up of lizard men are close to the truth," Dawn let out a rueful chuckle. "But you said elves are only in Golden Land."

"Right. Like you can only find a Jigglypuff on Route 115 in Pokemon Ruby."

"Giselle, please use plain adult English. Why are three elves in New York City now?"

"Well, Princess Tristabelle just came to live a normal school girl slice of life manga. But she had a brother who tried to usurp the throne. She kind of foiled his attempt and not like Scooby Doo and the gang kind of foiled but like near decapitation foiled, and he got exiled. So he's promised to kill her, and he's maybe in America, or that's what Princess Maggie's locator spell says, but I'm just gonna be honest for a moment, I don't think she's a very good witch."

"There are witches?"

"And werewolves, and sorcerers, and orcs and doppelgangers and dwarves, and gnomes, and—"

"Stop!" Dawn shouted so loud Giselle thought she would rattle the night sky painting off its hook. "Did that Anika woman know what these girls were before she put you in this situation?"

Giselle fell back on the bed as if shot. A grand reaction, the type she usually gave when Dawn pressed her and she couldn't bring herself to lie.

"I'm going to kill that woman," Dawn decided.

"Killing will not bring you peace. That's what Professor Xavier told Magneto in *X-Men First Class.*"

"Pack your bags. It's time to go home."

"What? No!"

"No? Did you think I'm going to let you stay in New York after you told me this? You just got attacked by a... a... a...demon!"

Giselle picked her body back up. She had to be brave and mature,

"I can name four mothers who would let their daughters stay."

"Are those going to be the four moms hugging me at your funeral and telling me how I had such a beautiful and brave daughter?"

"I'm not going to die," Giselle said, pumping her fist in defiance.

"No, you're not going to die because you're coming back to California with me and away from this... this... this... utter insanity!"

***

Fleur slammed back her second shot of brandy then slammed the glass on the monochromatic island that was the centerpiece of the condo's luxury kitchen.

"I ain't apologizing," Fleur decided.

"Where's your brain, you redhead idiot?" Fleur had barked at Sofi.

"The hell you ain't," Dusty snapped as she too took down a second drink. Only hers was a Capri Sun.

"You wanna bet I'm gonna apologize?"

"That there is a bet you can't win, Fleur Flannagan. I swear to god you're gonna apologize."

"Swear to god all you want, it won't matter because I'm a demon."

"You put our address online so your followers could send you shit and look what happened! You left us open to an attack from every fuckface and shithead in New York," Fleur had yelled at Sofi which sent Sofi running out of the condo.

"I've been alive for a century, and never in one of those days did I say sorry," Fleur grumbled.

"Today ain't like yesterday, it ain't like the day before, and it ain't like the day before that. Because today you're gonna apologize."

"Why should I?"

"Because we got a lot of enemies out there and we ain't got a lot of friends. How many friends do you have?"

"In the immortal words of Tupac Shakur, I ain't got no motherfucking friends."

"My name is Dusty Blackwood and I ain't got no friends neither 'cept the ones in this condo. Now rather it's tonight or rather it's next week, Dusty Blackwood is gonna get her hands around Prince Gorick and whoever else has been messing with us, and I'm gonna do it with you by my side, and I'm gonna do it with Sofi by my side."

"You wanna bet?"

Dusty almost threw her Capri Sun at Fleur but controlled herself to say, "I ain't betting you on whether I'm gonna fight someone. Go find Sofi and apologize, and before I get real mad!"

Fleur buried her head against the island, letting her chocolate locks fall all over the place, "Jeez, okay, okay. I'll apologize."

***

"But, mom!" Giselle whined.

"But, mom? Wake up, Giselle, this isn't a video game. You don't get to hit the reset button when things get bad."

"Video game consoles don't have reset buttons anymore and haven't for a long time."

"Who cares about that? Honestly, Giselle. Why would you even want to be in a world where you are in danger of being attacked by demons, werewolves, vampires, and who the hell knows what else? What could be the benefit of you, Giselle, living in this world?"

Giselle took a sharp intake of breath before stating in the softest of tones, "I defeated a demon. I mean, he was just the principal demon of Sloth, so I'm guessing he was pretty lazy but I beat him."

Now it was Dawn's turn to take a sharp intake of breath.

"I threw Big Stense pills into his mouth and choked him back to hell."

For a moment Dawn blinked in astonishment, "The erection pills they sell at the gas station?"

"Anika says I shouldn't have been able to defeat him, but I did."

Dawn didn't move an inch. Not her grey eyes. Not her clasped hands. Not her mouth. Nothing.

"It was at the carnival the school had. He was trapped in the mirror universe but was reaching for me. I was scared. But I beat him."

"And you think you can beat this Prince Gorick? Because you have penis pills?"

"I'm not going anywhere near that guy! I'm helping to get the Dark Objects we need to magically imprison him."

"Why does a girl who wet the bed until she was twelve—"

"Eleven!"

"Twelve. Why does she need to help the gold standard of supernatural do anything?"

"Because I'm resourceful, mom. I got the two Dark Objects we have, and it was my idea that got them working. The pure elves are like, uh, what's a reference you would get. They're more like The Hulk; they wreck things. They don't figure out things. They break things and people."

"So we as humans are at the mercy of an all-powerful country of omnipotent pagan elves?

"Fleur says to be glad it's not an all-powerful country of radically Islamist elves."

Dawn didn't want to, but she smiled anyway.

Giselle was about to lay plain her defeat of the goat monster when the sudden swinging of her door trampled that. Mother and daughter turned their head to find Krisdane, body tensed with worry, standing in front of them.

"Your Highness?" Dawn asked, confused.

***

The restaurant at least had the awesomeness to be playing "Jumpman" by Drake and Future as Sofi sat outdoors underneath a yellow umbrella and sipped on a mimosa.

The restaurant was named Ellen Choo's. Orange umbrellas were placed in front of the diner and stood behind pots with an angelic motif and pink shrubbery. The way the shrubbery was set made it look like the trumpeting angels were expelling pink bursts of color. This establishment had marked the start of the girls' adventures with the cursed millionaires and billionaires.

It had seemed odd to Sofi how they had been forced off the trail of that curse and into a war with an exiled prince.

But, Sofi didn't have to worry about that any longer. She looked over at a table of wrinkled old women who blended into each other forming one wrinkled face and thought about how she'd never grow old. She would be eternally beautiful, like her mother. When she reached her mother's age, would she have forgotten about her brief friendship with the vampire-succubus hybrid, the pure elf, the pixie and the human that had just come to an end?

It had to come to an end, because obviously, Sofi had endangered them all putting up her address for followers to send her things.

Sofi was half paying attention to a report on the Youtube channel "Hemera Highlights" about the freshman camping trip—a trip she would miss as she was about to say a bitter farewell to New York City and Hemera.

That's why she was surprised to see Fleur Flannagan in her daisy dukes, Motorhead shirt, and black ribbon in her hair approach. Fleur gave the impression of being a rocker from the '80s. Sofi always assumed the '80s had been Fleur's favorite decade.

"Sup," Fleur said, her big pale blue eyes cast downward.

Sofi's long pink lips tried to form a smile but failed.

Fleur sat down on the chair backward, which made her look like a delinquent from an '80s teen comedy.

"I said some shit," Fleur began. "that was uncalled for. So if you got smoke for me then I deserve it."

"Are you saying sorry?" Sofi asked, shocked.

The Hemera Highlight news report switched to discussing the fifth anniversary of the Psycho Wave killings.

"I don't think I'm physically capable of speaking those words but the spirit is there. So, look, just come back to the condo. I don't know what time Dusty and Tristabelle are on but we're in way over our head. You don't fight Belephegor, SKM, Mermeut, The Ice Rider and Gorick Golden and not take a loss somewhere. We are overdue to get our asses beat. You're the only one of us who can't actually die, which makes you pretty useful."

"You said it was my fault we got attacked by that biker."

The restaurant began to play "Fucking Problems" by A$AP Rocky and Fleur's doll face lit up.

"I say a lot of shit. You know I'm not allowed in the Philippines because I told the president he had a small dick. I've never seen his dick but I said it. But look, you're the Drake of this arrangement."

"I am?" Sofi asked.

"Hell yes. We're all on the track but it's you, Drake, you're the star."

"I am the only one who can shapeshift."

"Yes!"

"And I can shoot flames from my tail."

"Yes!"

"And I'm immortal!"

"Yes!"

"And I'm hot."

"I love bad bitches, that's my fucking problem."

Sofi shrugged and said, "I guess I can come back to the condo. You girls do sort of need me."

Fleur pounded the table in delight so hard the mass of wrinkled faces looked over at her.

Fleur commented, "Fuck Drake. You're the GOAT, you're Larry Bird."

"Who's Larry Bird?"

Fleur shot up out of the chair like Sofi told her she gave her an STD, "Who the fuck is Larry motherfucking Bird?! Uh..forget that...let's just stick with the Drake thing."

Sofi's long pink lips finally managed to form their smile.

***

Prince Krisdane took a knee and pulled Giselle's hands into his. They were warm and soft and felt like taking a bath with a mug of hot chocolate,

He said, "Giselle, I was told over the magic mirror by Tristabelle a demon attacked you. The Christian underworld smiled upon that beast for if I had been present, we would have danced to the lengthy opera of his death throes."

"Don't worry about it, Prince Krisdane. Your sister stomped him out. I was just telling my mom pretty much everything. I mean everything."

Krisdane tugged on his brown curls, eyes shut, deep in thought.

"Lady Dawn, your daughter is under royal protection. Myself, and Princess Tristabelle have sworn to be her shield. Even...Prince Trygyrr shields Giselle. Somehow."

"Why?" Dawn asked sharply. "You're the most powerful people on earth. What do you get out of worrying about one human girl."

Giselle had a sudden, unexplainable, excellent feeling about this. Like she was hit with a meteor strike of red roses.

"She is not one human girl," he stated with his hand to his heart. "She is Giselle Nyfall."

Dawn seemed to have a tidal wave of understanding sweep over her as she nodded for what seemed like a very long time. Finally, she said, "Two questions. What do I tell your father? And how can I help your fight?"

Giselle's heart-shaped lips formed a shocked O.

Chapter Ten: Donations, donations, donations!

Giselle Nyfall peered at the Jay Copeland building on the Hemera Campus. The same semi-gothic, semi-modern structure that housed the office of Dean Lorne Pederson. Her bold blue eyes took in what she considered to be a video game dungeon. In her mind she knew she had the perfect party for a quest.

Dawn Nyfall. Class: sage.

Princess Maggie Elvrina. Class: witch.

Prince Krisdane Elvrina. Class: knight.

Princess Tristabelle Elvrina. Class: dark knight

Giselle Nyfall. Class: MOTHERFUCKING HERO, BITCHES!

"Squeal!" Giselle shouted as she clung onto her mother's arm.

Some mothers and daughters went on shopping trips. Some went to the hairdresser together. The Nyfall girls were out to snag themselves a Dark Object.

After that hot furious surface that was Dawn's anger had been cooled by Kirsdane the previous day, it was left to Dawn to do an about-face with Stephen Nyfall, Giselle's dad. Dawn had to recommend their daughter stay in New York. Generally, Stephen was accepting of any and everything his wife told him. Thus he gleefully accepted Dawn's declaring it would be best for Giselle's mental health and her prospects that she attend Hemera. He didn't even bother to ask why Dawn had come to that decision or what influenced the sudden switch of opinions. He merely wished his daughter luck, told her to take lots of pictures, and decided to increase the limit on her credit cards. Just in time for the start of the fall semester.

There was a question in Dawn's mind of how exactly the royals would protect Giselle from the vile elements that bubbled around the girls. When Princess Tristabelle summoned her magic sword, Msitlewoe, Dawn's worries abated.

Being the inquisitive sort, Dawn pressed the royals for all the information she could gather on their family and the species of elves. Prince Krisdane said the elven race was old enough to be fossils. They were once revered and feared by the Germanic people as gods. Maggie said that pure elves could not tolerate vileness, which thanks to the humans' destruction of earth meant they could feel the pain of the planet.

As for the royal family itself, Princess Tristabelle said they inhabit a world of sexual excess, sibling rivalry, petty intrigues, militaristic sadism towards evil; a world where dwarves were tossed, monsters were battled for sport, criminals were beheaded, where humans were executed without trial, and peasants prostrate themselves for favor. Yet it was a family that had kept the earth realm safe for more than a millennia.

Prince Krisdane explained that the Goldeb Land government functioned with the crown as an all-powerful ruler. Succession was typically hereditary. However, the ruler was free to choose his or her successor from any one of the Elvrina lot. Great clans ruled over specific territories with the only cities in Golden Land being the seats of power of those great clans. Some clans were elves, but others were ruled by vampires, werewolves, witches, or dwarves. They began in Golden Land merely as tribes who immigrated to be free of the human world and rose to power at the will of the Elvrina kings and queens.

"Squeal, squeaaaaaa!" Giselle shouted, still gripping her mom's arm.

"Giselle, if you don't take this seriously I'm going to send you back to the condo. Now can we review the plan? I'll distract the dean and lure him out of his office. You four will enter his office and search for a Dark Object?"

Giselle nodded eagerly.

Dawn added, "He probably has an assistant you would have to distract."

"No problem!" Princess Maggie exclaimed, with a toss of her golden curls. "Big ol' sis has the solution and his name is Prince Charming."

The thought of Prince Krisdane charming another woman almost turned Giselle into an obstreperous wreck. But as they say in hockey, "you have to take a hit to make a play," so Giselle kept calm and quiet and focused on nice things. Like Princess Tristabelle's hooters. That was until Dawn caught her staring at them and nudged her.

"And you know Dean Pederson has a Dark Object because Ashley the witch told you?" Dawn questioned.

"Not exactly," Giselle responded. "Ashley was looking for Dark Objects and dropped a personal note from the dean. So two plus two equals four, five times five equals twenty...wait no that's not right!"

"Nevermind," Dawn said, following with a sigh. "Are we ready?"

"Lady Dawn, you are the bait upon our hook," Princess Tristabelle stated firmly. "You should take the lead."

"Right," Dawn started. "And Giselle behave yourself."

Solid advice. However, Giselle was too busy staring at Princess Tristballe's boobs to hear it.

***

Dean Lorne Pederson's office was presided over by a chubby but cute student named Anita Cotton. The office she sat in was surrounded by pictures of the dean with various celebrities, politicians, and socialites, some of whom had graduated from Hemera. Between these pictures were framed poems written by the dean.

Dawn felt a tinge of revulsion bubbling up as her searching grey eyes took in this ode to the dean's ego.

Nonetheless, she was able to pleasantly tell his chubby assistant, "My name is Dawn Nyfall. My daughter is attending Hemera for her freshman year. I'd like to talk to Dean Pederson about my husband and I making a substantial donation to—"

As if the Kool-Aid man burst through the wall, a short round bald man with beady eyes burst through the door behind the assistant.

"Donations?" The beady-eyed man asked, turning his round head around the room. "Donations! DONATIONS!"

Dawn stepped back toward the door on nervous instinct, "Yes, my husband and I would like to make a gift to the school. And my daughter would like to start an e-sports team."

"Gifts! Gifts! GIFTS!" the man exclaimed, rubbing his hands together like a dope fiend.

Then he did something Dawn never would have expected. His cracked, chapped lips began planting kisses from her hand up to her elbow. As he pulled back, it was only then he noticed Dawn milk wagon's in a low-cut top. His beady eyes nearly bulged from his rotund face.

"I donated twenty dollars to the student meal assistance program, Dean Pederson, " Anita said with pep in her voice.

"Next time make it twenty-five," Dean Pederson instructed with a finger wag. Then he turned onto Dawn, those ugly lips filling into a big grin. "Allow this humble, humble, humble man to take you on a tour of Hemera and show you all the great things I have accomplished. I kept the students safe during the Psycho Wave murders. I have designed the campus to make it so we're good stewards of New York City. I made it so students from poor backgrounds could attend my prestigious institution. Let me show you all the great things I have done."

Dawn felt she was about to puke, but managed to smile and nod.

When the dean took his arm around hers, her urge to puke rose to the highest heights since Giselle made that tuna casserole. Yet off they went with Dawn's stomach roiling.

It took about a minute after the dean left for the most handsome man Anita had ever seen to slide through the door.

Prince Krisdane fluffed his brown locks as he innocently peered about the room.

"Forgive me, I think I may have entered the wrong room. But now..."

Prince Krisdane was so hot that the woman could only amass words that possessed no vowels. "Ghdhdh? Bhdhddh?" Anita stammered.

"I am sorry I will leave in a moment. But, well, I hope this is not too bold," Prince Krisdane said, purple eyes cast down demurely. "I need you."

Prince Krisdane was wearing a black and white polka dot polo shirt that clung to his hardbody and glamoured his elf ears away along with slim-fitting black pants.

Prince Krisdane was so hot that Anita's words were reduced to incoherent mumbling. She sounded like an eggplant might if it could talk.

"You can help me complete my current song. I feel a beauty radiating from your spirit. A beauty like no other. Please come with me."

Prince Krisdane extended his hand forward. She took it in an instant, matching Dean Pederson's donations inspired smile. Though if Prince Krisdane extended a bag of shit she would have taken it. Together they left the room and Anita's duties behind.

Within moments the blonde triumvirate—or what Fleur had deemed the supernatural Aryan Nation—swooped in.

Maggie's huge crystal blue eyes, which slanted more than her sister's looked around the room, "Let's take a simple approach and tear everything to pieces! If anything bad happens, I'll protect all of ya like I protected the King Olafgar Port from those zombie pirates."

Princess Tristabelle asked, "Would that be the time you overflowed the bathtub playing with rubber ducks and destroyed a 700-year-old painting?"

"That time exactly!" The ditzy princess declared.

"We all break things when we're little, Princess Tristabelle," Giselle stated.

"That was three weeks ago," Princess Tristabelle noted with a disparaging shake of her head that waved her blonde bob.

"Let's try and be careful," Giselle commented. "Dean Pederson might be the employer of the SKM who is looking for Dark Objects. He might even have a patron demon of dark magic!"

"Eh, I doubt we have much to worry about," Maggie commented with a shoulder shrug.

"Death flag alert! Death flag alert!" Giselle shrieked. "Take that back, take that back!"

Princess Tristabelle just sighed as if asking the Allfather what she had done to be saddled with such dramatic, such inapt help. The almond set eyes of the princess were rolling as she pushed the door to the Dean's office open.

The office was a less than humble ode to the man who sung his praises continuously. He had nerve enough to have a statue of himself resting in the far right corner. It stood near a bookshelf that housed many books he owned to look smart but never actually read, and his series of leadership books, which in turn had been read by about 30 people total. Across two decades. And the readers were related to him. And six of them were illiterate.

"We should be quick," Giselle stated. "I don't want a similar incident to my disasterbation of senior year."

"Disasterbation?" Princess Maggie responded.

"I thought the drama room was gonna be empty, and that IG model was looking so thick. But then those pesky middle schoolers showed up, and kind of different but sort of the same."

No. Not the same at all.

The bookcase was the first place Princess Maggie explored, taking care not to enact her hazardous plan of turning the room over.

Giselle carefully searched the dean's desk to find him hoarding bundles of hundred dollar bills. Each bundle had a sticky note that read: "DONATIONS! DONATIONS! DONATIONS!"

Princess Tristabelle studied the statue. It was repellent, despite being of excellent craftsmanship. Her vast experience in the supernatural world told her the statue was more than just a monument to the dean. It needed to be tampered with to betray the dean's secrets. Her almond set eyes appraised the statue even deeper, as her mind processed just how she might make it forsake its duty to its master.

"It's not a golem," Princess Maggie quipped. "You can't have sex with it."

"Silence!" Princess Tristabelle barked. "That was one time. You would have done the same thing if you saw how it was equipped."

"Look at all these donations," Giselle whined. "People give donations, and it goes right to his pocket. We should tell the *Times* what he's doing with the donations."

Flick!

That sudden noise, like a flipping switch, brought the statue to immediate life; it stepped gingerly to the left. Princess Tristabelle had the composure of a cyborg and did not react. And Giselle and Princess Maggie even mirrored her reaction.

"It moved," Giselle stated plainly.

"Indeed," Princess Maggie responded equally plainly.

"Ahhhhhh! That's crazy!" they both shouted, screams shattering their once empirical tranquility.

"That's bad!" Maggie whined.

"Super bad!" Giselle groused.

The statue returned to its normal state of being as it stood next to a small door with a gold and black striped pattern.

"We did it!" Giselle and Maggie celebrated a victory that was not in anyway their doing.

Immediately Princess Tristabelle tried to push the door open. But even her pure elven might could not leave it unhinged.

"Very well then," Princess Tristabelle said to someone. Someone who clearly wasn't there. "My sister and I shall bare our breasts for your delight."

"Huh? What's going on?" Giselle asked, looking to Maggie with confused raised eyebrows.

"And go!" Maggie shouted.

In an instant, Giselle treated to four cannonballs like tits of boobage excellency. It wasn't as if the Elvrinas' tops posed much of a threat to their exhibitionism, given how slinky they were. But they did come away with shocking ease.

"Uh? What?" Giselle muttered.

"Back to back!" Princess Maggie yelled suddenly.

Within moments like they were robots called to do duty, the princesses released themselves of their bottoms. Pair sof rock frim sticky buns swayed into Giselle's view.

The girls stood back to back and flexed their legs for God knew what reason, Giselle decided. Though she was more than happy to see those banging Scandanvian tushes. Damn, Giselle thought, they knew just how to stand on those muscular legs of their. They highlighted the steeply jutting slope of their butts and good od what butts they were, Giselle thought.

"Now, door fiend, savor our Elven beauty!" Princess Tristabelle shouted.

"It's not a door fiend. It's just a door," Giselle grumbled.

"Down in front!" Maggie barked.

"Holy mother!" Giselle yelled at the pose Maggie called down in front. Tristabelle dropped to her knees, which Giselle decided she had lots of experience doing. Maggie seductively crossed her leg across Tristabelle's shoulder, dominating her with a fierce pose and a cocky smirk. Princess Tristabelle wore a mock shocked expression as if striking oil while she glided her hand up her sister's leg.

"Pleasure yourself to your comeliness, door!" Princess Tristabelle demanded.

It didn't.

Because it was a door.

Nonetheless Maggie called, "Face to face!"

Princess Tristballe laid herself across the floor, inviting a kneeled Maggie on. That was all Maggie needed to put on a slick smirk and crawl toward her little sister. After slow agonizing moments, Maggie reached little sis. The witch rolled her long fingers up Princess Tristballe's golden thighs, journeying the viewer, which they assumed was a door, up to the princess' sweetest spot. In a second, Princess Tristabelle purred as her sister explored her silken skin.

"Wait," Giselle said, laying her hand on Maggie's shoulder. "I've seen a door like that before in the library. It's plain to see this is one of those puzzles where both doors have to be opened at the same time."

"Opened at the same time?" Princess Tristabelle asked. "Ah, group spread eagle!"

"No," Giselle said before a sigh. "Open doors, not legs."

"How confusing!" Princess Tristabelle exclaimed.

"Ten-four, good buddy!" Princess Maggie shouted, using that phrase to inanely express her understanding. "I'll take Giselle to the library. We'll get on the magic mirror and open the door while you open this door, kiddo. Easy-peasy-lemon-squeezy!"

"Sounds good," Giselle said with a nod. "But what will you do if the dean comes back, Princess Tristabelle?"

"Most likely engage in some form of low-level torture."

"As they once said on The Simpsons, 'it's funny because it's true,' " Giselle commented.

***

Giselle used her junior varsity cross country skills to lead Maggie to the library as fast she could, which wasn't very fast in comparison to a pure elf's normal speed.

Those JV cross country skills weren't what they used to be (despite only being used months ago) and Giselle took a moment to heave and wheeze in front of the library. Princess Maggie was kind enough to pretend it wasn't obvious why Giselle consistently finished last in her races and patiently waited for her friend to recover.

Once Giselle was good to go the pair entered the school's library. There wasn't much activity with the semester yet to start. A few tours were being conducted, which Princess Maggie interrupted to tell everyone the school was haunted and they were all going to die gruesome deaths.

After Princess Maggie dispensed that very likely to occur prediction, she followed Giselle to the roads and transportation floor where Giselle found their original Dark Object.

There was the door of gold and black stripes that Giselle was annoyed she hadn't investigated in the first place.

Unfortunately for the girls, in front of that door stood two burly bearded men who, unsurprisingly, wore all black with the letters SKM stitched onto their polo shirts.

"Now, I know why Fleur drinks all the time," Giselle moaned to herself.

But Princess Magalinda who was as chipper as a morning talk show host, batted her crystal blue eyes, and said, "Ashley sent us here!"

"AAH sent you?" the one on the right said.

"Indeed she did, awesome friend!" Princess Maggie bellowed, hands on her hips, nose held high. "Not only are we master ninjas but we're famous magicians. We're The Magnificents and Ashley told us to relieve you and entertain you!"

I see why the queen doesn't like Princess Maggie to leave the castle. She's gonna get us killed!

"Naturally, I'm the leader. And this is my much less attractive assistant!"

"Why does it have to be much less?" Giselle griped.

"Quiet, ignorant and useless fool! Now let's debut our special dog trick!"

"We have a special dog trick?" Giselle wondered

"YOU IGNORANT WHELP! IT'S TIME FOR ME TO BEAT YOU!" Princess Maggie shrieked while leaping up and down on her zebra print sneakers.

The two SKM members looked at each other in confusion, their mouths hung open without anything to say.

Finally, one guard spoke and said, "Yo, we'll leave this door to you two."

The SKM goons broke away from the blondes as quickly as possible.

"Awww, I wanted to show them the dog trick. It's where I turn you into a flower that barks like a dog!" Princess Magalinda exclaimed with a flip of her blonde locks.

"Does that actually work?"

"Hmmmm. The last guy I tried it on exploded. But I had a good feeling this time!"

Giselle just sighed and told Princess Maggie to contact Princess Tristabelle over the magic mirror. Once the princesses were in touch, opening the door was coordinated between the two.

"Magikadabra!" Princess Maggie shouted as the doors gave way on both sides.

"I see nothing," a frustrated Princess Tristabelle announced. "Are you certain we are not meant to perform group spread eagle?"

"I'm game!" Princess Maggie announced.

"And I see..." Giselle trailed off, "Four books, one red, one green, one blue, and one a yellowish pukey kinda color. And there's a note." Giselle scooped up the note and grazed her eyes over it. "Organize the books in chronological order of their release to reveal the treasure."

"These books have no titles and are torn apart on the inside," Princess Maggie complained. "All they have in them is one page of writing. But who cares anyways? Puzzles shouldn't be reduced to silly things like solutions."

Uh, that's literally what puzzles are meant to be reduced to.

Giselle added, "It looks like these might be all Shakespearean quotes."

"Splendificent!" Princess Tristabelle declared. "Read them to me at once, please."

Princess Maggie put on a theatrical voice, moreso than her already theatrical voice and read from the red book, "The red book says 'Caesar's spirit, ranging for revenge, With Ate by his side come hot from hell. Shall in these confines with a monarch's voice. Cry 'Havoc,' and let slip the dogs of war.'"

"That is obviously from Julius Cesear," Princess Tristabelle stated.

Giselle read next, "The pukey book has this: 'Revenge should have no bounds.'"

"Ah, yes, that is Hamlet. A marvelous quote," Princess Tristabelle declared.

Princess Maggie spoke up, "And here's the berry blue one: 'Vengeance is in my heart, death in my hand, Blood and revenge are hammering in my head.'"

"I believe that is Titus Andronicus," Princess Tristabelle mused.

"The green book," Giselle started. "Reads like this: 'If a Jew wrong   a   Christian, what is his humility? Revenge. If a Christian wrong a Jew, what should his sufferance be by Christian example? Why, revenge. The villany you teach me, I will execute, and it shall go hard but I will better the instruction.' I know that one! Merchant Of Venice! In eleventh grade I wrote a paper on if the play was anti-Semitic and it was so good I got invited to my teacher's daughter's Bat Mitzvah."

"How fitting these quotes are on vengeance when I shall have my fill of it when I best Gorick," Princess Tristabelle mentioned icily. "Now let us arrange these books forthwith. Place Titus Andronicus first."

Giselle stashed the blue book back onto the shelf.

"Then," Princess Tristbelle began, "place Merchant of Venice."

That was the green book which was situated next to the blue book.

"Next you shall place Julius Ceasar."

The red book was plopped down third. That only left the yellowish book which Giselle carefully set at the end. She was about to note the puzzle was very Silent Hill Three when she and her princess pal saw the shocking sight of the bookshelf disintegrating into grains of dark sand. The sand shifted and swirled like volcanic ash being moved across the earth until there was no sand at all.

In place of the mysterious shelf sat a skeleton, whose skull bore a stone that swirled with what Giselle swore could be interstellar gas and dust.

More concerning to Giselle was the three charges of black smoke that sped from the skull into the hallway.

"Shit! Something got out!"

"Something did? These adorable blue eyes didn't see anything," Princess Maggie commented.

"You're telling me you didn't just see three balls of black smoke shoot outta here?"

Princess Maggie shook her head. Then she stated, "But cha-cha-cha-cha we have found our Dark Object and it's already charged with Dark Energy."

"That is capital news!" Princess Tristabelle declared. "We are a locator spell away from finding and destroying Gorick. Maggie, how are you progressing with it?"

"I do like curry. Thank you for asking," Princess Maggie stated.

"I asked how you are progressing with the locator spell."

"You're right. Americans do call football soccer because they play nude except for their socks."

"Again, how are you progressing with the locator spell?"

"How are you progressing with getting pregnant by a golem?" Maggie snapped back.

"Grrrrrr!" Princes Tristabelle hissed.

Giselle interrupted, "Why don't we make it through the first day of school without being attacked and then worry about the locator spell?"

"Good thinking, Giselle," Maggie exclaimed, flipping her golden curls. "You can't rush perfection!"

"But I can surely rush a fool," Princess Tristabelle responded through gritted teeth.

Chapter Eleven: Of Conquest, Revenge, and Llamas

A smile broke out above Prince Gorick Elvrina's chiseled chin. But not because he was fucking Ashley Alison Holtz from behind; that was a mere diversion. The smile broke out because his lead intelligence officer, Vaan Filma, vampire, had run down his sister, Princess Tristabelle's allies. Five teenage girls, Princess Magalinda who couldn't fight her way out of a paper bag, and Prince Krisdane who couldn't get out of the way of his weepy chivalry.

His sister, Princess Tristabelle, hadn't even thought to give him a challenge. Revenge would be too easy.

She defeated him once with luck as her sword. Now she wouldn't even manage to slice off a strand of his shaggy golden hair.

Gorick laughed again as he gripped Ashley's ass cheeks atop the bed. They were red from him spanking her earlier. An action he did again to elicit a yelp and a squeal from the raven-haired beauty.

His laughter ripped around the stately hotel room his still vast fortune had provided him. The room had designs inspired by New York City's art décor culture—dark wood accents, and vintage artwork. There was even a terrace overlooking New York's skyline. It cost $895 a night. Mere pennies for The Golden.

"We have always been told a witch can summon a demon," Prince Gorick stated to Vaan who had told him of his sister's friends as well as the two SKM goons who accompanied him. "But they need the right amount of human sacrifice to do it. You tell me this Sofi Poe had been 'tweeting,' as they call it, about a Hemera University camping trip? I will stain my sister's heart and soul and we will use every single student who ventures to the woods as a sacrifice to raise a demon."

"Oh, baby, I like bad boys!" Ashley shouted as his bulk continued to fill her.

"I am no bad boy. I am the celebrated Prince Gorick "The Golden," the rightful heir to the Golden Land and the one true protector of the earth realm."

"I'm just glad the earth protector didn't use protection!" Ashley claimed. "But, daddy always told me told elves are against raising demons."

"Never question The Golden, woman," he barked, spanking her again. "My kingdom is the eldest government in Midgard. I require great power to take it."

"Ohhhh, Ashley likes a powerful man! Reminds me of sweet old dad! And guess what? Llamas can communicate by humming! Incredible!" Ashley shouted to a confused head shake from her fellow SKM members.

Gorick continued to pound her like the helpless, horny girl she was. He spanked her once more to force out another cry that was half-pain and half-delight.

He hadn't even properly bothered to undress the young woman. Instead, pushing her schoolgirl skirt above her nice ass and pushing her panties to the side for easy and quick access. Though calling her underwear panties was giving it far more credit then it deserved. It had merely been a waistband attached to some thin strip of fabric.

There hadn't been any foreplay of any sort either. The pure elf had never seen the woman until about ten minutes ago. Ashley had merely accompanied an SKM ninja providing intel and Prince Gorick, as the rightful heir to the throne, decided to take what he wanted then and there.

Gorick situated his strong hands on her slender hips. His eyes that rested beneath a prominent brow bone sparked with pleasure. A pleasure he increased by yanking Ashley back and forth on his massive member. She became like a sleeve, a tool to get the most dangerous man in the world off.

"Most of these dorks just use me as fap material. I like a take-charge guy! And did you know Llamas can take charge of a herd of sheep?" Ashley commented.

Prince Gorick could do without her commentary but decided to let her have her fun. Her walls quaked around his huge shaft as he continued to jerk her back and forth against his powerfully built body. Her muscles clenched together with surprising vise grip strength to milk the nectar from his very being.

But Prince Gorick was far from ready to cum. Moreover, a woman had to earn the right to have his seed inside her. This girl, who's named he had forgotten, had failed to do so.

Eventually, he grew bored with just taking her from behind. After all, he'd taken countless beauties from behind. She was nothing special to him, But she giggled with glee as he flipped her over and hung her head over the bed. Her crow colored locks sagged towards the floor.

"If SKM doesn't have a witch capable of demon summoning, scour this city for one," Prince Gorick ordered the goons.

"Perhaps it would be more efficient to use an SKM demon sorcerer. Then we would not need the blood magic and human sacrifice," Vaan stated.

"Silence, clodhopper!" Prince Gorick bellowed. "You will do as the rightful heir to Golden Land commands."

An angered Prince Gorick turned upon Ashley and planted himself in her mouth as she lingered upside down on the bed. He didn't give her a second to acclimate to all that bulk in her mouth. Instead, he started fucking her mouth, his jewels slapping off her pretty little nose.

Spit and mucus rolled out of Ashley's mouth and down her pretty face, some getting in her eye. Even though it stung, she couldn't help but get wet at the animal throat-fucking Prince Gorick was giving her. His rod was thick in her thin throat. It cut off her ability to breathe, a wall against the constant gagging noise.

The visual alone was amazing for the attending ninja, Ashley's head trapped between his thighs, unable to do anything but take him however he wants.

Prince Gorick felt as dominant as a lion as he looked down and watched the young woman drool from the force of his pounding.

His brief pause amplified her lusty, untamed gurgling noises. After he took a moment to savor her savage noises, he pressed on, pushing her body to its bursting point.

Ashley was driven wild with lust, her sex soaked with juices. Her body shuddered, both from pleasure and from the force with which Prince Gorick assailed her mouth. She grunted and groaned, sounding more animal than supernatural. There was a climax here and a climax there, too many to accurately keep track of.

Prince Gorick had a change of heart. He decided she had earned his seed. A massive amount of it flooded into her. Her warm lips sucked and sucked, coaxing even more of his juices into her waiting and willing body.

Finally, when she got all she was going to get, Ashley told Gorick, "You're much more fun than my current employer. All it is is Dark Objects this and Dark Objects that. She's such a bore."

Prince Gorick ignored Ashley's complaints. Instead, he turned to the attending ninja and said, "We will be needing a cabin in the woods. It seems I will be attending Hemera's camping trip. Where can you hide, little sister? Where can you flee? The Golden is everywhere."

Chapter Twelve: School'd Ya

Faith healings, resurrections, exorcisms, control over nature. Religion had a monopoly on miracles, Giselle knew. But the greatest miracle the earth had ever beheld was now secular.

Giselle Nyfall was going to Hemera University after all, and she couldn't believe it. Even after her mom had assisted with Dean Pederson, there was still a certain doubt that hovered in Giselle's mind about her being allowed to attend Hemera. Instead, her mom had lauded Giselle's resourcefulness when told about the door puzzle. Not only that, but she also called her a "sometimes mature young woman." That was worth a squeal, which made Dawn roll her eyes and say "those times still weren't all that often."

The only reason Giselle wasn't being accompanied to her first class by her mother was that Prince Charming, Krisdane Elvrina, had promised to deliver Giselle safely and timely.

So timely the duo was able to stop at a McDonald's near Hemera's Law School for breakfast.

Prince Krisdane munched an Egg McMuffin as he held the door open for Giselle who sipped on coffee.

"I have found a new pinnacle in taste!" Prince Krisdane announced loudly enough to attract a curious stare from a passing police officer.

Giselle noted, "You so need to try the double croissan'wich with sausage from Burger King next."

As the two journeyed underneath a construction overhang a pair of college-aged girls in yoga pants and tank tops gasped in appreciation at Prince Charming. One even shot Giselle a jealous frown.

"So that's what's it like," Giselle marveled. "In those few romance books I've read or those supernatural books, there's always a scene or two where the main character gets dirty looks from other girls for being with such a cute guy."

Prince Krisdane smiled bashfully with a mouthful of 760 mg of sodium sweetness.

"Or I could say such a mind-bendingly handsome guy?"

Prince Krisdane's smile was broad and effulgent, the kind belonging to one who welcomed a sincere compliment while also welcoming the savory deliciousness enriched by flour, yeast, yellow corn meal, USDA Grade A Egg, and Canadian Bacon.

Giselle thought back to her first walk with Prince Krisdane, the walk meant to fetch Sofi from the men whom they would soon find to be cursed. She remembered his easy charm, his rich kindness, and her loathsome klutziness.

Today he was still charming, but her aversion to coordination and penchant for mishap were kept at bay, despite an irksome mime's pantomime of the New York Knicks' worst defeats around 86th Street nearly air balling a shot into her face.

"So, Prince Krisdane..."

"Call me Krisdane. I insist."

"You can call me G. Shorter, looks cooler when I sign my name G. So anyway, Krisdane, I showed you some of my world."

"Maggie had made note of American reality televisual shows. Yet nothing prepared me for the reality show Game of Thrones!"

"That's not a—"

"Where might I find a land where a mere human rides a dragon?"

"At the New York Public Library," Giselle quipped as they rounded the corner to come upon the Arts And Sciences building. "Like I was saying I learned ya on the excellence of Jamie Lannister, even if you said you could beat him in a sword fight. Not gonna argue. So you owe me. Tell me about your world."

Krisdane finished the last of his Egg McMuffin with eyes fluttering in joy, then asked, "What might I tell you?"

Giselle rounded upon Prince Krisdane, just as a tall bald-headed forty-something male was appraising the prince with an appreciative nod.

Not only was Prince Charming stunningly good-looking, even his fashion was on point. Especially for someone who was dragged, without a change of clothes, through an unnecessary gauntlet of magic portals to New York by a witchy sister that was failing her portal class. While it took Princess Maggie more than a few tries to reach the proper portal originally, she took to shopping with Tristabelle's allowance the way Fleur took to illegal gambling dens. Princess Maggie bought more than could possibly be necessary for her stay, while Princess Tristabelle bought a few things for her brother. Some of which he wore today — dressed in a navy polo with a red shoulder trim and khaki shorts.

Though how long Krisdane and Princess Maggie would remain on American shores was a nebulous thing. Prince Gorick was at large and Princess Maggie's locator spells were as schlocky as any other spell of hers. Furthermore, the pair had snuck out of the country, forcing Princess Astrid to use some legendary big sister skills and cover for their absence. Princess Tristabelle surmised the headmistress of Lady Chevalthorn University of Witchcraft, where Princess Maggie attended, would be a fiercer authority for Astrid to tame than King Fenrisson.

"So, Krisdane, almost all the Elvrinas have a magic something they can use," Giselle reminded herself as she adjusted a backpack weighed down by a sketchpad and art supplies. "Not Princess Maggie or Princess Constantina, but you do. So what is it? I bet it's a badass sword that's strongest in daylight."

"A magnificent guess. Mine is the sword Phoebus, which sparkles with sunstones and gains immeasurable power during the day."

"If Princess Tristabelle's Mistlewoe goes to the fairest princess and Prince Gorick's Chosen Spear goes to the Elvrina with the best leadership stat, what got you Phoebus?"

"Though I might dispute the gods' choice, it was my gallantry that earned me my sword."

"I swoon!" Giselle announced, after which she swooned and nearly fell into a bicycle messenger.

Krisdane asked in a merry tone, "If the gods were to give you a magical tool, what might it be?"

"An indestructible suit of armor because I'd need it because I fall a lot."

"There's a certain charm in that. And I would know charm," he decided with a tilt of his head and a grin.

"So how's it all work? Like the gods show up all badass and Thor: The Dark World are all like 'Here's Phoebus oh gallant Prince Krisdane Elvrina?'"

"One might wish for such a euphoric anointing. But no, the weapons materialize when the gods have chosen. That could happen at any time truly. I am fortunate they chose me right as that wyvern wished to eat me. On the other hand, Rodgir was given Internal Flame when he was passed out at the bar of a brothel."

"There's something to buy a round of drinks over! But I bet Internal Flame and The Chosen Spear are nothing compared to Phoebus. That sun-powered sword sounds so awesome. And I'm so not just saying that because you're my favorite prince ever.

"It is a most helpful tool when fell beasts slither and crawl to Midgard, our world, from the outer realms or the Corrupt Forest. "

"So what's Princess Astrid's special weapon?"

Prince Krisdane's face sagged a bit, "She wields Pendelum, granted to the princess with an iron will, which gleams and shines like fire but is said to cause a great evil. Thus she mostly uses a bow."

"And she's in the Air Force?"

Prince Krisdane's sagged face rose into a smile, "She is the commander of the Wild Pegasus. Astrid 'Iron Wings' riding the Pegasus Bucci."

"Yooooooo, she rides a Pegasus? Yooooooo, yooooo, yoooo! Do you ride one?"

"Tristabelle says you could not handle knowing what I ride."

"All right, I'll drop it for now. But just for now. That Corrupt Forest you guys always mention...you're always so spooky about it. Was it just POOF!—little squirrels and woodchucks and other woodland creatures became elite menaces or what?"

Krisdane took a long breath and his hands found his pocket. Bold eyes went up to the sky in time to see a jet zip by.

"Human technology. Marvelous. Less durable than what I ride though—though less temperamental," he stated then cast his eyes downward. "As you know, Golden Land was risen from the sea by The Allfather long ago, perhaps far too long for time to record. The Allfather entrusted the land to the Elvrinas so that we may protect the earthen realm. It was assumed we would be protecting the earth against fell beasts from the other realms, but now we have to protect it against humans as well."

"Totally sorry about that."

" Long ago we had stewards by the name of Clan Bathild."

"Were they pure elves?"

Krisdane nodded and then went on, "As is the story, the Elvrina king did not take kindly to Lord Bathild's humble suggestion to unite their families by marriage thus turning Lord Bathild's daughter into a future queen. Rebuked, Lord Bathild stewed in his home until he had a visit from an explorer. Who this explorer was has been lost to time. Or perhaps many characters have become one. Regardless, this explorer informed Lord Bathild that he would find all he needed to usurp and ruin Clan Elvrina in the unexplored northern forest of Golden Land."

"Uh-oh," Giselle said, voice a whisper. Her phone was buzzing. Most likely her mom but this story was too intense to endure an abrupt halt.

"In the northern forest Bathild and his household found...we do not know what they found except merely a treasure chest. The legend goes... the trees pointed them to it." Krisdane shook his head as if the thought of it all caught him with pain.

"Lord Balthild advised caution in their approach. Yet his daughter, eager for revenge over the slight, opened the chest. When she did so, she unleashed unfathomable darkness that corrupted the forest."

"What do you mean by darkness and corrupted?"

"It was a miasma that came from that chest. Or it might have been a mist. Whatever it was...it killed all plant life, darkened the sky, and released foul beasts that poured into the country as a whole."

The girls had often made passing mentions of monsters but gave no origin for their existence.

"We are plagued by trolls, harpies, orcs, and much more because of Clan Bathild. Making their home in the dark forest denied them sunlight, and the generations of Bathilds and their household grew pale with pitch-black hair. They became known as the corrupt elves. Today they are led by Emperor Grim Bathild."

"That is so the name of a dude you do not want to tangle with. Have you met him?"

"Few have, fortunately. The Bathild goal is the exact opposite of the Evrina goal. They want the end to all life on Earth."

"Except theirs."

"Who's to say? Death can be a welcome kiss for some people."

"So lemme think for a second," Giselle massaged her temples, firing up her brainpower. "If Prince Gorick chased Emperor Grim into the Corrupt Forest, do you think he got some miasma mist thingie that corrupted him? Like supernatural chicken pox?"

Prince Krisdane rubbed his chin then spoke in a resigned tone, "Constantina spoke of that possibility. Though she said there was no way to prove it as no one ever returned from the Corrupt Forest but him. And it never occurred to her until after his attack. What happened to him exactly we never knew. But he changed."

"So maybe he's not the bad guy. He's just sick."

They had arrived at the building of Giselle's first class. She felt oddly calm about it. Relaxed even. The nerves of the first day at college couldn't exist in a world with serious threats like Emperor Grim and Gorick Elvrina.

"A sickness perhaps," Prince Krisdane began. "But after what he has done and the lives he has taken he is but a tragic figure. He is not a sympathetic one."

"The enemy of the state Prince Trygyrr talked about last week that was supposed to be in Golden Land was Gorick?" Giselle asked to a nod from the prince. "But why would Princess Tristabelle's loyalty ever be doubted by Prince Trygyrr or King Fenrisson? It sounds like Prince Gorick hates her."

Prince Krisdane's beautiful eyes found the sky again and he spoke in a weary tone, "Tristabelle was his favorite."

Giselle rubbed Krisdane's shoulder, it was firm and lean with muscle. "I gotta get to class. Are you gonna be all right?"

"Father says, 'Fine, good, all right does not matter. You are Elvrinas that is what matters," he said, though his smile didn't match his tone. But then he added cheerfully, "And Sofi has agreed to meet me for coffee."

A date? I have found my rival!

***

Art 151 aka Drawing The Human Body section 1004AB at 10:05 am was Giselle's first class of her college career. It was a chance for her to show her extraordinary artistic talents.

Giselle breezed through the classroom door the way she imagined Sofi would do it, head up, eyes fierce, a swagger in her step. If you were going to be somewhere, be the most noticeable, so went Sofi's thinking.

But as soon as Giselle stepped into the classroom, the sight that greeted her made her want to expel Art 151 from her schedule. There at the head of the class was her professor—a mocha-skinned beauty with full lips, elegant nose, a bundle of brownish curls, and an aristocratic stance.

She was Diana Mironov. Wife of Russian millionaire and formerly sex cursed Val Mironov. Only previously sex-cursed because of an orgiastic intervention on the part of Giselle's housemates.

Giselle sulked in the seat nearest the entrance; memories of testy visits from the wives were potent.

Diana flounced past the array of students to a sorrow-eyed Giselle and painted her once cloudy day with rainbows and sunshine as she dotted her forehead with a kiss.

"This is Giselle and I love her!" Diana announced, getting a confused Giselle a few jealous stares from the other students.

Perhaps an easy "A" secured the first day of class? And all it took was sex? Giselle gave serious thought to unleashing her Hot Squad in her biology professor's bedroom. Science never was her strong suit.

Giselle's moment of delight was shaken and stirred into a rainbow whirl of confusion when Dusty plopped down right next to her. Dusty's bra busters were busting through her Hemera Volleyball T-shirt and she wore rainbow-themed earrings and necklace as accessories along with a cowgirl hat.

"Dusty? You're not in this class."

"And who is, missy?" Dusty retorted, waving to a grinning Diana. "Nate Myers? No sir-ee-bob, not after I kicked him right there in his dang shins and sent him crying back to his dorm."

"Oh my god, Dusty, you just go online and register for classes. You don't have to attack innocent people."

"You oughta be thanking me, Giselle," Dusty pointed out, tilting her head up high with her happy, cute circular lips in a satisfied smirk. "My pixie dust in Professor Diana's coffee was all it took for her to go from mean ol' wife to havin' Giselle for WCW World Heavyweight Champion! And I mean World Championship Wrestling not Woman Crush Wednesday. Cause today is Monday."

"Wow, that's so useful," Giselle said, shocked. "I mean, don't ever use pixie dust on me for that because it's an incredible violation, but yeah, mega-useful."

Dusty flashed another cute pixie smile that made her chipmunk cheeks look like they were storing every acorn in the state of New York.

Giselle realized she only had a rudimentary rundown of Dusty's abilities. The pint-sized pixie was a factory for that magical dust. The effects were startlingly medicinal, but the hows of production escape Giselle.

Fleur informed Giselle fairies and pixies boasted the power of nature manipulation. If it fell under the four elements of earth, wind, water, and fire, pixies and fairies could harness it. Dusty, as claimed by Fleur, was an exceptional Elementalist. The "Paul Pierce of fairies" was the Boston Celtic great Fleur compared Dusty to. Giselle thought to call Dusty the "Kobe Bryant of fairies" was more fitting but she kept her mouth shut.

"So, like, why are you in this class anyway?" Giselle asked Dusty. "You're a parks and rec major, and you think most art is the devil's work."

"Fer one thing maybe we can get some information outta Diana about any suspicious people her and her husband may have done been around before Val got cursed. You may have forgot about the sex curse but I ain't. Fleur thinks her dad is responsible and bet me an ice cream cone he did it. If Professor Diana's happy, then she'll get to yappin and maybe we can figure out if we're dealing with Prince Gorick or Saint Lazarus or someone else for this curse. We can't get to Val Mironov so this is what we got. But the real reason I'm right here with ya..."

Dusty's big doe eyes directed themselves to the door—and shortly everyone else's did as well, while their jaws directed themselves to the floor. For Princess Tristabelle arrived in all her babe-nificence. Her rounded chin was held high, her cupid's bow lips formed a polite and small smile. If this golden skirt and abstract floral print top wearing princess was in the middle of a succession crisis and held designs on brandishing a magical sword against her brother, nary a soul would guess it.

"Dusty, you're gonna let your clearly homicidal, brother-killing, crush pose for a 100 level art class when again she's clearly homicidal?"

"Hush up, Giselle. My pa got my mom with me right before he defended his Fairy Revolution Wrestling World Championship at Nymphomania Eighteen."

"The only words I understood in that were hush, up, Giselle, pa and mom."

Princess Tristabelle spoke over her shoulder, "I have made a commitment. When an Elvrin commits an Elvrina commits..."

"Lemme guess, King Fenrisson said that," Giselle remarked.

Princess Tristabelle flashed Giselle a thin affirming smile.

"I noticed she didn't deny the clearly homicidal part," Giselle lamented as she dug out her art supplies.

Dusty did the same which led to Giselle face-palming because Dusty's art supplies were Crayola markers.

Diana welcomed the students to Art 151 and handed out the syllabus as Tristabelle took a seat on a stool in the front of the classroom. The students introduced themselves to one another with the pudgy but cute Anita Cotton going on an unsolicited and long-winded spiel about her thoughts on what constituted a "real female artist."

"Class, I want to see what level we're all at so we're going to hop right into the drawing," Diana announced. "And as a special treat, you get to draw authentic royalty, Princess Tristabelle Elvrina of Golden Land."

"She's not a real princess," Anita complained, shaking her head vigorously.

Before micro-aggressor Dusty could unleash a micro-aggression on Anita, Giselle slammed her hand over her mouth.

"One more word against my noble bearing and I will be forced to hurt you," Princess Tristabelle joked with a little chuckle. Everyone else chuckled with her except for Giselle, who knew Anita was close to hurting for certain.

"Today," Diana began, placing her hands on Princess Tristabelle's shoulders, "is a simple day. I just want you to draw the beautiful princess' upper torso."

"I thought this here was gonna be nude modeling," Dusty whined.

The class began their task of putting the perfect princess on paper. Except for Dusty who just drew doodles of scenes from Fairy Revolution Wrestling. Shockingly, when class ended Diana held up Dusty's work and declared, "A thrilling ultra-modern look at the tumultuous nature of international politics that plagues a princess' life. Amazing. I will hang this in my gallery!"

"What about mine?" Anita whined, showcasing her work to her unimpressed classmates.

"Yours? I'll be composting that at the co-op grocery store to help get me out of doing any hours this month," Diana stated,

"Mine? Instead of that crap that high schooler drew?"

"High schooler?" Dusty shouted, jumping from her stool. "You better pipe down, ya little bu—" But again Dusty was prevented from rifling out a torrent of offensives by Giselle's hand over her mouth. This time Giselle endured a Crayola to the ribs but her grip held.

"I shall thank you all to leave your drawings with me so that they may hang in Hildegard Castle, the royal seat of Clan Elvrina," Princess Tristabelle spoke in a sweetened voice. A sweetened voice and kindly request that added all but Anita to the growing list of Belle Ringers. Many of the students looked back at the youngest Elvrina princess with adoring sighs as they exited the room.

"Giselle, Princess Tristabelle, Dusty," Diana started, holding up her hand. "You three, stay."

Diana's lips were pressed together tightly as she went to the door, shut it, and locked it. Then she spun upon the girls with her eyebrows pressed down, her eyes narrowed, and her lips in a wild grin.

Her mouth spoke in a strong, deep voice Giselle swore could not belong to her, "Now class begins."

Chapter Thirteen: Dream On

Diana was a space station orbiting the celestial bodies of Giselle and her Hot Squad. Around she went, sizing up the tall Princess Tristabelle, the busty Dusty and the stacked Giselle.

"Oh, you wild, wild girls," Diana murmured. "This is just what I need."

"Uh, I have to be in biology in ten minutes," Giselle complained, looking down at the time on her phone.

"You have to be here with me for this private class," Diana responded as she sniffed Princess Tristabelle's blonde bob. "My husband and I are swingers, and I think it's time we swung."

"Gulp!" Giselle expressed without actually gulping.

"I see what makes you girls so special but I want to *see* what makes you girls so special. Do you understand me?" Diana asked, rubbing the royal's arm.

The corner of Princess Tristabelle's mouth rose just a bit. Fitting for a sister of Freya, who worshiped the goddess erotically.

"We done did this before and you missed out," Dusty informed Diana with a little sympathy pout.

"I won't miss out this time," Diana stated, hand on Dusty's shoulder. "Not at all."

"This one's all me!" Dusty hooted with an energetic fist pump more like she had been called into a volleyball game.

"Perfection!" Diana decided, closing her eyes and giving a firm nod.

"Yer tongue is bout to be flapping in the wind like a worn-out bloodhound," Dusty declared, and no one knew what the hell she meant.

Dusty's getting her shot with Tristabelle! Don't fail, Dusty! Don't have an allergic reaction to her perfume like I did with Shawna Pierce in eleventh grade! And don't wrinkle your nose if you smell something like I did with Jack Lambert in tenth grade because then she'll think you think she smells!

Dusty was quick to rid herself of her already revealing attire while keeping on her rainbow-themed accessories. Her thoroughly tanned milk bombs, as Giselle would term them, bounced free along with the generous flesh of her ass that had the pixie dust influenced professor nodding in respect.

"Ya'll like these all-natural jugs?"

She's still selling that all-natural lie. Points for dedication.

Princess Tristabelle at first set her mouth in a grim line. Then she said, "Dusty, don't you dare touch me with those filthy unseemly hands of...OHHHH HEAVENLY ASGARD!!"

If there were other students to hear the eighteen-year-old princess' shout, it would be sure to send them seeking transfers to colleges for the deaf.

It's was all due to Dusty's not-so-unseemly hands making a not-so-gentle grope of the royal's ample breasts. Princess Tristabelle's nipples responded to the firm raking and pinching Dusty delivered, quickly hardening. It wasn't long before Dusty was prying Tristabelle out of her ultra-expensive outfit without regard for the fact that it was ultra-expensive.

With sinful determination befitting one of the demons in Madame Wanda's tales, Dusty nipped, licked, and sucked down on the most excellent pair of boobs she'd ever come across. Princess Tristabelle's senses teemed with raw fervor, and if Dusty moved any faster she'd be shaken by a devastating orgasm.

"Oink! Oink!" Princess Tristabelle did truly, honestly, oink like a pig then had to hurry out, "The peasants will forgive their lady for sounding like Dusty's social circle."

"Forgiven," Diana muttered, her eyes wide, her body leaning forward as she soaked in the marvelous sight of Dusty at work.

The busty country volleyball star swept kisses all along the flawless flesh of the princess. Princess Tristabelle was lucky this wasn't Fleur she's dealing with as Dusty pulled at the bud with her sharp teeth causing pleasure to spring forth all across the princess' long, well-built body.

"Yes! Ravage me, Dusty!" Princes Tristabelle begged.

Dusty ground her teeth into the royal's nipples, causing alternate shockwaves of pain and pleasure to seize Princess Tristabelle. As Dusty suckled and nipped at her horny love the busty cowgirl ground two fingers against the desperate princess' desperate sex."

"Oh, Dusty, I shall forever be at your disposal to use and fuck as you will!" Princess Tristabelle promised.

Pleasure flared in Dusty's naughty little slit. She had three fingers jammed in there and they brought to her to an astounding climax. She swore she could see stars and the lights of the rainbow bridge that connected earth to the other nine realms according to Golden Land's religion. She would have to thank The Allfather for blessing the earth realm with such a fuckable horny creature as Tristabelle.

Dusty finger fucked her queen until the blond minx started to collapse from the pleasure.

"Oh, Dusty, you fuck me much too hard!" Princess Tristabelle whined.

Dusty didn't let up, letting Princess Tristabelle's delightful moans be a signal to add another finger to the two that were jammed in there. With relentless force in play, Dusty didn't back off from her finger bang. She pounded the blond tart until a gush of juice exploded from her slutty hole. The helpless princess came again when one finger invaded her tight tush.

"Oh good heavens!" The princess wailed.

Princess Tristabelle grunted like a pornstar, which led Giselle to note that all her roomies moaned like pornstars. Certainly, Princess Tristabelle moaned and cried as if she were on the set of "I Came Inside A Schoolgirl." More juices spilled out of her in response to the hammering in that perfect firm booty.

"Ohhhhohoh, so many fingers inside my slutty butt! Frejya save me!"

Nothing saved Tristabelle as an orgasm hit her like a hurricane. Dusty gave her no break as she attacked her with thrusts that knocked the breath from her. There were spikes of pain and pleasure as Dusty assailed her back passage like it owed her money.

"Don't get involved, Giselle," Giselle told herself. *"Your mom will obliterate you."*

The little cutie got massively aggressive with Tristabelle's pendulum-like boobs, lifting and pushing them together to form what should be an impossible mountain of cleavage.

"That's it," Diana murmured. "I know a place for you two pretty whores."

Dusty snagged Princess Tristabelle's cupid bow lips, sucking on the lower one, dragging it out and letting the princess' deep-set almond eyes go a fluttering and her Viking Barbie body quiver.

Princess Tristabelle was succumbing to Dusty moment by moment, and with the rush of exhilaration streaking through her nude body, she swung her arm out and knocked over a jar of pencils.

"Something tells me I'm gonna be the one cleaning that up," Giselle said with a sigh.

Princess Tristabelle's knees buckled and she started teetering sideways, carrying Dusty with her, a leaning tower of blonde hotness. Together they knocked over a pair of easels, which Giselle knew she would have to clean up.

Dusty seemed not to care if they were on unstable ground and Princess Tristabelle just knocked over Diana's smoothie. She was way too into having her electric tongue explore the mouth of the gorgeous royal, while her hands reached up to entangle themselves in the back of Tristabelle's wavy bob.

Dusty pulled back to say, "Queen Tris, I just gotta say, yer purdier than Uncle Clem's prize heifer, Stephanie."

"Dusty, should you ever compare your lady to a bovine, I will have your head removed and placed on a pike at JFK's runway to show all new arrivals to this city what happens to those failing to flatter their lady's charms."

"Mmm, I love it when ya make violent threats. Gets me hot!"

Dusty hauled Tristabelle's left leg up over her back giving her prime access to the most desired area in the free and not so free world. Dusty's ravening tongue caressed Princess Tristabelle's slobbering spot. Dusty gathered a heaping of juices from Princess Tristabelle's inner folds. The delicious taste would be one she'd remember when she was a well-aged fairy.

The tiny cutie thrust three fingers inside herself, letting out a loud moan against the love of her life. Dusty's sex was coated, dripping even, and she felt her body boiling. She savaged herself with a hard and relentless pace. It helped that Princess Tristabelle was hard and relentless in grounding against Dusty's adorable face.

"Dearest Frejya, I can not stand much more of this!" Princess Tristbaelle exclaimed, breathlessly.

Giselle wondered how Princess Tristabelle could manage to think to speak with how wildly she was flopping about and moaning. She watched as Princess Tristabelle grabbed onto Dusty's curled blonde locks and further rammed her face into her sex. That prompted

Dusty to increase the diddling of herself right before she was forced to remove her fingers to squirt onto Diana's floor.

Princess Tristabelle's body was vibrating with so many new and powerful sensations it could be questioned if her morning tea had been doused with pixie dust. Yet there was no magical substance at play, only the wild licks of the world's biggest and littlest Belle Ringer.

Unable to keep any semblance of her ladylike composure, the princess massaged her face, caressing flushed cheeks, patting down her rounded chin and square jaw.

"Ah, yes!" the blonde princess exclaimed. "I must tell Constantina how thrilling a lover a pixie makes!"

"So is telling your sister about your sexual escapes a normal thing in Golden Land?"

"Is it not in America?" the princess wondered.

"My sibling is a Yorkie, and he caught me masturbating once, and it was pretty awkward between us for about a week," Giselle commented with her head hung low.

Princess Tristabelle bucked against Dusty's face as electric currents of pleasure surged through her. Giselle figured anyone else might be hurt by the powerful thighs of the pure elf banging against their face. But Dusty was spurred to new heights of lust and furiously attacked her sex.

"Yer pussy is so slutty, my queen!" Dusty bellowed.

"It is not slutty if it is sanctioned by the goddess," Princess Tristabelle corrected.

I should have used that line when my mom discovered my Pornhub history.

Dusty was in a far-off zone, a highlight reel worthy display of oral sex that brought the princess to a classic orgasm. Both girls' bliss and lust for one another reached proportions no human could dare survive. Their bodies rumbled in unison, Princess Tristabelle's quaking like a wave traveling thousands of miles.

"Yowza, she really did learn a lot from 50 Shades of Grey before her mom burned it!" Giselle observed.

Princess Tristabelle slumped backward on her butt and threw her head back with a wild laugh.

"Kama Sutra twins, Giselle." Diana said, rubbing her eyes as if waking up from a dream. "Let's all talk."

Princess Tristabelle panted her way up to Diane along with a styling and profiling Dusty, who fluffed her hair and did a little strut.

"Hey, Giselle," Diana started, "Can you clean up the mess while we talk? Pretty please."

"I knew it," Giselle sobbed to herself, and she went off with sagged shoulders to do janitorial work on the first day of class.

"You two were amazing! My husband, Val, and I are good friends with a Pedro Gomez, who tends the grounds here, and Seamus McGrath, the Irish rapper back at the condo."

Seamus was one of the many men inflicted by the curse.

"We belong to this great underground club, if you know what I mean, and there was this woman we met there last time and she was wow! Just like you two. Same aura. Something about her. Then there was this man. Princess Tristabelle, he looked a lot like you. He even had your eyes."

Gorick!

"Truly?" Princess Tristabelle said with politeness, though her face held a subtle twitch.

"The 99th Degree is the name of the club," Diana stated.

"It's just a regular nightclub?" Giselle asked.

Diana chuckled, "It's everything in this city. It's the only place to be."

"So where do we find it?" Dusty questioned.

"If I told you the owner would never let me back in. I know one man who told who had his fingers broken. But it is marvelous. You never want to leave."

Dusty was indignant, "Woman, if you don't tell me—"

Giselle darted over from cleaning up pencils to cover Dusty's mouth before she took a nuclear warhead to this recently built bridge.

"But one of the men might have looser lips than me. Pedro, Val, Seamus. Most likely Seamus aka SeaSeaSea. I can't quite get into his music but he is hot. He'd probably tell you anything you could hope to know about the 99th Degree. Rappers love to brag, especially this one."

Giselle nodded to Princess Tristabelle, both girls pleased with nuggets of info Diana dispensed.

Diana produced a flier from her bag written in green and black lettering with a picture of a campsite and displayed it to the Hot Squad.

"On another note, the school is running these camping trips for freshmen throughout the fall semester. First come, first serve. You should go and mingle. I just know you're the type to make a hell of a first impression!"

"Yes," Princess Tristabelle responded, her face granite solid, her mood guarded like the Hildegarde Castle. "Perhaps we shall."

Chapter Fourteen: Psycho Wave

Giselle, Dusty, and Princess Tristabelle left Diana's class with the cliched pep in their step. Such pep was most boastfully displayed by Dusty who strutted into the hallway, swinging her arms and "whooing" to Giselle and Princess Tristabelle's embarrassment.

Princess Tristabelle was trying to both corral Dusty and explain to Giselle that if Princess Maggie could cast her locator spell at the 99th Degree where Prince Gorick had been, her spell's miserable success rate would vastly improve. Thus "light would shine on their sepulchral situation," Giselle had to pretend like she knew what sepulchral meant.

Dusty's blustery stroll was interrupted by her bumping into a black man with sunken, vacant eyes and tattered clothes.

Giselle recognized him as Tyrone Elder, the Hemera board member who the girls had saved from a sex curse during an orgy that left him zombified. But now his condition seemed somehow worse than cursed. The color was drained from his body, leaving behind a ghastly pallor. He looked less than human in this state. More than cursed, he looked ghoulish.

"Hey! Watch it, buster," Dusty chided the all-black wearing Elder.

Her demand earned no response. It was as if the vacant-eyed man could only focus on one thing. One person.

Giselle.

The only human of the three blondes halted, unable to bring herself to move out of Tyrone's path. Her big blue eyes tunneled into him as if the only reason they existed was to stare him down.

Tyrone kept shambling towards Giselle. His unsteady movement prompted a student with a green afro to quip that he was drunk.

Giselle knew better.

The strange man's expression was blank. As if nothing in the world concerned him beyond Giselle. And few would think Giselle concerned him beyond the alarmed woman herself.

He reached bony hands out to Giselle—fingers that should have provided only the scantest of grip seized onto her with incredible power.

"Hands off, urchin!" Princess Tristabelle barked.

She got no response. Though Giselle wasn't surprised. He wasn't here to listen.

His cracked, chapped lips spoke in a weak, distant tone, "Mother. I have arrived."

Then he collapsed and died like a black hole imploding. Or space-consuming itself. As his dying body curled in on itself he seemed to grow smaller, weaker. But somehow even more imposing to Giselle, who shifted behind Princess Tristabelle. Better to be behind the magical sword-wielding elf than in front of this alleged son of the night mother.

Confused students rushed over to bear witness to the death of this bizarre character. The green afro'ed student asked everyone if they knew where to get what the dead man was on as it had to be "some powerful shit."

Giselle watched, still clinging to Princess Tristabelle, with wide blue pools of horror as a ball of black smoke rose from Tyrone's body and flew down the hallway. Somehow she was the only one to see it.

"What in the hell was that?" Dusty snapped, poking the dead man with her sneaker. "We just saved this fella," she moaned beneath her breath.

Giselle, though, wanted nothing to do with the intrigue of this dead man. She merely clung to Princess Tristabelle, instinctively pulling her away from the scene of the death.

***

Anika's chin was steepled above her hands, her elbows resting on her black obsidian desk. Her snow grey eyes passed across what

Giselle had dubbed (against their will) the Hot Squad. Giselle, Sofi, Fleur, Dusty, and Princess Tristabelle.

When you dedicate the time, weather the vicissitudes of the supernatural world, and collect a radiant treasure of supernatural aristocracy, you were due a reward. You were not due your plans being thrown astray. You were not due Trygyrr Elvrina's meddling. You were not due Mermut the tornado. You had a collection of supernaturals as beautiful as a curlicue, as mighty as a typhoon. They were not to be wasted solving curses, fighting washed up exiles, and posing you questions about recently deceased bums.

"It's a shame Tyrone died an oh-so ignoble death," Anika lamented, her voice rife with sarcasm.

Fleur, leaning against one of Anika's limestone warriors, quipped, "It was a real smart idea of you three to haul ass immediately after he died. That's not suspicious at all."

Dawn Nyfall, on speaker on Giselle's phone, added, "You were smart to leave if you saw something leave his body."

"It was one of the same things I saw when we found the last Dark Object," Giselle noted, while getting a shoulder rub from Sofi.

"Great," Fleur grumbled. "Giselle, you attract problems like Sofi attracts VD."

"Fox spirits can't get VD," Sofi said plainly, not realizing she just got insulted.

"After we saved him from the One Night Curse," Princess Tristabelle lamented, staring out the window at a boy playing the ukulele. "He has died never to bloom again. Could this be the resurfacing of the curse?"

"First African American Hemerea board member, Tyrone Elder, dies suddenly in campus hallway," Sofi read off her phone. "Wow, I had sex with a trailblazer. I feel like Coretta Scott King."

"You're making something out of nothing," Anika commented.

"Something out of nothing? No need to talk about Giselle's sex life," Fleur joked.

"You don't seem to be taking this very seriously, Fleur," Dawn chided.

Princess Tristabelle fretted, "I fear we might throw our lives away chasing some bizarre plume of smoke that may not have killed anyone but may surely kill one of us!"

"This, my dears, has nothing to do with killer smoke. This is is a copycat killing," Anika began as she rose from her chair. "We are on the fifth anniversary of the Psycho Wave killings. I assume we're all familiar with them?"

"I ain't," Dusty spoke, and Dawn added that she wasn't as well.

"They were a series of awful brutal murders that took place around Hemera during the fall semester," Anika explained, "The exact dates escape me, but the nature of the murders was sensational. There was a professor found burnt to a crisp in a chemistry lab, whose body was impaled on a broken stop sign. There was a homeless woman whose stomach was bloated from being full of pennies and nickels. What you've found is someone imitating the Psycho Wave killings for their own sick and twisted enjoyment. The killer was never caught. So much for our tax dollars being put to good use."

"Didn't they have a suspect at least?" Sofi asked.

Anika shook her head, "Nothing. Not even a single lead."

"It's obviously something supernatural in nature," Dawn decided.

"That is what human paranoia sounds like," Anika claimed, taking a seat with perfect posture. "It could have simply been a vicious human at work."

"So, we have another mystery to solve?" Giselle questioned.

Anika stated, sharpness thick in her voice. "You're not the police, you're not the FBI, you're not even the Fairy Best Investigators.

If you chase everything, you'll catch nothing. The police will solve this eventually. "

"It's quite disturbing that in all my research of this damn institution, I never heard of a Psycho Wave," Dawn grumbled.

"Don't worry about it. I'll protect Giselle."

"You?" Dawn asked, sounding almost incredulous.

"Sure. They don't make white asses like that everyday!" Fleur quipped.

"WHAT?!' Dawn bellowed so loud one would swear the power could emerge from the phone and rattle these walls.

"Mom," Giselle blurted, "EEP!" She shouted. Fleur had snatch as much of a handful of Giselle's rear end as she could handle.

"You felt these cheeks?" Fleur asked Dawn. "Whooooo,"

"Whoooo!" Dusty felt the need to scream.

"Do not be offended, Lady Dawn," Princess Tristabelle hurried to state. "They are glorious glutes. And Fleur is not wrong? Giselle is Caucasian, so that would simply make them glorious Caucasian glutes."

"I feel like someone's culturally appropriating my hook," Sofi bitched.

Dawn spoke tightly. Very tightly. Very, very, very, very, very tightly, "Giselle, meet me at Central Park after you're done with classes," Dawn stated. "It's time we just had a little mother-daughter fun."

"What will the rest of you do besides classes?" Giselle asked.

Sofi, looking at her phone, cooed, "We're gonna see SeaSeaSea in concert!"

Chapter Fifteen: L-L-L

Positivity! Glorious positivity.

"Keep positive, Giselle," Dawn had texted her the words of encouragement after her Math 101: "Math in Baseball" class.

Yes someone had died in front of her. Again. Yes, there were malevolent balls of smoke on the loose. But she had to be positive! She was with the Avengers of the supernatural realm. So positivity had Giselle twirling in wide, wonderful circles just outside of Central Park this evening.

Unfortunately, she fell over a Golden Retriever out for a walk and almost cracked her skull on the pavement.

But positivity! Isn't this what she always wanted? To be part of something extraordinary? Now she had the freedom to submerge herself in this dangerous schoolgirl anime that had become her life.

Adoration. Admiration. Affection. Giselle had the three A's for her doting mother. And her mother had given her the freedom to live the life no other human college student in the world could ever experience.

So why was Giselle starting to feel like a noose was being placed around her neck?

Mother and daughter were set to meet in Central Park, to take in the expansive and historic spread of land. Giselle had arrived after her Biology lab where she inexplicably yet predictably started a lab fire. Yet Dawn was nowhere to be found.

Considering the dangerous cast of villains Giselle had been introduced to, this sparked a flame of worry in Giselle's heart.

Princess Maggie had dramatically regaled Giselle with tales of horrors that roamed this realm. Water hags, grave hags, necromancers, incubui, wolfmen, wraiths, grave fiends, SKM ogres, and many more Maggie didn't get to introduce. That was thanks to a stern admonishment for scaring Giselle from Princess Tristabelle.

But what if a water hag crawled out of the sewers and dragged Dawn to a murky miserable demise. Giselle had fought water hags in The Witcher games. They were serious business!

As the fires of worry were about to consume a pacing Giselle, her phone rang.

"Mom?"

"Giselle, here we come!" her mom noted with an unusual amount of pep in her voice.

"We?"

Dusty was at a volleyball game in Connecticut surely committing a litany of micro-aggressions and possibly outright crimes.

Princess Maggie, Sofi, Princess Tristabelle, and Fleur were at SeaSeaSea aka Seamus McGrath's rap concert. Prince Krisdane was at the consulate trying to convince Astrid to provide more big sister cover to shield him and Maggie from the wrath of King Fenrisson for being across the ocean.

So, who was we?

"We" was Dawn and Mister Blowjob Hair, Lazarus of Bethany.

They looked perfect together. He in his navy polo shirt, an expensive watch, and khaki pants. Her in her capri pants and lavender and cream striped shirt. They looked too perfect. Like their carriage ride should end with Lazarus proposing to Dawn instead of ending in front of a white-haired eighteen-year-old who had enough fury in her trembling fists to cow a grave fiend.

The noose was tightened by Giselle's own hands. In the rush of explaining Dark Objects, Golden Land and Prince Gorick, Giselle had never bothered to express that Lazarus was the bad guy in the Hot Squad's story.

"Mother."

Giselle never called Dawn mother.

"Giselle, sweetie, this truly is a beautiful, beautiful city," Dawn spoke as Lazarus helped her down from the carriage

Every video game in her collection. Every single fucking one Giselle would trade for a stake to drive through this scumbag's heart.

"There's a definite charm in this city," Dawn expressed, "that you just don't get anywhere else."

Giselle disliked how Dawn's searching grey eyes found Lazarus.

Dawn was halted from speaking by the ringing of her phone. She pardoned herself leaving her daughter, her human daughter, alone with the original vampire.

Giselle hated how beautiful this man was. He owned eyes that matched Fleur's pale blue ones yet claimed a sharpness hers lacked. Stubble lined a diamond-shaped face that would put him in his twenties if Giselle didn't know of his ancient age. And his hair flowed in endless streams of brown. Befitting Fleur's small height, he stood at 5'6", perhaps 5'7" if Giselle was being generous. But he had the presence of a giant.

"What are you doing with my mother?"

He stood silent for a good moment. His sharp eyes bearing down upon Giselle like an oppressor.

"Well?!" She snapped.

He pulled his gaze away from Giselle and stated in a low rumble, "Riding."

"Stay away from my mom."

"Send my daughter back to hell."

"Never."

He clasped his hands onto her shoulders, behind a still-chattering Dawn's back. His grip reminded Giselle of her dad's golf grip had Stephen ingested every bit of HGH in California. His eyes bore into her with a strange and awful force. Unimaginable horror was laden in his stare. Yet Giselle felt an indestructible wall form in her mind as he instructed: "You will kill Fleur Flanagan."

"I just said never."

"My...but...what?" he squeezed her tighter. Probably tight enough to bruise she guessed. "You resisted? What are you? A werewolf? Unlike other vampires, I can be a friend to wolves if they are friends to me."

"I'm a pissed off daughter. And a pissed off friend. Stay away from my mom! And leave Fleur alone! She doesn't deserve to die."

He pulled back from Giselle, his grip, his stare, even his words came from a distant place, "Doesn't deserve to die. Do you know many she's killed? How many souls she's taken to hell?"

"Don't try and act like you're doing this for the greater good."

"I see Fleur taints you. Such a shame you're not more like your mother. Do you understand who I am? The things I am responsible for?"

Giselle stood with her arms folded, "I don't care."

"When everyone else was trying to get away from Satan, I'm the one who came to meet him. He found me in Syria, 'come have a seat with me. I need you.' Yes, that's me Saint Lazarus of Bethany he needed. Lazarus of Bethany, the man who's wined with kings and dined on queens. Saint Lazarus of Bethany. I gave him a granddaughter and it's cost me. It's cost this earth. I am prime, ready, willing. The earth is prime, ready, prepared for Fleur to be killed. She is the worst woman in the world today. She has a heart as black as pitch, a mind as corrupt as a politician, and a victim list deeper than the Bible. I want her to be ended in a spectacular, betraying fashion!"

Giselle responded simply and fiercely, "I've seen what Fleur can do, and you'll be the one going down to hell."

A laugh. All Lazarus did was laugh a sweet, terrible, lovely, awful sounding laugh.

He walked off, leaving Giselle wondering if the sky above had darkened in the past few minutes.

***

It was a bright explosion of supersonic trap beats and violent swirls of golden and blue lights in the Sky Reach for Seamus McGrath's up and coming hip-hop alter ego, SeaSeaSea's concert. Students and non-students —who discarded their inhibitions the second they bought a ticket to see the charismatic Irish rapper—thrashed and raged to his magnetic personality and effortless vocals. He prowled across the stage, a hyena in a pink skirt and shredded black leggings.

"Some shadows kill, some shadows steal, some shadows made their dirty deal," the red fork-bearded rapper spat on stage. "Was an angel in this world, died doing not what he was told."

Princess Tristabelle, Princess Maggie, Sofi, and Fleur were on the investigative prowl. The girls had merely wanted to know how to get to the 99ᵗʰ Degree. But Seamus had told them he'd tell them after the concert and also inform them of the mysterious woman he met who he stated now haunted his tumultuous dreams. Princess Tristabelle surmised this woman might have been the sex curse caster. The real question would be who she was working for, Lazarus or Prince Gorick.

Princess Maggie, who wore a pink mini-dress with a glittery finish, announced while twisting round and round, "No one ever said Maggie is guilty of not knowing how to party! Party too weak and you're as fun as sour milk, so you gotta party strong!"

Princess Tristabelle, who could almost pay someone's tuition with a $2,000 black ruffled cocktail skirt, and a $3,500 see-through black star embroidered ruffle-sleeved top, dug a $1,400 pair of heels into the ground, "This is a matter of serious importance," Tristabelle chided her elder sister.

Princess Maggie snatched her sister's ruffled skirt. Before Princess Tristballe could shout," praise Odin" Maggie slid her sister's skirt down her smooth legs, revealing her sparkling white thong. Only when an acne riddled freshmen looked over in open mouth shocked did Maggie utter "oops" and pull them back up.

"Serious importance!" Princess Tristballe whined.

Princess Tristabelle rifled through her custom-made ice white purse, which boasted the glittering image of House Elvrina's sigil: a dancing maiden on a field of a white. Bandages. She needed bandages. Not for her or Maggie—elves so rarely needed them. Not for Sofi, who was off somewhere on IG Live. Nor were the bandages for Fleur. A vampire can heal in seconds. These bandages were for Fleur's dinner, the wrist of freshman Veronica Diaz

Sofi was the first, and so far, the last of the Hot Squad daring enough to be bitten by Fleur. She described it as "a whole lot of WTF then a whole lot of OMG."

Miss Diaz was an orgasm and a pint of blood into the OMG side of things.

An annoyed shake of the head from Princess Tristabelle prompted Fleur to extract her fangs from Veronica's wrist finally.

Veronica's mouth oozed a satisfied moan. A far contrast from Princess Tristabelle, whose mouth emitted "tsk-tsk-tsk" when Fleur licked her full lips and fluttered her big baby doll eyes to taunt Princess Tristabelle with her mini-bloodgasm.

"Listen to the Witch of Waverly Place over there," Fleur instructed Princess Tristabelle. "She knows how to have fun."

"That's good because I'm normally the most serious Elvrina we've got," Princess Maggie lied through her thin lips.

At that blatant falsehood, Princess Tristabelle couldn't help but laugh.

Princess Maggie declared with a twirl and flip of her curled hair, "You're all seeing why Elvheim Magazine named me most fun princess four straight years."

It was a rare thing for anyone from Golden Land to hear rap music live. Aside from a siren off the western coast who was temperamental about performing, rap talent was rather dim in Golden Land. The most popular music in Golden Land was a hybrid of opera and trance EDM that often told the tales of heroes past and present.

Sofi arrived, commenting, "Maggie, you have to put the brakes on Fleur." Her green eyes watched Tristabelle spin bandages across Veronica's wrist. "When we first got here, we saw two Bloods beat up a Latin King and throw him on the subway tracks, and Fleur just jumped in to get some blood for later. Totally violating the rules of the consent pamphlet the school gave us."

"This one gave me consent," Fleur countered, and what she meant is that she used the wicked vampiric power of glamouring on Veronica. "It was either drink her or a Red Bull. And I ain't paying eight dollars for that piss swill then twelve more bucks to put vodka in it. Fuck that; I just lost twelve bucks in a dice game in the Bronx. And I got shot afterwards."

One more glamor from Fleur captured Veronica's entire human soul and infiltrated it with the orders of, "Its been real, but forget this."

Mind and soul stripped clean of Fleur, Veronica left without a word.

"Ya know, I've been thinking," Sofi started.

"We're fucked," Fleur announced.

"I was having a little fun with my Musical Theater teacher until I used Icy Hot as lube on him, so I had a lot of time to think while he cried. And 1 thought 'what if Prince Gorick and Lazarus aren't behind all this weird crap going on? What if there's someone else in the mix?"

"I buried all the wrongs I've done," Seamus bleated. "Still you know I'm coming after you. Your heart of gold, my soul of ice, this is the story of a kingdom told..." He went on, fans spellbound by his words.

Sofi pressed an imaginary "Like" button, wrinkled her nose, and declared "I have a good point! All of us have other enemies, right?"

Fleur quipped, "My dad's been paying child support for a century. His hard-on trollops movement has been trying to kill me and my mom for decades, why wouldn't he fuck with people around me to kill me? He probably wanted to weaponize Seamus and the others to fuck me up. But anyway, what's with these sad songs? This shit is awful. I came to hear about some potato farmer fucking a bad bitch on top a pot of gold."

"I bet the Elvrinas have made lots of enemies," Sofi offered.

"Ah, yes! There was the lazy gardener with the glass eye that Rodgir threw a rock at when he was 18 elven years old," Princess Tristabelle declared. "Truly, he had no hope of advancing in life so seeks his revenge upon us all."

"Uhhhh, think a little bit more on that, Viking Barbie," Fleur ordered. "Could it be a corrupt elf thing?"

"There's an easy answer for that, little vampire, the corrupt elves are barricaded in the corrupt forest," Maggie announced.

"So there's probably other people who hate you. I'm sure you guys have shut a lot of bad shit down for a long time," Fleur noted.

"Shut shit down?" Princess Tristballe said, taken aback. "We have never interfered with anyone's bowels, Fleur! We are not madmen and tyrants!"

Fleur face-palmed.

Princess Maggie responded, "I think what my adorable little vampire is trying to say is that there's a ton of evil people skipping about who we made skipping about a lot harder for. We've killed bank robbers; we've killed slavers, we've killed necromancers, we've killed witches practicing blood magic, we've killed smugglers, we've killed humans, vampires, werewolves, mummies—if they exist we've killed em. There's melted bodies of our victims stuck on pavement, there's demon dolls buried alive, there's even a talking cow in the dungeon!"

"Yes, the dairy queen, the usurping cow," Princess Tristabelle lamented. "But the ice cream made from her milk is truly worthy of high praise!"

"I would love some ice cream!" Sofi decided.

Princess Maggie jumped in delight over the thought of the tasty milk which made her own milk makers bounce around.

"What about Dusty? Sofi wondered, "What's her mom do with all those kids' teeth she collects anyway. Creepy!"

"I believe they're used to make the magic wands," Princess Tristabelle noted. "Some such manner about childlike exuberance being the key to making the wands work."

"I doubt a supernatural ninja gang would get mixed up in fairy business," Maggie commented. "Besides, the fae are sweet, kind, and mega-magically cheerful just like yours truly! Who'd wanna hurt them?"

"Speaking of mothers," Princess Tristabelle began, "what of yours, Sofi? Very few women's gold-digging has been galling enough to bring the end of dynasties in China, Japan, and India, and Gus The Mattress King of Miami."

"Daddy! Killed by a fox! Ironic, don'tcha think?"

"Uh-huh, it's like the time I went to Asia and got hella hammered and got a bad case of Indonesia," Fleur commented.

"Fleur, it's Bulgaria, not Indonesia," Sofi corrected her incorrectly.

"Oooh Tammy Mae!" Princess Maggie exclaimed, clutching Fleur's hand. "You haven't heard the story, little vampire. Tammy Mae is the original fox spirit. Word has it she's disguised herself as a concubine in ancient China to ruin a dynasty, posed as a young girl to win the favor of a Japanese emperor she doomed and led several U.S. presidents to scandals! One thing is certain, little vampire, each stop made her mega-magically rich!"

"My kinda woman," Fleur declared.

"That's my mommy!" Sofi shouted with a firm and proud nod.

Fleur looked at SeaSeaSea swirling in his skirt, giving herself a moment to think. "Forget Giselle," Fleur grumbled. "Her mother's pro-GOP tweet got a sorcerer in a Che Guevara T-shirt in his feelings? Her just dad's a tech nerd, but then again his shit crashed my old Galaxy."

"Should've got an iPhone," Sofi said with a cute little whistle.

"All this thinking is killing my brain cells," Fleur grumbled. "I'm gonna pop some Xans and Percs."

The girls hadn't settled the mystery that floated within their minds. Did a despoiled prince, whose name commanded fear across the supernatural community, need to torment his baby sister and her friends with these such tricks? Did history's original vampire need such roundabout mechanics to slay his daughter? For now, all they could do was enjoy the concert like everyone else as blazing beats hammered eardrums, pulling the fans into a frenzy that lifted them off the floor.

But then a blazing fast fist belonging to a black-clad black man hammered the eardrum of SeaSeaSea, pulling him into a terrible journey that lifted him off the floor then slammed him to the ground. Unconscious. Broken.

"He got knocked the fuck out!" one fan screamed.

"SeaSeaSea, more like L-L-L," another snickered

The figure was like a stream of water through the hands of security, avoiding their grasp with unerring ease. SeaSeaSea continued to lie on the stage. Unconscious. Broken.

Someone yelled, "Kill that nigga!"

"Fuck him!"

"Someone help Seamus!" Sofi demanded, while recording the chaos on her phone, purely for journalistic and not for social media's sake.

"Fleur," Princess Tristabelle directed, "maintain the safety of Seamus. Maggie and I shall pursue this ruffian!"

"You got it, kiddo," Maggie chimed with an enthusiastic rubbing of her hands.

Fleur nodded, and the princess/swordswoman/figure skater/rap beef settler ran off with her witchy sister.

Too fast for any human, this man escaped the gym with Princess Tristabelle's sense of justice gnawing at his trail. Rather than complete a rush into the busy streets, the man dashed through the doors of the school of chemistry building using his strength and momentum to burst through what should have been a hindering lock.

"Wait!" Maggie ordered. "Isn't that mega-magically a bad idea to follow a shady mystery man into a dark building?"

"The only mystery that man possesses is the mystery of whether I will disembowel him or behead him when I catch him," Princess Tristabelle responded.

Princess Tristabelle sped into the building far quicker than one wearing high heels should be able to do. Right behind her was her worrying, flats-wearing sister. But when they entered, there was no mystery man to mega-magically catch and mega-magically disembowel.

"Great," Princess Maggie whined. "Now how do we find him? It's not like we can sniff him out. We're not were...were...WEREWOLVES!!!!"

Princess Maggie's hand trembled as her finger directed her sister to turn around. Turn around to face what laid SeaSeaSea out. Turn around to see a man whose entire body was wracked with tremors. Whose dark skin was being overtaken by fur. Whose frame grew larger by the second. Whose entire humanity was eliminated as if it never existed. Because in its place stood a mammoth silver wolf.

A silver wolf that took the lead in front of two smaller black wolves.

"Maggie, be a dear and alert the others to what we have found."

"What about you?"

"Vampires, humans, witches, werewolves, we kill 'em all."

The second Princess Tristabelle finished that sentence Maggie was off, barreling through the busted doors to find help for a sister who was merely inspecting her nails.

"Shall we then?" Princess Tristabelle asked with a toss of her blonde bob.

This wasn't Princess Tristabelle's first dog show.

A previously unseen black wolf rammed the blonde from behind, pushing the pure elf into the chemistry room in a tangle of fur, heat, slobber, and expensive attire. The wolf barred a horrific row of fangs, dripping splatters of spittle onto an unwitting Tristabelle.

The princess pushed with her legs and hurled the werewolf off her into one of its approaching partners.

Yet as soon as she rose, she had to twist over a lab table to avoid the snapping jaws of one of the other black wolves.

Mistlewoe. She needed her magical sword that had shredded the lives of an impressive rogues gallery of supernatural foe. But as she stuck out her hand out to usher it in, she was met with a swipe across her wrist from one of the black wolves. Any other supernatural being would be gushing blood. A human would be dying but as a pure elf Tristabelle endured only a slight bloodletting.

At the front of the class stood the silver wolf, sitting with such patience and calm one would confuse him with one of the royal family's many well-trained dogs.

Princess Tristabelle rolled backward only to find a black wolf coming at her with bewildering speed. It was something of a minor miracle that she was able to press onto a lab table and twist herself backward in avoidance.

One of the black werewolves tackled Tristabelle so hard her eyes blurred. But they were not so blinded as not to see the row of terrible teeth that hovered above her.

Suddenly a tiny blur of brown and black thunder slammed into the werewolf before Tristabelle had a moment to stage a defense.

"Fleur!" Tristabelle spat through ragged breath.

Fleur had to spin to avoid the charge of the two other black wolves. They careened into each other, bouncing back as though they were shaggy pinballs.

"How many fucking wolves are there? This is a-goddamn-annoying," Fleur bitched.

Still, the silver wolf held his position. No movement. No expression. Nothing but grey stoicism.

Though pained and whimpering, a werewolf lunged for Tristabelle. Countering the charge, the girl known throughout her kingdom as The Bright Eyed leaped and then twirled down onto the wolf's head with a figure-skating style toe loop. There was a satisfying crunch; one Tristabelle hadn't expected given the might and durability of werewolves.

"You could have just punched him," Fleur noted.

"Now where would the art be in that?"

A wolf used the girls' distraction to barrel into Fleur with his side, sending her tumbling head over heels. Owing to her fantastical vampire agility, she came down on her Chuck Taylors, but soon had to use centuries of strength to prevent the wolf from biting her head off.

"Sofi! Where are you?" Fleur bellowed, drool from the werewolf pouring on her face.

A long, flaming shard of glass impaled the werewolf's neck courtesy of a throw from the fire-coated hands of Sofi. As werewolves have no fast healing factor like vampires, the beast whined a blood-curdling cry. His mass imploded on itself, his fur wasted away and he was left a weakened human.

The silver wolf hissed as he summoned a magical smoke bomb with a swish of the tail. He threw the girls into a hazy bout of confusion. One that aided the wolves' retreat, a notorious trick of a merc gang Fleur knew all too well.

"Fucking SKM!" she cursed. "I am gonna fuck them all up next time."

"Our fight was not for naught," Princess Tristabelle commented as she turned over her shoulder. "I believe we have a prisoner."

Chapter Sixteen: Sofi Time

Unconscious. Broken. This would remain SeaSeaSea's state for now, as Sofi read from The Shade Room, "Seamus is in a coma! OMG, will he be okay?"

"He got punched by a werewolf, dear," Anika noted, traveling into the battlefield of the chemistry lab. "If he regains use of his extremities, it will be a miracle worth sainthood."

"That guy is gonna die because of us," Fleur said, her pale blue eyes staring into someplace far beyond Hemera.

"He is going to die because a werewolf hit him," Anika corrected, a little more sternly than she would like. "You saved him from a curse."

"And then got him killed. I've killed a lot of people, I mean a lot of people, but I've never second-hand killed someone. When I kill, I kill."

Anika swept her long fingers across Fleur's face. There was a flinch at first but then a long sigh from the brunette.

Fleur kept her eyes downcast, avoiding Anika, "Don't think I give a shit about any humans because I don't."

Anika attached her delicate hand to Fleur's muscular bicep, "You've been lifting even more than usual," she smiled, not smirked. "Keep at it."

There was a calm in the room after that. Anika gave a nod with her usually smirking lips forming a grim line. The girls had contacted her before she entered her kickboxing class. Now they met with her as she wore yoga pants and a sports bra that all hugged her slender yet muscular figure.

"Can you fix him?" Sofi asked, pointing to the man she had stabbed with a flaming shard of glass. His breath was ragged, his body was sweat-soaked, and his slowly blinking eyes locked on Anika.

"I can certainly try."

"Splendificent!" Princess Tristabelle exclaimed. "There is a minor lordship at the end of this for you. Why yes, your land may be where that condemned gnome strip club is but it shall be your condemned gnome strip club."

With that odd bit of motivation to spur her on, Anika dug into her purse. Her fingers dug out a corked vial of an orange liquid. "Oriole Blossom.... for the cure of the wound," she spoke twenty-seven times over the vial.

"She's reduplicating the power of three and nine," Maggie informed everyone. "Mega-magically powerful numbers in witchcraft. I could have done that. I just didn't want to."

"Very good, Princess Magalinda. Someone is a studious witch in training. These are mega-magically powerful numbers. Now that should fix him long enough for you girls to torture something out of him."

"You know us so well," Fleur quipped.

Anika dipped the vial into the man's mouth, ridding half of its contents into the man's throat. The man took on a look of gratitude, eyes flashing, mouth almost smiling.

"Speak quick, wolfie," Magalinda ordered, "... or the little vampire is gonna CRUNCH, snap into you. Are you SKM?"

Not taking his eyes off Anika, the man gave a small nod.

Fleur demanded, "Who are you working for? Where is he? Where's the 99th Degree?"

"We're losing him," Anika said quickly and nervously. She hurried in dumping the remains of Oriole Blossom down his gullet.

But rather than stay in the world of the conscious, he morphed into a frothing, nonsense-spitting wreck. Foam pooled in his mouth then became an onrush that rolled onto his bare chest.

"Shit!" Fleur snapped, pounding on the man's chest in some futile effort to restore him to health.

Futile indeed. The foaming ceased, and the gibberish ended. What was left was a man drenched in blood and foam and sweat and absent of all life.

Dead. Broken.

Fleur felt a surge of rage roll through her body. It came out in the form of her stomping the dead man's head and hollering, "Eat a dick! Eat a dick! Eat a dick!"

Anika sat with hands on knees, head slowly shaking, "Oh, what a semester we're having."

"Wait," Sofi began, "we just had an SKM guy come back from the dead a few days ago. So why not him?"

Anika quickly asked, "What happened? In exact detail, s'il vous plait."

Sofi explained, "It was crazy. This guy died and he came back alive and was all 'lemme serve you, night mother, blah blah blah' to Giselle, then she fainted, then he died again. Aren't I hotter than Giselle? Shouldn't guys be coming back to life to serve me?"

"Sofi, this isn't funny," Anika chided, hands on hips.

Fleur took a seat on a lab table and said, "She ain't lying."

"Bringing someone back to life is a perilous very difficult thing. It doesn't happen casually," Anika reminded the others with a raised index finger.

"It did this time," Fleur mumbled while she sniffed some strange chemical in a tube. It smelled kind of like ghoul brains. Fleur loved ghoul brains.

Anika asked, "Where is the body now?"

Princess Tristabelle replied, "Why, we burned it of course. Ah, truly there is nothing finer in America than sitting about the campfire and burning a body among friends followed by a decadent orgy! America truly is the land of dreams."

"I just can not fathom how or why a body would come back to life unless it was spelled to. Certainly, that would make employee retention easier for SKM. But I've never heard of that kind of spell. As I said, it is murderously difficult to bring back anything and not have it be a shambling corpse."

"It's like preemptive necromancy," Maggie complained. "That's mega-magically terrible! You stake the crazy vampire hyped up on pixie dust and then he comes back to life in a second and bites your head clean off. Horror! Farewell, all! I just can't live in this world any longer."

"If that is true, may I have your hat collection?" Tristabelle asked a little too excitedly.

"Ugh, who gives a shit?" Fleur grumbled, hopping off the lab table. "We need to get to the 99th Degree and now we can't. Why? Because annoying shit keeps happening to us. It's only been a week, but every other hour some fuckery that doesn't happen to other supernaturals happens to us. Can't I drink some blood, can't I smoke some weed, can't I eat a sandwich, can't I get some peace?"

"Relax, pretty gal," Sofi said with a wiggle of her cute nose. "It's about to be Sofi Time!"

****

Stuart Logan sat on a bench next to Sofi in front of Hemera's Charles Shango building in the mid-morning, trying to make damn sure everyone saw he's keeping company with the sexiest redhead on campus. His lady love wore a beige off-the-shoulder top and glossy aviator glasses. Unfortunately for Stu, passersby only thought Sofi was an education major babysitting a troubled youth.

In truth, Sofi had met Stuart because of his claim that he had his ear to the pulse of Hemera. A pulse that hummed in the body of someone Sofi needed information on.

Pedro Gomez. Groundskeeper. Swinger.

Sofi asked, "Sherman, you know a lot about Hemera, and you were on campus over the summer. Did you hear anything about this Pedro Gomez person?"

Called by the wrong name? Stuart hardly cared, eyes affixed on Sofi's legs gleaming under the sun.

"I heard he's a bitch, a cheat and nothing but a sucka," he answered, "The game did not put a deposit of pimpin' in Pedro, so don't think you'll get a withdraw of pimpin' from him."

"You're too funny, Sam! Think about starting a podcast while I'm on the hunt."

"The hunt?"

"For Pedro."

"You wanna meet that guy? That loser doesn't deserve to talk to dem titties though!" Stuart bellowed, making a grabbing motion at Sofi's breasts.

"Ugh! I don't want to but I've got to. Because reasons. I need to know where this club called the 99th Degree is. And he knows."

Princess Maggie had "perfected" her locator spell to the point where if she could cast it at a location where Gorick was recently, it had a 45% chance of being accurate. The 99th Degree was just such a location.

"Maybe I could help you look for it," Stuart offered.

"Scott, you do way, way too much for us. Don't worry about me, it's Sofi Time!" Sofi stated with a wiggle of her freckle-dotted nose.

There was a pop-up shop Sophie needed to hit but this sucka Pedro had to be hit with Sofi Time.

Sofi Time, as Sofi's mom Tammy Mae stated to her daughter, was the time when Sofi accomplished what no other could. Be it winning a beauty contest or reducing a water hag to ashes, the world could always count on Sofi Time.

Fleur couldn't glamor anything about the 99th Degree out of Pedro this morning. It was if there was a wall shielding such knowledge and the bulldozer of a glamor couldn't break it down. That left Sofi to investigate the swinging groundskeeper, who also encountered the now fabled mysterious woman at the 99th Degree.

But what a waste of time when there was shopping to be done. If only an invisible voice would call out to her and guide her away from this hard work. Then she could hit that Gucci pop-up shop.

Suddenly Sophie's phone buzzed.

"Hello!" she answered

"Hey," Fleur grumbled, "I was thinking you don't have to follow Ped—"

"I don't have time to talk. I have to go find Pedro! Peace out!"

"Don't you hang up on me, you stupid fuc—"

CLICK! Sofi hung up.

"Okie dokie, Sven, thanks for your help," Sofi rose off the bench to her full-length beautifully-figured beauty. "It's Sofi Time!"

The redhead beauty broke into a sprint that curled her around the Charles Shango building. In an empty spread of land, Sofi's body shimmered with intense coloration until there was a miniature explosion of brilliant golden light resulting in one hell of an adorable red fox.

Sofi caught her reflection in a shard of glass and gave an approving wag of her tail.

Sofi's phone, lip gloss, keys, and stylish clothes were safely locked away in what her mom called the Kitsune Cubby system or an interdimensional storage unit. This was radically different from werewolves who obliterated everything on their body the moment they transform. Whenever Sofi summoned her human form, so too would she call back all the gadgetry and clothes she couldn't live without.

Free of her human accouterments or human limits, Sofi trotted along with stealth and speed as her asset. Unlike some other fox spirits, Sofi was just as comfortable in her fur as she was in her skin. The girl learned to walk as a fox before she learned to walk as a human and spoke her first words in fox form. All this was well beyond the ears and eyes of Gus the Mattress King of Miami.

Sofi prowled what greenery the school could claim for itself in the densely-packed metropolis of Manhattan. This was where Pedro and another groundskeeper shepherded not a John Deere but a flock of sheep. Urged to go green, the school had done everything within its budgetary power to be environmentally responsible. Sadly, that wasn't enough for a further campus protest movement, which shut down buildings until gas-guzzling lawn care vehicles were eliminated and sheep were brought in to tend the grounds of Hemera.

This should have presented a problem to any right-thinking fox. A fox would never get close enough to eavesdrop on Pedro due to the easily startled sheep. However, it was motherfucking Sofi time so the red fox strutted into the mix with a wagging tail full of swagger.

Just because she was a foxy lady didn't mean she couldn't still tell Pedro was a hottie. The twenty-eight-year old's narrow frame stood 5'9, a thin mustache streaked across an angular face, and he showed his flair for the striking with a dyed blonde pompadour.

"Come on, Pedro, take me to your swingers club," the other stumpy groundskeeper pleaded. "That'll show that nasty bitch to fuck the landlord."

Pedro just turned his head away and gave off a lazy laugh.

That's right when he noticed a red fox sizing him up.

"What in the hell? Matt, stay here."

Pedro armed himself with a rake, a seemingly harmless weapon, but enough to send Sofi scurrying away. Not content to just let Sofi beat a hasty retreat, Pedro pursued her and did not leave poor Sofi with many quality escape options.

Sofi darted through the legs of one student, taking them entirely by surprise, as evidenced by their books dropping to the ground. Then she scampered atop a bench, across the legs of a grad student and over their cheese fries. Yet Pedro was still on her fluffy tail. Off she went, interfering with two students kicking a soccer ball back and forth. Using some deft skill, she swatted the soccer ball at Pedro, which he was barely able to avoid tripping over.

The soccer ball kicking students watched in wonder as Pedro committed to a big swipe of his rake—one that was sure to doom Sofi should he land it. Sofi had plans other than a mauling by rake and deftly curved around Pedro so his rake slashed only where she used to be.

Where she was now was scrambling up a tree.

Though bested, Pedro was not about to sue for peace with a damn fox.

"What the hell kind of fox climbs a tree?" he yelled at her. "And that tree is right next to my barn!" he pointed, as Sofi's eyes went to where the herd was normally held.

Sofi could bring Pedro's young life to a quick end if she really wanted to. Humans tended to suffer an eternal demise when fox spirits started unloading lightning and fire from their tail. But he was such a cutie she couldn't bring herself to fry him or even maul him.

"Pedro? Oh, Pedro?" came a California voice Sofi loved so dearly.

Giselle cruised to Pedro in a pair of bombastic low-rise short-shorts that got Pedro's blood pumping, and a grey slim sleeve stripe polo that showed a generous amount of Giselle's King Kongs, as she would term them.

"Pedro," Giselle's heart-shaped lips moaned, "the townspeople have been telling me about an elite main character that's got access to a secret dungeon."

"What?" Pedro asked, his blood pumping a bit less.

"You know, the super-secret dungeon you're gonna tell me about, you super-secret stud."

"I don't know no secret dungeon," he responded, rubbing his thin mustache. "I'm just a simple groundskeeper."

"Uh-uh, Diana marked you as a quest giver. So tell me everything about the last time you went to the 99th Degree. And uh tell me where it is too....stud!"

Sofi observed from her tree, not appreciating Giselle's Youtube Gaming interrogation techniques. Perhaps if she was trying to pry an exploit to NBA 2k out of Senor Gomez this might not be totally embarrassing. As it stood, Sofi felt like chucking fireballs at her head.

Pedro crossed his arms, "What type of shit is this?! If you know about the 99th Degree, you know damn well you don't belong there or near anyone who goes there, girl."

"Get in the damn barn, Pedro," Giselle snapped. "Or, uh, or else! Sex is pain, Pedro, so get moving!"

Within seconds Giselle was hurrying into the barn.

"Wait! Damn it!" the pompadour sporting hottie barked. He followed Giselle into a barn that Dusty would be right at home in with its straw floor, wooden cages, and sun-lit illumination.

"Ah-ha! Name's Giselle. You're totes in for it now. I'm gonna turn up the heat well past 99 Degrees. Heh, that was kinda funny. Did you get it? Because you're not laughing and it was pretty funny."

Pedro looked Giselle up and down. Twice. "Turn up the heat? Sure you are, kid. How ya gonna do that?"

"Uhhhh, I hadn't thought that far ahead. I just kinda saw you chasing the fox while I was in American history and had to act...uh...stud?"

Crrrreeeeaaaaaak. As the barn door swung open, aches of panic grasped Pedro. Giselle guessed it was his supervisor coming to rid him of that pesky thing called employment. But the one who arrived was a voluptuous redhead parading across the barn.

"Giselle, don't hog Papi all to yourself," Sofi warned gently.

"Ta-da-da! Sofi has joined your party. What do you say, Pedro?"

Both Pedro and Giselle were leering at, what Giselle would term, Sofi sweater bazookas.

"Papi like," he declared, and his stiffening rod declared with him.

"Papi, Papi, Papi, what a man! I've heard a lot about you," Sofi cooed. "All these women can't possibly be right, can they?"

"Why don't you find out?" he dared.

"Yep, Sofi, you do that, and I'll just hang back here and be all cool and such. Not voyeuristic and all creepy and weird," Giselle promised, then stepped back and nearly tripped over a rake.

Sofi used her thick and long tongue as a weapon to hobble the cocky Latino as she forced it inside his mouth. The ever-voyeuristic

Giselle watched with hands rubbing as Sofi went wild within Pedro's mouth. Pedro kissed back, not to be dominated, and their tongues interlocked in a whirlwind. Sofi's squeezable jugs pressed right up into Pedro's shockingly toned chest.

"Who knew sheepherding equaled gains?" Giselle pondered aloud.

Sofi pulled back and asked, "So, Papi, are you gonna tell us all about the 99th Degree?"

Pedro sucked in a deep breath before announcing, "Hell no. If I told you anything about it, the owner would bust my skull open. That's the rules. Rules don't change because you're a freak."

"Papi, you're three tax brackets too low for me but you're gonna get Sofi's Magic Touch."

"Sofi's about to make the 99th Degree look like a meeting of the National Abstinence Education Association," Giselle declared.

With more strength then Pedro could imagine she had, Sofi pulled her Latino lover into a sitting position on a bale of hay. More excitement came bounding to Pedro as Sofi turned away from him and rid herself of her bottoms and frilly pink panties to showcase a perfectly thick ass.

"Catch me, Papi," Sofi demanded as she drooped to her hands and threw her legs back at his sides. His reflexes kicked in and saw him catch her powerful pins at his sides like they were about to do a wheelbarrow race.

Sofi promptly proved Giselle's claim correct as she effortlessly enveloped him with her soaked sex.

Giselle's heart-shaped lips wore a big brilliant smile, for even a deep dive into PornHub couldn't find a position as hot as Sofi's chosen one.

"Oh, lord!" Pedro shouted.

Sofi called back to her cheerleading days, "Ready? Okay! Let's fuck this hot pussy!"

Sofi rocked her hips, while her internal muscles clenched Pedro. The sensation was out of this world. Eyes shut, Pedro was mouthing prayers to avoid a premature and dreaded eruption. Yet with the way Sofi moved her shapely hips and tugged with a seemingly blessed sex, Pedro could feel the smoke ready to burst from the chimney.

"Oh, lord times infinity!" Giselle whooped. "This is so much better than American History."

Pedro was one hundred percent determined not to spill his juice into Sofi. He thought of his grandmother, he thought of his unpaid traffic tickets, he thought of the batting stats from the 1989 Detroit Tigers. But the redhead made that hard as hell. Each plunge onto his hard as a glacier self was done with a steeled vice grip designed to drain every ounce from him. The teenage babe knew exactly what she was doing, letting out smooth sexy laughter as she held his member in the grip of paradise. She was squeezing it, teasing it, and letting the nasty bolts of lust grip his body.

"Even though this isn't rich dick, it's still pretty good," Sofi informed Giselle who gave a thumbs up in return.

Perhaps even hotter than the heated pounding Sofi treated her sex to was the furious bouncing of her big lightskin booty. Pedro's eyes basked in the sight of the delicious and fantastic brown flesh that was launched into a furious jiggling spree. As the nymphomaniac rolled and bounced her hips, her juicy rear flesh jumped and clapped in ways that would put her in the VIP section of the 99th Degree.

Sofi murmured, "Pedro, you're taking me to heaven, Insha Allah."

Giselle's eyebrows raised.

"I'm showing how attuned I am to my progressive values with my cultural appropriation," Sofi announced.

"Actually you're showing how unattuned you are to your progressive values with your cultural appropriation," Giselle responded.

Pleasure pooled around her body, from shin to forehead. It was rich and heady and had her tongue absent mindedly wagging.

"There's a selfie," Giselle decided.

Sofi didn't lose her purpose though. She continued to slam back against Pedro with a horny, desperate need. It was though she could never live without his meat and was desperate to claim it as her own. How she needed this steel to blaze through her everyday of her life!

"Oh my gosh!" Sofi exclaimed. "Pedro, although you're poor in money you're rich in dick. Wow, everyone can be rich in something. Giselle, I grew today."

"Well, you didn't use a condom so you just might."

Again and again, the eighteen-year-old redhead bounced onto Pedro. Again and again, Giselle sweated in a glorious erotic heat. Her mind was locked onto what was happening in front of her; a fiery sword wielded by a blue-collar Latino lover slicing through her voluptuous roomie. Sofi was shameless in how she threw it back on Pedro. The biracial beauty was upon his dick as if the damn gods demanded it!

And, oh, how her huge honey buns rippled endlessly. Rolling waves of golden brown flesh crossing the ocean of hotness that was Sofi's ass.

As Sofi's glorious ass heaved and rippled, Giselle could imagine taking big handfuls of it. Or perhaps even sandwiching her face between the hefty cheeks. That would be a treat for Sofi's Onlyfans subscribers and would probably excuse the outrageous 45 dollars a month fee Sofi was charging them.

Since they were already jiggling, and she had put a stranger's dick in her, it would be totally cool, Giselle thought, to spank her.

"That's degrading!" Sofi barked. "You're treating me like a cheap whore,"

"SorryIwon'tdoitagainreallysorryI'llstop!"Giselle whined as she bowed before Sofi.

"I didn't say stop," Sofi commented lazily.

So Giselle slapped dat ass again. Hard. Hard as fuck! Tina from Dead Or Alive hard! What a reward Giselle got when the bronze skin honey's booty rippled so greatly Giselle thought it was imploding.

"There you go, baby. You don't have to look anymore. You can touch it all you want."

Giselle bashed Sofi's ass with the force of someone who sometimes does Fitness Boxing on the Switch. But that was enough to send an earthquake through Sofi's hot brown ass.

"Yeah, bitch, you claim that ass!"

Giselle claimed it. Claimed it for all the ass lovers who follow Sofi's socials. For all the people who drooled over her bent over in a g-string on Twitter. For all the people who fainted after she posted herself only in a whip cream bikini on Instagram. For all the people who paid 10 dollars a month for her private Snap and funded her vacay to Monaco. That ass slap was for them.

"And I claim a discount on your OnlyFans!" Giselle bellowed.

"Yeah, but no. No you don't," Sofi noted lazily.

This wasn't as bad as when Fleur did it because it was a barn. Sheep lived in barns and rats lived in alleys. There was a difference.

"Yeah baby, give it to the vice president of The After School Slut Club!" Sofi shouted.

"I thought I was the vice president," Giselle whined.

Sweat soaked Pedro, whose mammoth member was bearing the full talents of Sofi time. His eyes were glazed over as though Sofi had fucked him into a faraway land. She couldn't see this but had to know her juicy love grotto combined with her bouncing behind was too much for any man to stand.

Pedro stammered pure gibberish. The bouncing of Sofi's giant ass was hypnotizing and brain-melting in its sexiness.

"Did English stop being your first language?" Giselle questioned

More gibberish.

"Your second language?" Giselle asked, concerned.

Even more gibberish seeps out of Pedro's mouth as his head lolled to the side.

"Your tenth language?!" Giselle blurted.

"Wow! Sofi admired. "I think I fucked him mentally handicapped! No, that's insensitive. Retarded."

"That's still insensitive!" Giselle corrected. "Pedro, just tell us where the 99th Degree is."

Pedro's head rolled forward then down, drool leaking from the corner of his mouth.

"Now he's not even speaking!" Giselle squeaked. "This is bad, this is bad. This is like date rape in reverse."

"Come on, Papi," Sofi pleaded, as she disentangled herself from his body. "Please tell us."

Sofi Time was not the time to shatter someone's mental faculties. Except for that grave wraith in eleventh grade. But that thing had it coming.

Pedro slumped to his side, eyes glassy, jaw slack. Yet he still uttered, "The corner of Cloister and Hubert. Deep in Tribeca."

"The 99th Degree?" Giselle responded.

He whispered slowly, "The 99th Degree."

Then he passed out.

Chapter Seventeen: And Rising

Blasé, plain, barren and dull. All words that could describe the forgotten section of Manhattan where the Golden Land consulate limo dropped Maggie, Tristabelle, and Dusty off at. The buildings that loomed over the girls were of a drab brick variety. The night sky hung like a sheet covering the corpse of this empty street.

Empty except for the 6'3 Asian man standing in front of a solid black door.

Luckily no one asked what the girls really needed to go to or why they needed to go there. No one was going to report it back to Trygyrr, or Queen Brunhilde, or King Fenrisson. Hopefully. It would simply be noted in a log and long forgotten about.

Unless something disastrous happened.

"That's it," Dusty declared. "That's gotta be the 99th Degree. And that there big sucker has gotta be the doorman. And he's gonna let us in otherwise I'm gonna let my foot go right up his ass."

"Dusty, I do not believe we wish to cause any more scenes. Delicacy and diplomacy shall win the day," Tristabelle noted.

"But-" Dusty started.

Princess Tristballe interrupted, "Delicacy and diplomacy."

"The prostitution rests!" Princess Maggie stated with a haughty nod.

"I am no prostitute. I do not accept money for sex. Though donations to the temple are welcome." Princess Tristabelle commented.

"Nothing to it, my queen," Dusty responded with a fist pump. "When he gets a shot of my puppies and goes into a trance, we'll waltz right through the door. Nothing more we gotta do."

With her "puppies" encased in a bright pink high-scoop dress with cut-out side panels to reveal pleasing amounts of skin, Dusty's plan just had to work. Though Princess Maggie and Princess Tristabelle were left looking around for members of the canine species.

Dusty moseyed up onto the doorman, who had sunglasses on despite the darkness. Tattoos written in Japanese reached from his arms to his knuckles. His beard was forked and his hair was slicked back.

"Howdy there, I'm Dusty Blackwood."

"Not on the list," he retorted without checking any sort of list. In fact, he didn't even have a list.

Princess Tristabelle and Princess Maggie shot each other worried glances. They were dressed similarly, with Maggie wearing a poofy-sleeved white dress with huge pink floral patterns, and Princess Tristabelle wearing a slinky, left thigh exposing pink dress that had huge white floral patterns. As always, neither bother to cover up much of their knicker bockers.

"Ya didn't let me finish. I'm Dusty Blackwood with the Double D's. Ain't they great?!"

Dusty lowered her top to reveal a sight that would make any man pant like a puppy. Instead, she got a dismissive wave from the doorman and the comment of, "Girl, I'm gay as hell."

Dusty nodded and cast her doe eyes downward where a rat scurried across her vision. Then, after a good ten seconds, she said, "Son, I just want ya to know my second favorite Fairy Revolution Wrestling tag team after The Music City Gunslingers are the homosexual luchadores Los Diablos De Feugo so this ain't a homophobia thing."

The man hadn't a moment to be confused by the statement. Confusion was halted by an overwhelming feeling of agony brought upon by Dusty's boot to the balls. The Tiny Terror of Nashville reached back, pulled the stunned man's jaw above her shoulder then fell to a seated position. This second sudden attack forced the man's jaw to drop down on Dusty's shoulder. The combo caused havoc for the man's health and his health insurer as the man was left splayed about the ground, foaming at the mouth.

"Oh! Goodness! Shocking!" Tristabelle exclaimed, with her hand over her mouth.

"In case you haven't noticed, kiddo" Princess Maggie began with a twirl, swinging her ruffled gold sequined dress around. "Now's our chance to get in the door!"

Without so much as a call to 911 for the doorman (or stealing his wallet as Fleur would do), the girls strolled into the 99th Degree. What they walked into was a short and bland hallway, filled with the haunting, dark noise of Lana Del Ray's "Dark Paradise" coming from the area beyond a black curtain.

"I'm scared you won't be waiting on the otherside," Princess Tristabelle recited the lyrics, confining herself in a very deep, very dark emotional place. "No, he will not be. Not anymore."

The haunting song reminded Dusty of music played in the Fairy Kingdom clubs of despair. Clubs which the usually happy fairies attended to get in touch with a darker emotions.

"Spooky, spooky," Princess Maggie decided, glancing over her shoulder.

The three stepped through the black curtain to enter a world that was far beyond the realm of the drab the immediate outside world ruled over. This was an expansive club with a brown marble floor with a large hexagon containing a black bat in the center. Paintings that must have been ages old and of priceless status hung along the walls. Many guided the viewer up a wooden staircase to two balconies. The lower possessed an empty throne while the higher balcony led to a hallway that stretched along three separate rooms. Gold and blue lights flashed across the club, bathing the club-goers and four sets of cage dancers.

The cage dancers made Dusty think of her mother, who was a dancer for Fairy Revolution Wrestling before meeting Dusty's father and becoming the Tooth Fairy.

"What do we do now?" Maggie questioned, gazing at two men making out.

"Our plans with this venture have been rather vague," Tristabelle determined. Then she was struck by a bolt of inspiration. Raising her hand high, she announced with a voice like a crack of thunder. "We shall make haste to the bar, ladies!"

And so, the girls strode to the bar, led by Tristabelle who did the walk Giselle thought should be in slow motion in a movie. They jostled their way to the bar, which was lit by neon pink and purple lights and featured a beautiful portrait of Nick Lachey for some odd reason.

The bartender, a tall woman with a shaved head and piercings decorating her face spoke, "You girls old enough to be in here?"

"I'm forty-four human years ol—" Maggie started then got elbowed in the ribs by Tristabelle. "What I meant to say is what I lack in age, I make up for in maturity, wisdom, and refined beauty."

"Sure you do. What are you drinking?"

"Ah yes!" Princess Tristabelle started. "Three glasses of milk from the finest cow in the village."

"There's no cows in the village. Just us gays," The woman flatlined.

"Give us three Red Bulls," Dusty said, throwing a rather large sum of money on the counter. "And keep the change. We got a future queen partying tonight."

The woman gave a laugh and went to work on getting the girls their Red Bulls. As they were supernaturals they didn't have to worry about the side effects of increased blood pressure and heart rate.

"My goodness," Tristabelle said over the dirge-like music. "This club rivals the Unlaced Corset in splendor. Rodgir would be truly at home."

"That's if mother ever lets him off house arrest. He's in deep trouble for sleeping with Trygyrr's wife."

Princess Tristabelle's almond eyes slammed shut, her Cupid bow lips grimaced, and her breath quickened. "You are a mendacious woman, Magalinda."

"I don't know what that means, kiddo. But I'm just the cute little Fluffy Bunny!"

"Why am I just hearing such terrible news?"

"No one wanted to worry you," Princess Maggie replied. "And it just happened."

"And what did Trygyrr do in response?"

"You'd have to ask Krissy. He was there. I think it involved knives and lots and lots and lots and lots of fire."

"Dang, was anyone hurt?" Dusty asked.

"Nah. Elves are fireproof, but Krissy says Lady Karlatta Liselotte was there and one of those kooky wigs she always wears caught on fire. They had to get three vampire guards to restrain Trygyrr."

"That fella didn't seem like the type to go all bonkers over anything."

Maggie noted, "Trygyrr and Rodgir have never got along. Trygrr is big on the duty of Elvrinas and Rodgir is a freewheeling rogue. If mom was gonna spit out two kids after Gorick, couldn't she have picked two who were more alike?"

"Oh sweet Asgard!" Princess Tristabelle whined. "The King's Deputy on house arrest for sleeping with the chancellor's wife?"

Tristabelle's mood was as dark as the song. "The Elvrina cloak is being stripped away to reveal fool's motley!"

Instead of the nine siblings her lady love had, Dusty claimed a mere one on her branch of the family tree. An Eleanor Blackwood, an agent with the Fairy Best Investigators and All Fairy Kingdom Girl, for her sincere, cheerful air, and adorable smile. She and Dusty only sometimes got along. Dusty had a propensity to practice their dad's, Brady Blackwood's, signature holds on poor Eleanor. Brady Hammers, Cock Blocks, and Stiff Kicks were all served to Eleanor who eventually learned from their Uncle Baron (Brady's tag team partner) to serve Dusty a few Music City Elbows as a receipt.

"Just thinking about all them kids is making me dizzy," Dusty responded after sipping her Red Bull. "Even my favorite hen didn't have that many chicks. What's the birth order?

Maggie answered, "It goes Bernhard 'The Bear,' Astrid 'Iron Wings,' Gorick 'The Golden,' Trygyrr 'The Stalker,'" Maggie went on as Dusty counted on her fingers,"Rodgir 'The Grandson of the Bitch,' Constantina 'The Wise,' 'Prince Charming' Krisdane, yours bewitchingly Magalinda 'The Fluffy Bunny,' and lastly and most beautifully Tristabelle 'The Bright Eyed.'"

"Math and numbers ain't my strong suit but ya'll keep saying there are ten of you. So the tenth one really is…"

"Dead," Princess Tristabelle stated flatly.

"But you're elves! Elves don't kick the bucket easy," Dusty said, then drowned the last of her Red Bull.

Before anyone could answer Dusty's question a black man with dreadlocks who looked to be in his late twenties sauntered between Princess Tristabelle and Dusty with an apologetic glance to the latter.

The man took a sip from his glass before a chuckle. Dusty could see his dark eyes darken as he said, "There they are. The youngest princesses of Golden Land. The Fluffy Bunny and The Bright Eyed. Or the slaughterer of Hildegard Palace." Dusty watched Tristabelle go stiff. The man continued, "A man can't lose everything. He can lose his home to exile, his brother to murder, his wife to shame, but something remains, and that's memories. Mostly the bad ones. The ones where his brother, only sixty years of age, is cleaved through his shoulder to his heart. A man remembers seeing that and running for his life. Running for his memories."

"Do you know where Gorick is, Vaan Filma of Hilenborg?" Princess Tristabelle asked tightly.

"Sir Vaan, Your Highness, your brother knighted me before the attack on the Palace."

"Do you know, Sir Vaan?"

"Aye, I know. Is such information valuable to you? Valuable enough to give a man his home back?

"It is," Princess Tristabelle answered sharply.

"He is further north. In this state of New York. The humans have these things called campgrounds. Woods where nothing terrible dwells. Except these woods have something terrible. Gorick the Golden whose had quite some time to think of the loss you dealt him."

"We thank you, Sir Vaan."

"I wouldn't do that."

"Do what, Sir?"

"Thank me."

Vaan waved at the princesses like he was waving a white flag and took his leave.

"My Queen," Dusty started, "you ain't gonna trust a backstabber like him, are ya? He could be leading you into a damn trap."

"That's right!" Maggie declared with wink of her huge crystal purple eyes. "And it would be terribly terrible to fall into a trap." Maggie walked away from the bar, drink in hand, others behind her. "But, well, it's probably a mega-magical bad idea to just start a locator spell out of nowhere when we're not supposed to be here. We just need someone to do us the favor of providing a distra—YIKES!

Maggie exclaimed a bit of shock because a thin woman with heavy black eyeliner, pale face, black-coated lips, and disheveled black hair walked right into her.

"Sorry, sorry!" the woman hurried to state.

"I'm a benevolent Fluffy Bunny, so I forgive you."

"Thanks. I can't believe my luck. I just, well, I just, well, I just had sex with a prince!"

"Oh, dear," Princess Tristabelle muttered as Cradles by Sub Urban began playing overhead.

The black clad woman swayed merrily, "His name is Rodgir, and he's a prince from a country called Golden Land."

"Motherfucking shit!" Princess Tristabelle exclaimed. "I shall endure no more of this. Tell me where I might find this Rodgir so I may gaze upon his noble person and perhaps offer my appreciation for his presence."

"Well, I don't know if I wanna just introduce him to a different girl."

"Hey, hey," Maggie interjected, "at least tell us what he looked like."

"Well, he had coal black hair, green eyes, a thick beard."

The song began speaking of living in a world of make-believe.

"You have encountered an impersonator," Tristabelle said flatly without much sympathy in her voice. "Rodgir Elvrina of Golden Land has golden hair, is clean-shaven, and has purple eyes much the same as mine and my sister.

"How do you know that?"

Tristabelle ignored the question, "How did this man speak?

"Uh, he was kind of short on words. The silent type."

"You have indeed encountered an impersonator," Tristabelle stated again, this time her hands formed tight fists.

"Are you sure?"

"My sister and I are residents of Golden Land."

"And so your dreams of being a princess come to an awful end!" Magalinda announced, distressingly holding her hand to her forehead.

"You oughta find this here Rodgir impersonator and give 'em a piece of your mind," Dusty encouraged. "You wouldn't be a real woman if you didn't. You can't let some stinking punk make a fool outta you. Go get 'em!"

"Go get him?" The woman asked unsure as the song spoke of honesty being a one-way gate to hell.

His bearded face endured a hellish punch that packed more power than the thin woman should have owned. Another punch bombed across his face, flinging him into a painting of a dignified black man. The third punch caught the notice of a few club-goers who turned to view the outrageously violent spectacle.

Yet it wasn't enough to create the sorely needed distraction.

"Dang, if that happened in the Fairy Kingdom we'd be talking about it for months," Dusty groaned. "Here, don't a single soul care."

"Perhaps these people need to be served a sweetened dish," Princess Tristabelle surmised. "My dancing ability is a feast for the eyes, no one can resist. Allow me."

"Save Me" by Omri began playing in the club. The song's male singer barked at their subject not tell to him he was sorry then implored someone to save them and never break them.

"It's the witching hour, girls," Magalinda cooed.

Princess Tristabelle sauntered to the center of the dance floor, already gaining the attention of several sets of eyes. She swayed back and forth and raised her arms in a long, luxurious stretch that highlighted her pendulous breasts.

The singer talked about their target being the thing that made them fear themselves. As Princess Tristabelle picked up the words, she began to sing to herself as she walked her hands down to her ankles. Her dress rode up her thighs, almost bearing her toned ass. It was a sight that demanded attention.

It got it.

The youngest Elvrina princess ran her hands through her wavy blonde bob, as she swished her hips to and fro. It was a seductive grind that had some watchers licking their lips.

The music blared, the crowd cheered, but Princess Tristabelle was in a world all of her own. She twirled on her heels in tight, sensuous motions that earned a round of applause from a muscular black man with a thin goatee on the balcony.

Meanwhile, The Fluffy Bunny dug into her purse to produce a map of New York State, a bottle of water, a lone button, a pendulum, and henbane.

"You sure you can do this?" Dusty asked, her doe eyes already rolling, her hands on her hips.

Princess Tristabelle sank to her knees then swiftly exploded into a back-bending pose of sexual triumph as she ran her hands along her slender waist.

"I'm mega-magically sure!"

"And how accurate is this thing?" Dusty couldn't hide skepticism.

"It's hugely accurate now that we're where Gorick has been. Like 58 percent accurate. Huge!"

Maggie worked fast, laying the map on the floor. As Dusty stood to shield her from any onlookers, Princess Maggie laid the lone button on the map. From there she ground up a specific amount of henbane and dumped it on the map along with a few drops of water.

Hurrying up, she faced west with the pendulum in her hand.

"Let the water show the location of Prince Gorick Elvrina of Alfheim, Golden Land," Maggie said twenty-seven times.

"You sure you used the right amount of that stuff?" Dusty asked to a head nod from Maggie.

The lights above pulsated into orange and red. The colors of fire. Mirroring the same fire Dusty felt was consuming her queen.

Maggie squealed in shock, watching the water gather the button in a bubbling miniature torrent. The liquid carried the button to a place in upstate New York—a place Dusty knew all too well.

"That's where the school's camping trip is!" Dusty exclaimed, doe eyes taking a close look at the map.

Dusty watched in sadness as she thought she saw Princess Tristabelle's entire face darken underneath the swaying of bright orange light.

Chapter Eighteen: Breaking Dawn

Normalcy had returned to the Hot Squad's Upper East Side penthouse. Giselle was in her room with Stuart streaming Persona 5 for PlayStation 4 for 60 or so watchers. Sofi was recording bikini try-on videos for sale for fifteen bucks on her website. Though for twenty bucks you could get a special blooper bonus video with promises of a nipple slip!

As for Fleur, the boy-short wearing vampire was on her phone, pacing down the marble foyer, roaming beneath a Shakespeare quote stenciled in delicate cursive on the ceiling.

"Hell is empty and all the devils are here," it read.

"Where the hell am I supposed to send you?" Fleur snapped. "Well aren't YOU a picky girl.... It's costing me a lot of money to send you there.... No you can't be like me... Hell no I don't need your help against my dad," Fleur looked up at the quote—how true it was. "And you're not as good at fighting as me.... If you run away one more time I'll pay a hunter to track you down.... Yeah, yeah, I'll send you some money.... I love you too. Bye."

As soon as Fleur clicked off her phone she found Dawn Nyfall, covered in sweat, clad in a sports bra and red yoga pants, looking at her with an arched eyebrow.

"That conversation sounded, I don't know, motherly," Dawn's thick lips suggested before turning into a small smile. "Those pale blue eyes are shining. You're happy. That was someone you love very much."

"She's a pain in my ass," Fleur said with a big smile filling her baby fat filled face.

"Aren't they all?" Dawn quipped. "By the way, I had lunch with your dad."

Fleur couldn't keep her full lips from forming a malevolent sneer. Though Dawn didn't notice. Instead, a dreamy state flashed through her eyes.

"He was so mysterious," Dawn reminisced, "but then again, so is his daughter."

"I'm not mysterious," Fleur countered, shoving her phone into her shorts. "I hate everyone I meet and there isn't any secret about that."

"Moody, sullen, depressive, but built like a fitness model with the face of a doll. Mysterious."

Dawn swayed her way into Fleur's room. Her movements so airy and light reminded Fleur of the way her mother, a succubus, would sway into men's hearts and bed. Fleur was more of a bulldozer, wrecking any one's inhibitons or sense of propriety.

The grey eyes of Dawn Nyfall scanned the gloomy room thoughtfully. She settled upon a stone podium where a journal of Fleur's conquests was held up by a twisting gnarl of stone branches.

"So, Fleur, do you have a boyfriend?"

"Nope."

"Good," Dawn spun around to Fleur as she pulled her red locks out of a ponytail. "You know I have a husband, but I bet you don't care."

"As President of The After School Slut Club I also don't care that your daughter is in the next room playing games with that rat-faced weirdo."

Dawn swung her arms around Fleur's neck, and with a dazzling gaze that hammered Fleur, she whispered, "I'm not playing any games, Fleur."

What was going on, Fleur wondered. *Where was the shining example of Republican family values Dawn embodied?* Fleur thought that for a second then decided she didn't care.

Tristabelle had explicitly stated in the Extraordinary Young Women's Code of Conduct that the fucking of another housemate's parents was forbidden. But as Fleur always said, "I'm a demon and I'm gonna get up to some demonic ass shit."

Fleur dove into a kiss, plunging her tongue into Dawn's mouth. She tasted of cherries. Fleur's favorite taste outside of blood. Her scent, her beauty, her breath hit Fleur in her perpetually needy place. The vampire-demon knew Stephen Nyfall had no clue what to do with this type of woman but Fleur did. She just had to figure out why her stomach was burning.

Fleur broke apart from the kiss to have Dawn beam back a sweet smile and an innocent tilt of the head. Surely not the smile of one who had stabbed a century-old vampire-succubus with a silver cross. And yet that was the smile Dawn gave as she had a silver cross piercing Fleur's shredded stomach.

Agony, with the heat of the bottomless burning, surged through Fleur. Blood dribbled through her open mouth, baby droplets falling on her bare feet.

"Saint Lazarus hopes you die slow," Dawn said in an unnatural saccharine littered voice.

Her dad had weaponized Dawn, glamoured her, used his daughter's promiscuous succubus nature against her, and was on the verge of achieving his century-long dream: banishing her to hell permanently.

With an effort that rivaled moving a golem, Fleur shoved Dawn to the ground. With Dawn went the silver cross, layered to its very top in blood.

"Saint Lazarus hopes you die slow," Dawn repeated in that same sing-song voice.

Free from a now-healed wound, free of all things silver and all things holy and Jesus related, Fleur could reclaim the speed and agility a supernatural owned over a human. Dawn was fit and quick, but she made a poor attacker with Fleur rolling beneath her attacking arm.

Dawn took a dizzying fall onto Fleur's bed, crashing against the sleek purple comforter and losing grip of her cross. Still, her expression was loaded with a sunny smile.

Fleur hurried to her BDSM box and snatched out a pair of fluffy black handcuffs. They had been a graduation gift from her mom, Lotus. And now they were wrapped around the right wrist of Giselle's mom affixing her to a bedpost that featured carvings of bats, ghouls, golems, and all sorts of nasties. All of whom Fleur would rather face than the prospect of telling Giselle that Dawn had been glamoured to kill Fleur.

"But Saint Lazarus said he hoped you'd die slow," Dawn said, her eyes big in wonder.

"Wait here," Fleur said in a panic. "I'm gonna get Giselle."

"That's good thinking, Fleur. She can kill you because Saint Lazarus hopes you die slow."

***

This was a new day in video game streaming excellence. In Giselle excellence! She had shattered her record of 50 viewers with a jaw-dropping, utterly miraculous 75 people to watch her play Persona 5. Sure Stuart, who was sitting next to her, got into a heated argument with someone in chat who said Persona 3 was better than Persona 4 and threatened to "blow up his block." But other than that things were going great!

She even had a guest appearance when Fleur burst into her room.

"Giselle, come here."

"Not now, Fleur," she then mouthed the words "75 people watching."

"Come here!"

"But we just got some new weapons and we're about to go to the third palace," Giselle whined.

Fleur's teeth bit her full bottom lip, and her eyes got big in panic. With no other recourse available to her, she snatched the PlayStation power cord out of the socket with such quickness that sparks flew.

"Fleur!" Giselle snapped. "You can't just unplug the PlayStation. You have to select power from the function screen—"

"Argh! Who gives a shit!" Fleur barked, stomping her feet in a very Dusty like manner.

Sofi strode into the room, red hair in an updo, bronze skin on nearly entire display because her string bikini was more string than bikini. She folded her arms below what Fleur had dubbed her "torpedo tits" and voiced, "Oh my god, keep it down. I'm trying on all the bikinis my fans sent me and recording it so I can sell them the video."

Fleur took off with enough speed she wound up sliding into her room. The others arrived just in time to see a handcuffed Dawn swipe at the sliding vampire-succubus.

"Why is my mom handcuffed to your bed?" Giselle asked hurriedly. "Mom, what are you doing handcuffed to Fleur's bed?"

"Giselle, sweetie, perfect timing," Dawn noted with more cheer in her voice than Giselle had ever heard before. "Saint Lazarus wants Fleur to die slow, so please take care of it for us."

"Stuart, can you wait outside?" Giselle asked, voice soft, face absent of color.

"But, I'm—"

Fleur gave Stu a shove out and slammed the door behind him.

"My old man glamoured her to kill me," Fleur informed the others.

"Mom, is that true?"

"Let's kill Fleur slow so Saint Lazarus can be happy and take us out to dinner," Dawn said perkily.

Giselle dropped to her knees and beat her fist against the floor. Beat them hard enough Fleur's book of victims wobbled. "No, no, no, no! We told you to stay away from him! Why didn't you listen? Why did he do this to you? How could he?"

"Fuck, we should have sent her home when she first mentioned my dad," Fleur groused.

"She just outright tried to kill you?" Giselle questioned.

"Uh, sure. Yeah. Just popped up and stabbed me" Fleur lied well enough to convince Giselle.

Sofi watched Giselle inch closer to her smiling mother, "Can you, I dunno, unglamor her?"

"Pretty much impossible," Fleur groaned, her hands again tugging at her brown hair. "The only way to unglamor her is for her to kill me."

"Great idea!" Dawn nodded her head with maniacal eagerness

"Not an option," Giselle announced with hard finality. "We can ask Princess Constantina what to do. That big mirror in Princess Tristabelle's room is a magic mirror so let's use that."

Sofi wrinkled her nose then gave a firm nod, which Fleur met with an uneasy, slow shrug.

"Good, Giselle, lead her away, then kill her slowly!" Dawn ordered before forming a smile too wide to be healthy.

"We're gonna help you, Mom."

The three girls left Giselle's raving mom to find a raving Stuart, in the middle of speaking to Tyr and wildly waving his hands in front of him. "I saw through the one percent's usage of numerology to control me, and now they're using tricknology on Giselle's mom to get to me. They don't know how I can fight the engineering of my captivity!"

Stuart kept on talking utter nonsense, and the girls just moved by very slowly and full of confusion at his bullshit into Tristabelle's room. Tyr followed.

All the girls' rooms were fantastic marvels of interior decorating, but Princess Tristabelle's wore the crown for opulence. There was a handcrafted high headboard of her bed with its engravings of elven warriors. The bed faced a splendid view of New York, the best of all the girls' rooms. Then there was her dresser mirror with its intricate ornate carvings that displayed various women that Giselle recognized from fairytales. Only they were portrayed as elves.

"How does that elven skank work this thing?" Fleur grumbled as Tyr rubbed against her leg.

Sofi stepped forward, "It goes like this; Magic Mirror, oh Magic Mirror, Princess Constantina Elvrina, oh pretty pretty please."

Their reflection vanished, overtaken by a purple mist. The mist faded away to reveal a room with looming tower-like bookcases, holographic images of swords, knives and assorted weaponry, and glowing monitors above various artifacts such as a golden breastplate, and a green helm in the shape of a dragon's head. Positioned in front of the monitor overlooking a veil decorated with a vine motif was Constantina in her wheelchair with blonde hair arranged into a series of braids on the right side of her head.

"Uh, Princess Constantina?" Giselle greeted her.

Princess Constanina swung around in her wheelchair, becoming instantly recognizable to Giselle. Giselle remembered seeing her head on Princess Tristabelle's compact magic mirror. The elven princess had wider eyes than Tristabelle, bejeweled eyebrows, a square jaw, and an older yet more sympathetic look than her little sisters Maggie and Tristabelle. Sort of a glamorous kindergarten teacher look.

Giselle had just remembered that a curse bound Constantina to a wheelchair. A curse Princess Tristabelle blamed Prince Rodgir for inadvertently causing.

"You must be companions of Tristabelle. I am rather glad to meet you," Constantina said, finishing her sentence with a kind smile of her long pink lips. "Though I know little of sexual matters, I can already tell she can find no better concubines than you."

"My mom was a concubine to a Chinese emperor," Sofi announced. "He died in a mysterious fox attack. So sad and tragic."

The Hot Squad and Giselle introduced themselves and their particular, or in Giselle's case lack thereof, supernatural species.

"You all make quite the group. And I see Tristabelle is influencing your choices of swimwear," Constantina commented," However, may I help you?"

Sofi spoke, "There's a glamoured human we need unglamored fast as fuck."

Constantina let out a heavy sigh and slumped her shoulders that were bare around a golden tank top. "A vampire glamor?"

Giselle nodded.

Constantina spoke, "The very nature of vampire glamor has been debated in lecture halls and castles for centuries. It may well be illusion magic. But if it is, it is no ordinary illusion spell. For illusion magic wears off while a glamor holds a firm root in the human's brain. But there's no real science behind magic. Magic is sometimes simply magic."

"Hey, Red Fox," Fleur turned to Sofi, "can't fox spirits cast illusion magic? Can't you overwrite the illusion?"

Giselle looked up with hopeful blue eyes at a nose wrinkling Sofi who spoke, "I've never tried any illusion magic though. I think I'm too young to do it t-b-h."

Constantina leaned forward and quickly added, "And layering an illusion over an illusion very well might create disastrous effects on the human mind," Constantina leaned back in her chair and swept a golden curl of hair from her kind eyes. "Now then, it is only a theory that a glamour is illusion magic. Had I the human with me, perhaps I might investigate their altered nature further, or take them to Clan Davenkiss, the leading vampire family in my country. All I can offer you is that the other theory labels a glamor as dark magic."

"So, we find a dark magic sorcerer and boom we fix her," Fleur offered, her voice rising with hope.

"Far from it. A dark magic sorcerer inflicts only malaise," Constantina warned. "Though perhaps a witch specializing in spells and brews that use a dark magic base could be of some help. It would most certainly have to be a powerful witch. And a well-practiced one for the inexperienced witch could make this situation all the worse."

"We've got one," Fleur chimed, her face lighting up with hope—a hope so infectious that Giselle's face lit up too.

Chapter Nineteen: Serenity

Dawn Lisa Nyfall passed away on September 12. Beloved wife

of husband, Stephen. Cherished mother of daughter, Giselle. Dawn was

a graduate of the Massachusetts Institute of Technology. She co-

founded Night Fall Technology with husband Stephen. She proudly

served as Chairman of Night Fall Technology's board for many years.

Dawn tirelessly worked as a liaison, organizer, and fundraiser for the

Republican National Committee. She was a wine connoisseur, and avid

tennis player, and enjoyed playing golf with daughter, Giselle. She was

"the best mother in history."

There was no hope.

There was hope.

There was no hope.

There was hope.

There was no hope.

There was hope.

Giselle stared vacantly at the door to Fleur's room. Behind

that door sat her mother, glamoured by Saint Lazarus to kill Fleur.

Dawn could be cured. Dawn couldn't be cured. Giselle's heart tumbled

and flopped with waves off crippling hopelessness and fierce defiant

hope.

Her head felt hot. Hot as a furnace with heat that boiled over, spilling into her guts and making her nauseous. She was about to slump to the ground, melted down by the painful heat, when she saw Fleur approaching with Anika, dressed in a smart business attire of black skirt, black suit coat and white blouse.

Trailing Fleur and Anika was what Giselle thought was a K-pop idol. The woman was blessed with wide eyes of round black pools, a perfectly rounded face, pretty thin lips, and wavy brown hair down to the shoulders.

"Giselle, this is the woman I was telling you about," Anika started. "Doctor Hannah this is Giselle."

"Doctor and genius," The K-pop woman said very flatly. "And also a white magic sorcerer."

"Really?" Giselle asked, her head now hurting worse.

"Do you not know what a white sorcerer is?" Doctor Hannah asked. "I can wield healing magic, heal wounds, erase scars, purge diseases. It's a more advanced form of light magic. Both are considered close to the heavens if you believe in that sort of thing.

"And Hannah doesn't," Anika said with a mocking tone.

"I can quantify my magic. Can you quantify the heavens? No," she said in a bored tone. "But that is beside our point. I find arguing with lesser minds boring. Giselle, it's possible to use this light magic to reverse the dark magic of the glamor."

"Only possible," Giselle muttered.

Fleur poked her with her bright yellow sneaker, "Pessimism ain't very main character."

Giselle had to put every ounce of strength in her body and soul to rise up off that floor. When she did, she led Anika and Doctor Hannah into Fleur's room with Fleur herself lingering behind.

Dawn was still handcuffed to Fleur's purple comforter covered bed. Currently, she was enlisting Tyr into the fight against Fleur, "Little things can do big things, Tyr. Look at Tom Cruise or Kevin Hart. You can be the Kevin Hart of murder and kill Fleur," she blabbered in speedy tones.

Tyr decided grooming his paws was more productive than homicide.

"Quite interesting," Doctor Hannah commented as she listened to Dawn ramble.

"Mom," Giselle started, each step painful, like walking up a volcano. "This is Doctor Hannah. She's come to help you."

"Possibly help. Though leaving her like this would produce an interesting study."

"Excellent news, sweetie! Right now I don't have a stake, but I think you can fashion something and use it to kill Fleur."

Her clothes thick with blood, her hands rife with blood, her face covered in blood. Giselle could picture her entire being coated with the blood of Lazarus. The blood she forced him to shed. Giselle did not like the feelings or strange out-of-body visions that vengeance brought her.

"Everyone, move out of my way," the doctor said in a not so soothing tone.

Doctor Hannah's hand thrust out as she stood as proud as the finest of statues. Concentration was spelled across her face with a set jaw and narrowed eyes. Her slim body began to tremble as her hand began to glow with white luminescence.

"Heal!" she shouted, then expelled a thick ray of white light from her hand. It struck Dawn like a bolt, jerking her upwards and forcing her head to snap back. But then Dawn sat still, her expression unreadable.

Giselle could still see the blood on her hands.

"I smell her!" Dawn shrieked. "I smell Fleur! Kill her! Make sure she dies slow!"

Giselle felt like she was drowning in blood. She couldn't tell when or how, but when she snapped back to reality, she was standing in the hallway getting her shoulder rubbed by Dusty.

"I just gotta make stronger pixie dust," Dusty told Fleur, Anika, and Doctor Hannah "You combine that with your white magic and everything'll be fine."

"A good insight, pixie," Doctor Hannah noted.

"Name's Dusty."

"It doesn't matter what your name is; I need an enhancement. Something of the day to fight a glamor which is considered of the night," Doctor Hannah stated.

"Do you have that something?" Fleur asked.

Doctor Hannah's shoulders sagged. "I did," Tyr scooted across her feet to reach Giselle. "I had a lock of Amaterasu's hair. She's a Japanese sun goddess. It was gifted to me by the most powerful white magic sorceress in Japan on her deathbed, but it was stolen from me by a man named Kabuso."

"I know that name," Giselle spoke slowly as Tyr nuzzled her. "I think we met at Belephegor's party."

"So if he stole your shit, then we have to steal it back," Fleur noted.

"I detect overconfidence in your voice," Doctor Hannah warned. "Stealing it back will be incredibly dangerous."

Fleur flashed—not a big happy grin but—a wild smirk and declared, "Good."

***

It came in waves.

The headache.

It felt like a dance.

Giselle's head was doing a dance of death.

Somewhere in front of her was the living room of the Upper East condo she now knew was her personal hell. In that hell were a gaggle of supernaturals. There was one vampire-succubus hybrid, a fox spirit, a pixie, three pure elves, a witch, and a white magic sorcereres.

One of the elves, a female with crystal blue eyes that slanted more than the other female elf, said, "I'm not a fighter, and I'm not looking forward to facing a Gorick whose got revenge on the mind and a nasty spear in his hand. So I'll just help with the heist. Bunnies are famed for their cowardice."

Giselle was shivering.

And hot.

Fiercely hot.

"You haven't escaped the fire, Your Highness," the witch warned. "You just jumped into a different flame."

"Flame shlame, no one is roasting this bunny," the elf with the eyes more slanted than her sister pronounced.

The pixie was determined to fight by her queen's side. The elf with the blonde bob flatly stated, "No one need place themselves in harm's way for a family feud."

The fox spirit said, rather coolly and bad-ass like, "If the family feuds, then the family feuds."

It was decided the elf with the blonde bob, the pixie, and the fox spirit would face Prince Gorick. Face him the same night they went to a camping trip for the school Giselle now knew as the goliath that ruined her life.

The white magic sorcerer said that Kabuso kept a lock of a goddess' hair where there were traps only a human could disarm.

The heat settled.

The shivers stopped.

Resignation.

Serenity.

"I have to go," Giselle stated. "She's my mom. I have to go."

The male elf said she couldn't. The danger was too high. The vampire-succubus hybrid argued they had no other choice but to bring this human. The male elf pledged his service to protect the human during the heist. The female elves, shockingly, agreed it was better he protect Giselle than fight Gorick.

Serenity.

Chapter Twenty: I am the resurrection and the life

"Pizza was always good pre-felony," that was Fleur's thinking.

"Fuck that white bitch that rolled through here and stole my shit with a pizza stain on her shirt. She ain't this, she ain't that, she ain't shit. Fuck her and her pizza, on god."

So, Fleur pulled the pizza from the pizza oven and sat it atop the monochromatic counter.

"A real American treat!" Maggie exclaimed. "Good thing elves can't get fat because I'm gonna eat the whole thing!"

"You need three things in your body to commit a successful robbery," Fleur stated as she lifted a gooey slice. "Protein, carbs, and ice water in your veins. I got my three."

Prince Krisdane stared at the pie like it had herpes, whereas Maggie smiled around a mouthful of pizza.

"Why do you talk different than Prince Charming and TB?" Fleur wondered.

"Ohoho! Good question, little vampire," The ditzy princess exlciamed. " Finally, someone delves into the mystery that is Princess Magalinda! While the others were training to fight frost giants and orcs and corrupt elves, and other scary baddies, I was busy in the palace watching all the American movies and shows our international knights would bring me. So I just kinda wound up talking like... me!"

Doctor Hannah moved her iPad away from Fleur's cheese and pepperoni beauty. Then she pulled up a Brooklyn street that owned what looked to be a narrow apartment building.

"This entire building is Kabuso's headquarters," Doctor Hannah informed the others.

Giselle's heart was terrorizing her chest; it was slamming with such intensity it wouldn't have shocked her if it burst through her body and landed on the pizza.

"Who is Kabuso?" Giselle questioned. "Why does he need a headquarters?"

"Kabuso is a thief who uses his powers to rob people of supernatural valuables. He is a master of illusion," Doctor Hannah answered

"I don't give a fuck if he's the master of the universe," Fleur remarked. "He's got it, I want it, and I'm gonna take it."

"How are we supposed to get in?" Giselle wondered, peering down at the iPad.

"Easy," Fleur commented. "We'll take the roof from the building next door. Hop on over to his roof. I'll carry Giselle on my back and go in from there."

Doctor Hannah noted, "I'll draw the security's attention by causing a scene out front."

"You cause a scene?" Fleur spoke her skepticism and showed it with folded arms.

"Yes, me. It is simple to cause a scene. Raise your voice. Swing your arms. A scene is caused. But you'll still face dangers inside. Illusions, traps, more security..."

"I don't want anyone to get killed," Giselle demanded. "They're just people doing their job."

"You will either kill these men or kill your mother," Doctor Hannah spoke in a bored tone.

Fleur downed her third slice of pizza then commented, "Fuck that no killing rule. Prince Charming, if someone comes after Giselle, you take that magic sword and gut them."

"Giselle, I will do what I must to protect you," Krisdane stated, tossing a heavy gaze upon Giselle. It made her feel as if a brick wall had been attached to her body.

"It's circumstances that make the murderer; that's what dad says," Princess Magalinda noted to a nod from Krisdane.

"I understand you're elves and vampires, but Kabuso has guards and traps that would test all of you and take off your head," Doctor Hannah noted.

"But I like my head," Princess Magalinda whined.

"We'll just have to duck," Fleur followed up her quip with a smirk.

"None of you are invincible," Doctor Hannah stated. " All of you can die."

***

Giselle was nervous.

Not butterfly in the stomach nervous. As she sat trembling in Fleur's arms atop an Eastern Parkway building in Brooklyn it was like maggots had infested her stomach. Maggots that kept growing in number as the seconds to the jump to Kabuso's building neared. Maggots that threatened to rise through her esophagus, into her mouth, and then spew violently on Fleur's black and white striped T-shirt.

"Fleur? How many people have you killed?"

Fleur frowned for a good while, then spoke softly, "I stopped counting after 100."

"What's hell like?"

"What?"

A gust of wind swayed Fleur's chocolate-colored locks.

Giselle expected a quip, taunt, a mocking comment, or at least a big happy grin. Instead, Fleur flatly stated, "You'll never see it."

Then they were in the air. It was over in seconds. It felt like hours. The grace of an elegant leap. The brutality of the expectation she might die. The perfection of Fleur's landing. Giselle hadn't a moment to process this all before Krisdane was gently pulling her out of Fleur's arms.

"Breathe easy, Giselle. No harm will come to you," he announced as he stroked her cheek.

"Ack! A touch from Prince Krisdane!" Maggie shouted. "There are girls in Golden Land who will pay twenty gold pieces for a skin sample of that cheek."

Fleur was busy staring at the grey door atop the roof, "You ready?"

"Don't we need more of a strategy?" Giselle questioned.

"I'm too lazy for that," Fleur countered. "Let's just beat who we see to death."

"No one dies, Fleur," Giselle said sharply, pulling herself away from Krisdane.

There was no response from Fleur on the no dying rule. Instead, the muscular babe placed her hand on the doorknob, and with a mighty yank, she broke the door and lock entirely.

Ever the chivalrous one, Prince Krisdane took on the danger for himself in stepping first into Kabuso's lair. What greeted him was a dimly-lit stairwell and a hailstorm of bullets fired from a ceiling based turret. The bullets slammed into him, shredding through his navy polo with white stripes.

"Krisdane!" Giselle shrieked.

But they were not shredding through Prince Krisdane's body. The noble prince stood calm in the face of what would be a regular man's death. The machine kept up its deluge; its weapons only being absorbed into Krisdane's body. As the turret continued to unleash what should be lead hell, Prince Krisdane reached forward and shouted, "Phobeus!"

Yellow sparkles began to surround Krisdane's outstretched hand. They coalesced first into a white hilt embedded with a runic script, then formed a crossguard made of a miniature, glowing sun, then created a blade that dazzled with tiny yellow sparkles. Though beautiful, the sword was not to be trifled with; when he leapt, he used it to obliterate the turret.

"Human weapons are so charmless," Krisdane bemoaned. "It is safe to enter."

A trembling Giselle brought up the rear, her wheat gold Nike's crunching bullets beneath her.

"Wha…what if there are more turrets?" Giselle stammered.

"I wouldn't count on that," Fleur commented lazily. "It's a bad idea to put death machines where your easily killable help can be easily killed."

"Are you invincible?" Giselle asked Princess Maggie and Prince Krisdane.

"I wish!" Princess Magalinda exclaimed. "Then I wouldn't be such a scared rabbit. Pure elves can be killed by fell beasts, metal worn from fell beasts, or other magic objects. But it's still a toughie to kill an elf. For a human, it's mission never accomplished."

The foursome stepped down the short stairwell, past the shattered remnants of the turret and into a hallway lined by a wall-length mirror.

Krisdane pointed out, "Doctor Hannah gave no note of where we might find the lock of hair."

"I guess," Fleur started, "We just have to stumble like assholes until we find it. And..." Fleur cocked her head to the doorway. "Someone's coming. Elves, take Giselle down that door behind me. I got who's coming."

Giselle gripped Fleur's arm, "Are you sure?"

"I'm always sure," Fleur declared, letting her full lips rise into a smirk.

Behind a fist-clenching Fleur the others sprinted to the door. They made it through just as Fleur was pierced through the throat with a wooden stake.

The stake had exploded through the mirrored wall. Now Fleur was painstakingly bringing it out of her throat. She wanted to scream but her voice box was torn to shreds. The surface wound was already regenerating. As for her voice box, Fleur had little idea how long it might take to heal.

The impact of a knee to her toned stomach dropped Fleur to her knee. It hit with the force of a sledgehammer. It could only belong to a vampire—one older than her.

Fleur's pale blue eyes lifted to see a vampire who couldn't have been any older than seventeen when he was turned. His face was round, his eyes big and a spare little mustache stretched above his lip.

That mustache was disgusting. It was hideous. If vampires could vomit, Fleur would vomit on it. She hated it with every bit of hell-born energy contained in her fit body. All that disgust was unleashed in the form of a leaping headbutt. Battered, the vampire staggered backward. It was just enough of a misstep to open Fleur's window to strike.

Fleur slammed the stake into the other vampire's eye socket so hard her knees trembled. The man's youthful face erupted with blood, his mouth pushing out a torrent of screams.

Fleur knew from experience that that injury would take a while to regenerate. She decided to slow the process by snapping his neck.

A bullet pierced Fleur's heart. But only a silver bullet; a bullet constructed for werewolves. The hapless guard who shot it cursed and fired again, as though the bullet somehow got it wrong and should have killed the teenager.

He was lucky Giselle instituted the no one dies rule. Fleur merely knocked him unconscious rather than tear out his heart.

Two more guards rushed her, each holding wooden stakes. One circled to her back, while the other lunged at her. Fleur made a quick slide through his legs. Then she came up with a backflip kick that sent him crashing into his partner.

"I think the no-killing rule is off when you try to stake me."

The same lunging guard made another lunge for Fleur. He was far too slow, and Fleur broke one of his ribs with her knee.

"Ah, nothing sounds as sweet as a breaking rib. Except Tristabelle's oinking."

Fleur scooped up the stake, just as she rolled through the remaining guard's swipe.

She spun towards him and bashed him in the face with an elbow so painful it seemed to blind him momentarily. That was all Fleur needed to get his stake then permanently blind him with two stakes through the eyes.

His scream was delicious.

***

Pure white-hot horror. It spread through Giselle like a virus. It crippled her. Her trembling body had to be helped into the oak furniture decorated office by Princess Magalinda. She had seen Fleur get impaled through the throat. The painting of red splotches on the office wall reminded her all too dreadfully of what befell Fleur.

"Don't you worry your pretty white-haired head, Giselle. I know vampires and that little vampire can't die from anything but a stake to the heart or heart being torn out."

It was precisely that stake through the heart possibility that made Giselle dry heave.

"Giselle, stay close to my sister," Krisdane ordered. "But please breathe easier. Vampires are a woeful chore to kill. To say nothing of a half-demon vampire."

Giselle nodded—though her nod was just a reflex as fear carved at her heart.

"Let's get this show rolling," Princess Maggie happily ordered as she peered through the oak desk. Her curiosity did not pull up a lock of hair, but rather a gauntlet encased in grey scales.

"Wyvern leather," Prince Krisdane muttered, his hand clenching tighter to his sword. "There is no way Kabuso should own that. The export of fell beast items is punishable by death in Golden Land,"

"Hi there!" Princess Maggie whistled in front of a bookshelf that contained a box featuring intricate Japanese lettering. "I present to you…this thingie!"

Maggie pried open the box very carefully.

The bookshelf on the far office wall parted in half to give way to a secret passage.

"Oh poopie," Giselle groaned.

That was the only statement she could muster as she and the others watched a battalion of humans pour through the entryway.

Except they weren't human. Not exactly. Some were missing eyes, and others had skin stripped to the point you could see skeletons. Others had maggots crawling in and out of their bodies.

"Reanimated corpses," Prince Krisdane noted with a sneer.

"You mean zombies?" Giselle asked, knees trembling.

"Pretty much!" Princess Magalinda added.

Prince Krisdane brought the glowing blade of Phobeus in front of him to impale one zombie through the throat. The next one got its torso detached from its lower half thanks to a sweep of the mystic sword.

"The only way to really kill these things is to kill the necromancer animating them," Maggie offered. "I'll go find him!"

As Maggie sprinted through the office door, Giselle was amazed at how a so-called coward could summon such strength of will.

Krisdane gave Giselle a hard shove to protect her from a lunging zombie. Rather than catch Giselle, the zombie caught the pommel of Krisdane's sword. Quickly, Prince Krisdane cleaved the arm off another zombie then swung his blade around to scalp the zombie that had made a move for Giselle.

Krisdane flourished to his left, cleaving one zombie at the cheek and mouth. Another zombie ate a boot to the gut; this put enough distance between it and Krisdane for Prince Charming to swing about and behead one closest to Giselle.

This is the worst season of The Walking Dead ever!

The zombies groaned, roared, and moaned. Yet so little of it affected Prince Krisdane. He attacked and slashed with calm, relaxed precision.

He kills them like he's whacking weeds on a Sunday afternoon! I'm more intense pouring milk into my Lucky Charms.

In an instant, the calm swordsman disappeared, replaced by a man who howled so loudly Giselle covered her ears.

Then seeing the bite mark, she yelled, "You're bit!" There was blood on his arm as he flung off his toothsome attacker.

He was in no shape to fight at the moment. Worse yet, the zombie wanted an even larger taste of him.

Later Giselle wouldn't know what blocked her fear, but she bravely snatched Phoebus from an ailing Krisdane, and with speed she never knew she had, she implanted the blade through the biting zombie's brain.

"Giselle!" Prince Krisdane's voice was thick with panic.

Right as two zombies were about to converge on her, they all dropped dead. For good.

Princess Maggie must have killed the necromancer. An elf versus a necromancer is like the main event of Nerdmania.

"Uhhh, here's your sword back, Prince Charming," Giselle extended the glowing weapon to Krisdane, who stood with his eyes wide.

"Giselle, you saved me from that fell beast."

"And you saved me from all the other fell beasts, so I'm not even close to even. But, Prince Krisdane, in uh human lore, when someone gets bit by a zombie they turn into a zombie."

Prince Krisdane chuckled hard enough to make himself grimace. "I'm lucky it is human lore and not a universal fact. As we are taught in school, great tides are sweeping throughout the realms. Some men are smart enough or evil enough to master them. Necromancers sacrifice their soul in exchange for harnessing the cold black currents of the universe. They take the waste products of the realm, corpses, and fill them with that black sludge to control them."

"You know what I learned in school? That sniffing the scented markers can take you to places you really don't wanna go. Let's get you patched up, Prince Charming."

Giselle tore off a part of Prince Krisdane's already torn shirt. Thinking of herself as something of a medic from a fantasy novel, she began twirling the fabric about his wound.

"You should not have been able to hold Phoebus. It should have disappeared the moment it left my hand."

Giselle looked at him with sorrowful blue eyes, "Is something wrong with me?"

"You wield a holy weapon, and you think something is wrong with you?" he smiled, raising a hand to touch her cheek but then holding back.

"Are all elves good-looking?"

"If you're referring to Tristabelle then, excuse my bias, no supernatural creature is as beautiful as she."

The blue eyes were downcast, this time out of embarrassment as she whispered, "I wasn't talking about Princess Tristabelle."

Something was coming out of Krisdane's mouth. Something Giselle hoped was a profession of love. But it was cut short by a Fluffy Bunny bursting into the room.

"I saved the day, friends and friendettes! Just don't tell mom that big ol' sis put a sharp ol' knife in the bad ol' necromancer's black ol' eye."

"Maggie, Krisdane got bit."

Princess Maggie stated, "I have some Valhalla Bell at the condo. A sprinkle of that and you'll be a-okay."

"Giselle, be at ease. I have been bitten by far worse than what you call a zombie. These creatures were—what do you Americans say—child's play."

"And lookie here, this rabbit managed to wiggle out where Amaterasu's hair is from the necromancer. He says it's in the room down below us. And we'll need a human to get into the door. It's showtime, Giselle!"

"We should tell Fleur where to find us," Prince Krisdane noted.

Giselle responded, "I'll call her."

***

"Your phone is ringing," Lazarus told his only child.

"It can wait. How'd you find me?"

Lazarus fluffed his brown hair. Fleur adjusted her ribbon.

"A concerned party contacted me," he finally confessed.

Fleur looked around at the guards she had incapacitated in the weapons room. Certainly, she could have found creative uses for the crossbow, flail, war hammer, and the sai, but Giselle said no killing, and so after her eye-gouging fiasco, Fleur had snapped a few vampire necks, and put a few humans in comas.

"A concerned party?" she sneered.

"A concerned party. Bravo on besting my glamor without killing your friend's mother."

"You're pretty fucked up, dad. Dawn never did anything to you."

He fluffed his hair again then said, "Fleur, I have arrived at dinner with royalty wearing jeans, and a T-shirt. And they said to me, Saint Lazarus, come and sit down, take the head of the table. May you be served first. May you be served the most. May you be welcome. May we be honored. Politicians have rolled in the mud to get my favor. Human lives, interests, they mean nothing to me! And yet, they do to you. A demon and a vampire concerned about human lives! It's absurd to think about! You are such a disappointment as a daughter."

"You really know how to compliment your girl, dad."

"Now, Fleur, daughter of mine, I invite you, try hard and try long, try and try to avoid being sent back to hell."

"No problem, dad. I'm a high achiever."

Fleur threw a wild punch that connected with her dad square in the jaw. If it did any damage, Lazarus sure had a funny way of showing it. He smiled a fang rich smile, then wiped away a trickle of blood with his tongue.

He casually encircled his hand around Fleur's neck. Before she could think to struggle, she was being driven onto the ground with such an impact, it cracked the floor.

"Fleur, I am over two thousand years old! You are a hundred and ten! Yes, Fleur, try long, and try had to beat me!"

Fleur threw lefts and rights with wild abandon. All the punches Lazarus avoided with prizefighter like grace.

Growing frustrated, Fleur leapt into an MMA style superman punch that got her caught within her father's arms. Within moments she was thrown to the ground with such force it cracked the ground and spewed blood from her mouth.

"You are not only dealing with a legend, you are not only dealing with a saint, you are dealing with your maker! Your mother has poisoned the well! Turned you into a parasite that feeds off my resources! I had high hopes for you! A vampire who can walk the day! And you waste the gift I gave you by drinking, whoring yourself, gambling the money I give you. You are such a disappointment."

Desperate, Fleur scooped up a crossbow, which she had no experience in using. It took her moment to figure it out. In that moment Lazarus closed the gap between himself and her and hammered his daughter in her muscular stomach with a punch. It felt like shrapnel exploded through her intestines.

Still, Fleur recovered quickly and went across her father's face with the crossbow. She saw blood fly from his cheek. Yet, when he turned to her, his face had already healed.

Lazarus hit his daughter with enough force to cause her to drop the crossbow and send more blood seeping out of her mouth.

Fleur looked up at her father, the man prayed to by humans for centuries, the Biblical icon, the cultural legend, she looked up at that man and spat blood in his face.

He dug his hand through her chest.

Gripped her heart.

And yanked.

"Such a disappointment," he said.

***

"She's still not answering," Giselle complained.

Giselle's big blue eyes looked up from her phone that showed six call attempts to Fleur. She then gazed at the basement room with a rich cream-colored brick wall, scaffolding and hanging vines. It was worth remembering so she could draw later.

If she lived to draw later.

Directly in front of Krisdane, Maggie and Giselle was a vault. Its door was closed with its wheel-shaped knob encircled by a hazy green aura.

"Anyone know what type of magic this is?" Giselle wondered, staring with a hard gaze at the vault.

"No clue, boys and girls," Maggie chimed. "But I bet it's mega-magical illusion magic. The Necromancer said we'd need a human to dispel it. So batter up, Giselle. Heh baseball, Krissy. The great American sport where two teams equipped with wooden clubs and round projectiles fight to the death!"

That's not baseball at all! But it would probably be more exciting.

The knob beckoned with its foreboding haze. Giselle didn't want to touch it. She didn't want any part of illusion magic. But touch it she did, twisting the knob until—

Nothing happened.

"The Necromancer is a huge, awful liar of unbelievable evil!" Maggie wailed."Lies are called perjury in America, Krissy, and they're punishable by cutting your tongue off and getting your ears burned!"

"I don't understand," Giselle mumbled. "We're so close. My mom..."

She felt the anger Bruce Banner must have felt when he turned into The Hulk. If she could transform into a mighty monster, she'd rip the door off, get the lock of hair, and then take the door and use it to reduce Lazarus to a quivering mound of flesh and fangs.

A white figure appeared—a white figure that scooted with four legs across the beige floor.

"Tyr?" Giselle gasped, hands trembling.

Prince Krisdane shoved Giselle behind him. Roughly. Quickly. As if her very life was in peril.

Tyr stroked his body across Giselle's leg and went to kneel in front of the vault.

Giselle could only stare open-mouthed as the vault door faded away in a haze of green dust before Tyr.

"Come in, come in," the cat purred.

"Who are you?" Prince Krisdane demanded.

"I am your Tyr. Come in, come in."

"This is like a sweet treat!" Princess Maggie exclaimed. "Talking animals are always good. I should know. I've seen the Lion King. A great tale of a transgender kitten putting the PRIDE in the pride."

What the hell is she learning about America, and where is she learning it from?

Krisdane extended his sword forward which Giselle thought would be menacing if he weren't so beautiful. He led the other two in following Tyr into the vault, keeping Giselle behind him.

The vault was much different than the outside area full of plants and brick. This vault was a magical and technological marvel. A laptop floated in the rear of the room, flanked by two gargoyles with hideous snarling faces and sharp wings with blades protruding out of them. Inside a glass case stood things such as a piece of chest armor with two crossed swords embedded in the front.

"The armor of Achilles," Tyr said, puffing up proudly.

The cat turned to a case containing a laurel crown.

Tyr announced, "The crown of immortality."

"I repeat, cat," Prince Krisdane said sharply, "who are you?"

"Yes, yes, young ones, you want to know who I am. I was your Tyr. But always I am Kabuso. I am a master of illusion. Yes, yes, young ones. You are in my domain. Unwanted."

Giselle spoke slowly as she felt like her lips were made of lead. "Why?" was all she could say.

"Prince Trygyrr Elvrina paid me a good sum to get close to you, Giselle. Yes, yes, believe that, young ones. I know all things about you. Yes, yes. But you are common thieves. We can't have that."

"But you're a thief, too! Maggie declared, pointing a hard finger at Kabuso.

"Please! We need that lock of hair for my mom!" Giselle pleaded from behind Krisdane.

"Thievery is an awful thing, young ones," the cat purred. "If we allow thievery, we open the gates to rape, assault, homicide even genocide. We weaken the moral fabric of society. Oh yes. We make authority into an illusion. When I was born, a hand was severed from thieves. That will do for you, young ones."

"But you're a thief!" Princess Maggie noted. Again.

"I am also a hypocrite," Kabuso declared.

Kabuso's fur stood, making him look more hedgehog than cat.

There was a good reason for his alarm.

Prince Trygyrr Elvrina stepped into the vault, elf ears decorated with silver earrings, and gold rings on every long finger.

"Trygyrr, how did you…" Prince Krisdane questioned.

Krisdane's sword was pointed at his brother.

"I came through sacrifices best left known only to the lady of the icy depths of Hell. Kabuso, I am disappointed in you, trusted friend."

"They're stealing from me, yes."

"Father, King Fenrisson, says circumstances make the murderer. I wonder, Kabuso, will these current circumstances make me a murderer?"

Kabuso shrunk into a tight ball.

"But we are friends!" the cat whined.

"My hands are coated in the blood of friends. Circumstances."

Giselle felt a rush of cold across her body.

"Take the lock of hair. Just take it. Oh yes. Take it!" Kabuso wailed.

The glass case in the far right corner popped open to allow access to a single strand of gold hair. Princess Maggie swiped it in an instant and stashed it in her pocket.

Kabuso, now reduced to a meowing supplicant, trod off with head hung low.

"Prince Trygyrr..." Giselle started, lips still feeling like lead. "Thank you."

"Hold your gratitude, Giselle," Krisdane ordered, voice laden with ice. "Why did you have Giselle followed?"

"Giselle is under my protection," Prince Trygyrr replied rather plainly.

"She does not need anything from you, Stalker," Krisdane snapped in a voice Giselle never thought he could possess. She imagined it was what a tiger would sound like if it could talk.

"I am the chancellor of the most powerful nation in the earth realm." Again, his voice was plain. "Why would she not benefit from my protection?"

"Your hands may be stained with the blood of friends," Krisdane spat, his sword never moving, "but, your soul is stained with the blood of humanity."

Trygyrr reminded his brother, "What is it that Gorick used to tell us? 'Humans are worse than a blight upon the earth. They are a virus. If six billion humans must die so the rest of the species on earth may thrive, then six billion deaths there must be.' That is what Gorick would say to us."

"Now you would quote a traitor on humanity while offering to protect a human," Prince Krisdane snapped.

"Giselle is more than a mere human," Prince Trygrr stated.

Giselle couldn't handle much more of mandates, genocide, talking pets, and supernatural traps, so she just sat on the floor, sucking her knees very close to her chest.

"Oh fiddle on all that," Maggie said with a huff. "Trygyrr, you have to hear the latest word from the hood."

"The hood? You are not wearing a hood," Prince Trygyrr commented.

"Gorick is in this very state, and Tristabelle has gone to fight him!"

Krisdane scrutinized his brother's reaction. Or lack thereof. "But you knew that already," Prince Krisdane spat, stepping sword first towards his older brother.

"Soon," Trygyrr started with a giggle, "They will be but bones on the earth and spirits in Valhalla. I admire such a bold and brilliant move by Tristabelle! We can hope it does not lead to her death."

"What if it does?" Giselle questioned with her eyes held shut.

"Mother will grieve, the kingdom will grieve," Prince Tyrygrr held his eyes on an emerald embedded sword. "Tristabelle will be elevated in the eyes of all, having proved where her true loyalties lie. If Gorick should die, we cannot help but honor him for his many tremendous contributions to this earth realm while disdaining him as a usurper. And again, Tristabelle will have proven her loyalties. But should they nurse their mutually inflicted wounds, take each other in the other's arms..."

"Fleur!" Giselle hurriedly exclaimed. "We need to find Fleur."

Interlude

What can possibly be said about the noble Prince Gorick? He is called "The Golden." He wields the legendary weapon The Chosen Spear with both determination and menace towards the evil of the earth realm. One look at Prince Gorick, and one knows he is extraordinary. But even then, one underestimates "The Golden." One does not realize he is the best battle commander the earth realm has ever seen.

They do not realize his bravery in the face of impossible evil knows no end. They do not realize his extraordinary courage and unbreakable will has saved billions of lives across the earth realm, across every species of life. One can never truly comprehend how extraordinary Gorick "The Golden" Elvrina truly is.

Lord Hunfrid Andvari of Mount Nida, Golden Land

Chapter Twenty-One: The Golden

"Wake up! Wake up!"

Tristabelle tossed about in her sleeping bag. She had barely gotten to sleep, and now someone was bellowing beyond her tent.

"Wake up! Wake up!"

It was a panicked, voice-cracking Sofi.

Tristabelle sprung up at once. It wasn't the first time she had been dragged out of her sleep by a fearful voice in her life. Plenty of times she and her brother, Gorick, had been in pursuit of a monster or some fiend or scapegrace and an innocent victim had screamed in the night at the sight of the churl.

The youngest princess of Golden Land stepped out of her tent, curiously peering around and finally settling on Sofi.

"What's the big idea, Sofi?" Dusty barked from behind Sofi. "Don'tcha know my Queen needs beauty sleep?"

Dusty was clad in pink unicorn pajamas and an oversized "All American Prick" shirt from Fairy Revolution Wrestling. Still tired, she leaned against one of the many Norway spruce trees in the campground. The trees had flat splays of scale-like foilage the Hemera students had found IG worthy.

"They're gone!" Sofi shouted, sweeping her hand around the collection of tents, food coolers, benches, and an unlit campfire. "I've checked all the tents. No one is around. Not even crickets. I'm deadass serious."

Dusty started mumbling curses as her fist pounded into her palm. Yet she still leaned against the spruce tree.

"The condition of your rear-end matters not," Tristabelle decided, peering far into the woods.

"Do you think Prince Gorick did this?" Sofi pondered.

"Gorick has fallen into depths I could not have fathomed. But this...my goodness! I suspect foul magic. Perhaps blood magic. "

"Blood magic?" Sofi asked, voice small.

"Blood Magic's the worst kind of magic, Sofi," Dusty replied. "A witch can use human blood to do things they normally can't do. Like summon demons or create astral projections. Hell, Sofi, they use it for demonic possession too."

Sofi muttered a very Giselle like, "Eeep!"

"Ladies, nay, warriors," Tristabelle started, "I have the privilege of your assistance and bravery. It is time we paid Gorick 'The Golden' a visit."

The princess retreated into her tent to fetch the Dark Objects the girls had cobbled together across Manhattan. What she found in her suitcase were her clothes and nothing more. All their hard work had vanished into the night, stripped from them by mystery and woe.

"The Dark Objects are missing!" the princess exclaimed.

"Missing?!" Sofi and Dusty echoed, with Dusty punching the air.

"I simply cannot accept this," Princess Tristabelle whined. "We have...we have...no, I cannot accept this."

"My queen, yer gonna have to 'cause we got a busload full of freshmen to save.'"

"You are correct, of course," Princess Tristabelle stated. "But to defeat my brother? How shall we see it through?"

"We'll work that out on the way over," Dusty replied.

The situation was so grim that the three couldn't change out of their pajamas lest time was wasted. All they could do was throw on shoes to carry them into the woods where "The Golden" glittered in his hideout.

"Mistlewoe!" Tristabelle yelled towards the air, "Come to me!"

The sword was there in a sparkling flash—the hilt made of translucent ice, with veins of the same substance running through it. The pommel or end of the sword was a white ice magic crystal. A foolish human might mock the fluffy wings that served as the crossguard, until they saw those wings aid Tristabelle in floating. Finally, there was the blade of solid, horrible, gorgeous ice encased in mistletoe.

"This ice blade has served my brother for over two decades of human years. Now in a moment of human time it will serve him justice."

As the girls trod through the forest based on Maggie's map and spell, Sofi and Dusty used their phones for flashlights, whereas Tristabelle used a glowing orange stone known as an aura stone.

Tristabelle had explained that aura stones were magical stones which harnessed the power of a particular school of sorcery. To create, one needed a sorcerer and then a thaumaturgist to harness the magic through incantations, spell casting, and machinery. Everything must be precise, or as in the case of fire magic a severe accident could occur. Aura Stones powered most everything in Golden Land that electricity would power in the human world.

"So..." Sofi started, cringing at the crunch she made stepping on twigs. Far too noisy to sneak up on The Golden, "did Gorick return his special weapon to the front desk before checkout? Because I don't wanna go out extra sad."

Tristabelle paused and examined her aura stone. This one was made through fire magic. She'd had it since she was five elven years old. Gorick had given it to her when she complained of a troll hiding in the darkness of her room.

"I do not know what happened to the Chosen Spear granted to him by the Allfather. But Allfather granted that none of you may die and that I may not die until I have had my revenge upon him."

Princess Tristabelle "The Bright Eyed" knew what she asked of her comrades. Defeating Gorick once was hard enough, and that was with her sister Princess Astrid at her side. Now they had no Dark Objects, and their hope dimmed to darkness.

Dusty turned to Sofi and spoke, "That coward son of a bitch Gorick went and put himself in our state, took our Dark Objects, took people from our school, but as far as him killing us? Uh-uh! He can get on his dang knees, put his hands together, pray to the Allfather, pray to Allah, pray to Buddah, pray to Shiva, pray to any dang god he wants. It won't do him a lick of good, Sofi. 'Cause we're gonna go on and march to him, put fires of a fox on his face, the magic of a pixie through his punk mouth and a sword up his sorry ass!"

Sofi's freckled face brightened, her green eyes lit like an aura stone, "Yeah! Even us undergraduate bitches can serve that Ph.D. asshole!"

Dusty and Sofi exchanged a high-five. It made Tristabelle's cupid bow lips form a small smile.

"Indeed!" Tristabelle exclaimed. "Perhaps they shall sing of our bravery in EDM operas! Toast to our might in taverns! Perhaps the ladies in brothels will take our names! And not the ladies with unusual growths on their faces, but the pretty ladies. Our victory shall go down in supernatural legend."

The time for fighting came as the girls reached a luxury cabin, whose front was dotted by lit torches. What should have been a unique and romantic abode with its elevated balcony and wonderful views of a serene natural setting was now a formidable fortress overlooking an infernal battlefield.

Most chilling of all was the macabre sight of the Hemera freshman laid out, all faces up at the side of the cabin.

Princess Tristabelle first recognized Kimberly Kayley, one of her Belle Ringers. Her eyes were closed, her lips shut, and her body was rigid.

"Are they dead?" Sofi questioned, her voice shaky.

Darkness permeated almost all the home, but in short order, the front door slowly swung open. Now unleashed upon the party was the resplendent evil of the golden greatness that was Prince Gorick Elvrina.

"Dear, brother, I see you see still carry that scar I gave you as a parting gift. Come let your favorite sister welcome you with a little peck," Tristabelle invited through a distinct sneer.

Silence was golden.

If Giselle was present she'd make a quip about pressing L1 to analyze the final boss, so that's what Tristabelle did. He stood at six feet two inches, though he had the presence of a giant. His armor beamed more than gold. It beamed a legacy, it beamed supremacy over all living things. With his arms uncovered and his neck free, the typical supernatural arrogance of "hit me where you please" seemed to mean even more coming from him.

There was more to his armor. Through the left side ran the engraved image of a screaming woman named Kriemhild, whose Norse legends were varied tales of revenge.

Sofi felt the bite of familiarity in his appearance but was stymied in placing the recognition. Aside from the Mistlewoe-made scar on his neck, Gorick inhabited realms far beyond any normal man's beauty. He had a chiseled jaw encased in stubble infused with grey, prominent browbone, broad chin, a medium shag of blonde hair, and of course, those clear, bright purple eyes that resembled Tristabelle so perfectly.

Laughter. Prince Gorick laughed. Not from an amused place but from the dark recesses his soul resided in.

"Is this the way of it, Tristabelle?" he finally spoke. "You bring your latest conquest and your handmaidens to sneer at my exile, bully my gloom? Have you not taken enough from me already? To what ends of this earth will you not go to heap your scorn upon me? What more will you strip me of? Was my right to rule not enough? Were you not satisfied with the safety of my kingdom? Need you my dignity?! Will you not rest until I am left to crawl back home and beg for the headsman's axe?"

Princess Tristbaelle immediately replied, "You are lucky you are a prince, for if you were anyone else, you would have finished that monologue with a sword through the eye socket. You would dare claim to be a victim? After the horrors you inflicted? After what you have done to these innocent humans?"

"I am the victim!" Gorick yelled, tears nearly ripping out his purple eyes.

"Tell me, brother, after all the accolades you and I received together, all the battles we won together, the parades in our honor, how are you the victim of anything but your own delusions?"

"Was I meant to be a supplicating hound for a father who loves neither family nor kingdom, a brother who wound up refusing the throne, or a sister unfit to rule? Was that what it was all for?"

"We all must play our roles in life!"

"You were meant to be my queen! You were supposed to rule beside me!"

Reading the deathly scowl on his face, Dusty stepped forward for the fight but Tristabelle motioned her back.

"Pah! Tristabelle, you have always lived a life of charmed revelry," Prince Gorick noted. "You can figure-skate, you can twirl in your little ballets, fight your battles as you will. You will never know what it means to be the vanguard of the realm of men. Bernhard took the honor of the family and country and threw it in the mire! Astrid will do the same, yet you still stand by her side, hand-in-hand as the great ruin sweeps over the kingdom. Darkness! Darkness is in this realm already! Doom is upon us! Only I am fit to sit on the throne and save the realm from the lurking danger! And you were meant to sit beside me."

"You are the darkness!" Princess Tristabelle snapped. "You are the great evil sweeping across the earth realm, Gorick. You have kidnapped these humans, you have gathered the Dark Objects, you have cursed the men at my dwelling, and you...you...you killed Wulf, you killed our baby brother!"

"No! His death is not my fault. I was aiming for Astrid. You hit my hand, you caused the throw of my spear to be off! You killed him! You! It was all you! Would that I had any Dark Objects. Then I would truly make you suffer!"

"You don't have our Dark Objects?" Sofi questioned. She got no response.

Princess Tristabelle spat, "You killed our baby brother, Gorick. You are a kinslayer. You are the darkness."

"You...you...you...would dare lay his death at my feet!?! You have blackened my heart forever, traitor. It would have been far more sensible for you to spend your days twirling about in your dance studios! But now our father will receive his headless daughter draped in the banner of our country. You die tonight, Tristabelle, and may you never reach Valhalla."

The girls heard a series of clanks, troubling sounds that come from the smoke bombs that created a heavy veil of grey malice around the cabin. As it started to clear, the Hot Squad found themselves faced with a legion of katana boasting SKM ninjas.

"Now, I believe we are ready to fight!" Gorick declared.

The prince tossed his right arm into the air; hand spread open to receive a gift that would be anything but a present to his foes. Radiant splashes of golden light reached out, engulfing his hand. When they disappeared, there sat The Chosen Spear. The spear looked more like a ray of light than a weapon of war, minus its handle, which was engraved with a pair of wolves locked in eternal battle. Worse yet, it had a trident shape, allowing Gorick to add slashes to the stabs that dotted his deathly offense.

"You cost me a kingdom, Tristabelle, you cost me a brother. Thanks to you I will never love again. I will make you pay for these crimes."

Gorick aimed right for the heart. That was a tactic that Tristabelle knew he was going to do and so gracefully twirled aside. An SKM goon tried to hook her arm to make her an easier target for his boss. Such helpfulness cost him his life as Gorick shred his innards out with his spear.

"Gorick The Golden requires no help!" the disgraced prince hollered.

Too close to Gorick to properly cut him, Tristabelle punched him directly in the jaw. Big brother staggered against his cabin, jaw sore, pride wounded, and a mystical sword heading for his brain. He rolled out of the way, and The Bright Eyed sheered off quite a bit of his house siding.

The youngest Golden Land princess then had to make a quick recovery, forced to deflect his swipe at her sides.

"Your Highness?" Came the worried voice of Vaan Filma from the cabin.

"Ah, Sir Vaan, so nice to hear from you again!" Princess Tristabelle cheered. "Pay my brother no mind, Sir Vaan. I think his youngest sister proves too grand a challenge."

Tristabelle pushed on her back foot and sprung into the air, making a full revolution before slashing her sword towards her brother's face. Yet, Gorick The Golden was chosen by the Allfather and got his spear up at the last minute to block certain death.

"Damn you, Tristabelle," he snorted.

Gorick took a swipe at Tristabelle's legs, getting nothing but air thanks to her elegant side-step. Anger mounting, big brother slammed an armored shoulder into baby sister to stumble her backward and leave her on her knee.

"You fall so easily! If you cannot hold your footing, then pick up the bow like your precious Astrid."

Gorick's words goaded Tristabelle into lunging for his stomach. It was a blow he checked with the handle of The Chosen

Spear. White sparks of light spun through the air as their weapons were locked and their frigid purple eyes glared into one another.

The earth realm could bear no more grinding of their weapons, and the siblings were pushed apart, seething stares still connecting them. A roar escaped Prince Gorick's lips as he slashed at Tristabelle; but she checked his blow and spun around him only to get her arm caught with his. The pure elf warriors hissed like tangled serpents and twirled with each other as if they were in one of Tristabelle's court dances. They did this until they pulled apart, eyes shooting murderous hatred at each other.

"You look so youthful and refreshed. I see killing our brother causes you to lose no sleep," Princess Tristabelle taunted.

"Arrrgh!"

Elsewhere, Dusty was more concerned with her (hopefully) bride-to-be than the battle that consumed her, "We gotta help the queen!"

The silver werewolf who had been lurking on the outside rushed to tackle Dusty. The two gathered up grime and dirt in a furious snapping of fangs and teeth as fae and werewolf collided.

Dusty ended up on top, but that was a momentary advantage as the werewolf shook her off and caused her to go rolling into a tree.

Rolling into the tree the way an SUV might plow into a tree. The blonde beauty looked anything but beautiful as she groaned in pain.

An actual smile slid onto the werewolf's face, for mealtime had arrived.

His path to his dinner bowl was halted by Dusty hovering off the ground with the aid of neon pink butterfly-like wings. They were made entirely out of pixie dust floating just an inch off her back.

A primal roar escaped the werewolf's mouth, and he leapt at Dusty. That's when a branch of the tree reached down to snare his hind leg. Frightened and off-balance, the silver werewolf crashed to the ground. His struggles were made all the more monumental when the roots reached up at what he now realized was Dusty's command and circled his neck. That's all little Dusty needed to snap his neck.

Sofi was in kitsune form and scrambling away from the would-be killers, who unleashed a bevy of shurikens at her evasive figure. A hop, a skip, and a jump led her to the top of one of the Humvees. Yet, two katana-wielding ninjas joined her.

Needing to be at full size to handle this, she transformed human form, bringing shards of golden light with her.

The ninjas, who had been going for a fox, wound up banging their faces as Sofi jumped over their lunge.

"I'm not like Fleur, I like it when straight guys almost kiss."

Outnumbered and unequipped, Sofi tried to keep the ninjas at bay. One grew impatient and lunged at her, forcing Sofi to spring up and hit him with a pair of boots to the face. The ninja careened into his partner as Sofi landed on the hood of the car. That was when a brand new opponent—an SKM ninja who also happened to be a vampire—dragged her off by her red hair.

"Ohhhh.....THAT IS IT, BUDDY! YOU TOUCH THE HAIR, YOU DIE!"

A hurried transformation into a fox freed herself, and then the return to human form allowed her to uppercut the vampire. A second go-round of that trick, and she landed a right hook. A third go-round and left-cross bombed across his face. The battered vampire hadn't a clue as to how to grab hold of Sofi as he was put on a painful backfoot.

He'd have been best aided running away, as the irate redhead shrunk into kitsune form, her tail emitting an increasing heat. The tail became engulfed in flames which soon formed a fireball that screamed toward the vampire. Unable to move, the vampire was consumed in death's pyre.

A fearful young goon punted Sofi forward, tears in his eyes, breath heavy. He never thought he'd meet with flame-throwing forest creatures.

He'd also never think again as Sofi lit his head on fire.

Four goons and three ninjas, including the two who survived the tussle with Sofi, gathered in front of Sofi, katanas ready for the kill.

The goons stepped forward in a locked unison, landing their boots into a full puddle of splashing water that no one noticed crystallized into ice chips. No one noticed but Dusty, who suddenly fluttered in front of Sofi, one hand on hip, other hand cooling the water to the freezing point. The goons desperately wished they could escape. Yet, freshly made ice snared them in place then encased them in its frigid death trap.

The goons were now prey for Sofi, who descended on them in half-fox half-human form, tail alight, and fangs bared. The screams were ghastly, the dismemberment total.

The legendary courage of SKM ninjas broke with two of the men running for the safety of a Humvee, as an incomprehensibly fast punch of Dusty shattered a leftover's jaw.

Meanwhile, Prince Gorick was sending repeated stabs Tristen's way, with each one avoided with a spin or a twirl.

"All these twirls, all these spins, hold still and fight!"

Gorick repositioned himself while his mind begged The Allfather for a clear, easy shot at his baby sister's heart. All that came was a panicked Vaan, yanking him back from an overhand cut from Tristabelle.

"Call Ose. The witch has summoned him. The life of these students has been almost drained. We retreat," Vaan urged Gorick.

Gorick turned a scowl upon his loyal knight. It was happening all over again. Defeat. Embarrassment. Retreat. Twice at the sword tip of the same damn sister.

"Ose!" Gorick hollered, scathing purple eyes locked on Tristen, "Great President of Hell, in accordance with the contract...kill my sister!"

The large living room window broke into thousands of pieces as a roar worthy of a sonic boom ripped across the night sky. All of this was brought by the seven-foot-tall, muscled beyond all belief, two legged, ax-toting leopard twisting out of the cabin to land in front of Tristabelle.

What a sight he made, Tristabelle thought on her first encounter with a higher Christian demon. His eyes blazed with fire, a nose ring pierced his face, his ax decorated by glowing words written in Latin that Tristabelle couldn't understand.

"Tristabelle," Gorick called, hurrying back to his humvees with his surviving crew. "I will come back for your body. You are a princess, and you deserve a proper burial."

Vehicles darted off as fast as the drivers could move them.

Princess Tristabelle circled back to her partners. They might have once formed a formidable wall of supernatural might and aristocracy. Now they were dinner.

Dusty snapped, "Yer the same rodent that's responsible for the Ice Rider!"

"The biker who attacked us?" Sofi asked.

"Yeah! You get a problem with us, rodent?" Dusty barked.

"I'm glad you questioned me. Now you can die first," Ose stated.

Ose launched his ax at Dusty's head at alarming speeds—but not speedy enough as the little pixie dove below it to lose only a few strands of hair.

Seeing her foe unarmed, Tristabelle dashed forward, sword lowered, with Sofi behind her. Ose dodged the charge of Tristabelle, and for once she didn't have the grace to deal with avoidance and stumbled to her knees.

Ose hollered, "Where is the one who banished Belphegor? I will AAAAAHHHHH!"

A cluster of green pixie dust hit Ose's fiery eyes, blinding him and causing him enough searing pain.

"Die!" Ose bellowed, his eyes leveled on Dusty who was ill-equipped to protect herself from the surging demon.

That was why Princess Tristabelle sprung in front of her at the last possible second; Mistlewoe severing his arm from elbow to hand with a beautiful yet savage overhand slash. A liquidized form of black magic, like toxic sludge, gushed from Ose's wound. Yet, he remained unaffected except for mounting fury.

Ose's free hand grabbed the Princess by the throat. Tristabelle let out a pained croak before Ose proceeded to slam her into the ground. Filled with so much hatred, Ose picked Tristabelle up and tried to perform that attack again. Yet he was confronted by half-fox, half-human Sofi on his back.

"You die!" Ose shouted

Princess Tristabelle was released so that Ose could hurl Sofi off his back. Yet now Sofi was the target of his murderous intentions. Dusty refused to let Sofi feel the crunch of his jaws and called on the limits of her plant control. Branches formed tentacles on her behalf, skulking downward, her commands angling them to wrap around Ose's waist. Only for the moment though—Ose needed just a hand and a snap to break apart Dusty's prison.

Ready to resume his rampage, Ose gathered his ax, fully capable of swinging it with one hand. Sofi appeared the most vulnerable of the group. His ax was at the ready, seconds from slicing through her neck. But she wasn't the broken fox he thought she was—she launched a fireball into his testicles!

"Death to the patriarchy!" Sofi yelled, as Ose sunk to the ground.

He looked on in confusion, bewilderment, and most of all horror at Princess Tristabelle rounding on him, serving as his eternal judgment.

"I hope my brother comes back for your body. You are the great president of hell, and you deserve a proper burial."

Princess Tristabelle "The Bright Eyed" of Clan Elvrina removed the head of Ose the Demon with her sword. Body and head toppled to the ground before it all disgustingly crumpled into a rancid melting of liquid black magic. After minutes passed, it left behind an Ose-sized patch of dead land in its wake.

Dusty got to her feet with a heavy sigh. Sofi merely wagged her tail and wrinkled her fox nose over a job well done.

"Now, ladies," Tristabelle began, twirling her sword, "We heal our classmates and then…then…then…we prepare for war."

Epilogue

Fleur had a viewing fit for the supernatural aristocracy she was.

In the great room of the Golden Land consulate, her body lay in a 14 karat gold coffin, the sunset-lit sky of New York City hovering over her through a glass ceiling. There was a rich and lively garden of flowers that spread below and around the casket. There were blooms of pink and red with kisses of white and green. There was even a throne behind Fleur, which was constructed out of a base of twisting roots, carved into a wooden seat, then expanding into a golden-leaved tree that reached to the ceiling.

"My mom got healed," Giselle said, standing over Fleur. She was the only one there. "She doesn't remember being glamoured at all or wanting to kill you. I tried to send her back to California but she won't go. Not when she knows why I'm crying," Giselle held herself so tightly it was like she could crush her bones. "I'm crying because she can't tell you she's so sorry."

The emotions became too much for Giselle. They rolled through her forehead, down to her aching stomach, to her legs and manifested at a kick of Fleur's casket.

"Giselle," came Anika Lindgren's familiar voice.

No reply came from Giselle. She hadn't spoken much since her mother had been healed. The brave act she thought she had to put on wore her down, took her heart, and shattered it into pieces.

Giselle didn't even acknowledge her mom running her fingers through her daughter's white-gold hair.

"Mom, go home."

Anika spoke, "Giselle, we need to talk. The situation has become rather distressing. Dawn says you simply refuse to eat."

Giselle still said nothing. This was just someone talking to the husk that was Giselle Nyfall.

"Giselle?"

"Did you know this would happen?" Giselle said, her voice, her entire presence, coming out like they were in some far-off hell.

A golden leaf fell from the tree and landed on Fleur's chest.

"In the supernatural community few of us ever die peacefully surrounded by loved ones. I did not see this coming though. I was sure when you went on your mission that some pitiful soul would be grasping to the life Fleur would be about to take. That is why we need to talk. There may one day be someone pitifully begging you to spare their life."

"What do you mean by that?" Giselle asked.

Anika put her hands on Giselle's shoulders. Giselle noticed she smelled like warm vanilla.

Prince Trygyrr entered the room, elf ears unglamored, and body encased in black pants and black shirt that had a purple floral embroidery.

"Be at ease, Giselle," Prince Trygyrr said with a smooth smile, "for there is only good news for you on this day."

"They don't think you're human, sweetie," Dawn stated in the softest of tones—so soft she had to repeat herself.

"Giselle," Anika started, "you are not human. I always knew that. Do you remember that glowing device on my desk when we first met? It is a magical object that glows when it detects supernatural beings."

Giselle spun around and glared malevolently at Anika, her blue eyes sparking, "I am not supernatural. I'm helpless, I'm useless, I'm worthless."

"Don't you ever say something like that," Dawn said more sharply than she intended. "You are extraordinary."

"You used Phobeus," Anika rubbed Giselle's shoulders in the most tender manner she could. "We had to tell the king."

Giselle felt her mouth dry.

***

Hell.

Hell was different things to different people. Hell could be a cold night in Syracuse, New York, sleeping on the steps of a church. Hell could be the hungry belly of an orphaned child. Hell could be the withdrawal from a powerful drug.

For Fleur Flannagan Hell was home.

"Ah," Fleur sniffed the air around her. The distinct smell came from the garden of dead flowers, each "rotten egg" plant cursing the human slaves with a sulfur-like stench. These poor damned souls would be in this exact spot for eternity. They were working over crops and plants that would never grow. Beaten, burned, and tortured by low-level demons who were themselves beaten, burned, and tortured by higher-level demons. So went home.

Fleur had never been able to get used to getting people to do things without violence or the threat thereof. Yes, a human could be glamoured, but no supernatural could be. Thus Fleur had taken her Hell earned lessons with her to Earth and spent her early years killing, assaulting and pillaging in exchange for help. But the longer she spent away from Hell the further the lessons of mayhem and misery held on her. She fought more than your average supernatural, but she killed less than most vampires not to mention demons, and due to her ability to walk the day, she blended in with humanity.

Now she was back in Hell where no one liked her because to them, she was the demonic equivalent of a sell-out.

The royal castle was a testament to impregnable masonry, constructed by human slaves who were lorded over by demonic masters. Iron spikes exploded from the towers of the castle with numerous people impaled upon them to suffer for eternity. Soaring windows that were protected by bars of fire lined the walls. There were seven gates for entry, each protected by iron spikes, and fire.

The main entrance, which Fleur needed to pass through, was guarded by Lix Tetrax. He was a true abomination with the body of a snail that continually oozed pus and claws sharpened to a fine point.

His claws were toying with a forty-year-old human female.

"Lemme through," Fleur mumbled.

Lix cast his eyes downwards. His pupils were moons.

"The Princess Fleur. Surprising."

"What?"

"That you remember where you came from."

Fleur scowled and folded her arms.

"Hell isn't for human lovers," Lix noted, piercing the human woman's eye and eliciting a scream.

"I don't love humans. I don't give a damn about humans."

"Are you here to liberate them? Take them to Heaven?"

Lix laughed. Laughed and expelled more pus.

"Lemme through, I wanna see my granddad."

A group of crows took flight from the nearest tower.

"No."

"If you keep putting me through shit, I'll see my grandpa one way or the other, and I'll tell him you were mean to me."

Snitching on Earth meant one thing to the told-on criminal. Snitching in Hell to Satan meant a whole different, a whole lot more painful thing to the criminal.

"Enter, Princess Fleur," Lix said, keeping his face held high.

With a heavy creak, the main gate opened, allowing Fleur to pass into the courtyard. The usual sights were on offer. Ted Bundy was being flayed. Vladimir Lenin was having his eyeballs pecked out by crows. Stalin was being crushed by an elephant. All the good tormenting stuff was going on.

Fleur strode forward and made her way into the hallway across the carpet of fire. She noticed a few new demonic faces barking at the human slaves who were washing the tile floor with toothbrushes. A whip lashed across the face of a slacking Spanish man who Fleur swore she killed in 1993.

Ignoring all the familiar torture and misery, Fleur finally entered the throne room. The throne room was about the only "seminormal" looking thing in hell, resembling an earthen throne room in some respects. Portraits of the kings, great presidents, and dukes of hell lined the wall with their eyes moving to watch visitors. A staircase lined with red carpet led up to a marble throne.

On that throne sat a baby-faced young man with dazzling green eyes, a shag of unkempt black hair, and a bright smile. The only thing that differentiated him from a highschooler in suburban USA was his red horns and orange cape.

"Hey, grandpa," Fleur greeted.

"Fleur! What were you thinking?" Satan greeted his granddaughter. "On Earth they tell you that you can do anything you want. But the truth is that you can only do anything that you're good at it. And you're the worst at killing 2,000 year old vampires! What were you thinking?"

"Getting your ass kicked is a lot like pregnancy. You don't try but you get fucked up anyway."

"Heheheh, I'm glad to have to have you home. I've been pretty assholish since my favorite granddaughter's been gone."

Fleur sighed a heavy sort of sigh as she climbed the carpeted red steps. As always Satan's lap was inviting so Fleur took a seat on it. Her pale blue eyes caught the flaming eyes of Ose's picture staring at her.

"I've gone through a lot without you, Fleur! Hades lost control again and I had to deal with a whole mess coming from the Greek underworld. What a pain! I tore off Ivan the Terrible's nipples again, but even that didn't make me feel better.

Fleur turned her head away from her grandfather and spoke very slowly, "I need you to send me back."

"Send you back?"

Even the devil got surprised once in a while.

"I've got a daughter, grandpa. Your great-grandaughter."

"Poppy?"

Fleur was up off her grandfather's lap and on her knees, "She needs me."

"But, I need you too."

Their hands met. His were warm, furnace-level warm, while hers were the chilled state of a vampire.

"I don't want you on your knees begging," Satana commented. "Buuuuuut I'm a sucker for a good sob story. Buuuuuut, I need my favorite granddaughter around."

"She's only eighteen," Fleur whined.

"You're only eighteen!"

"Please! I'm begging you, grandpa."

"Huuuh, I suppose I can help my favorite granddaughter out. But I need you to bring me back a souvenir."

Fleur's baby fat-filled cheeks expanded with her smile as she nodded.

"I need the blonde girl you're rooming with. The one who banished Belephegor."

Fleur's happy grin immediately sagged as if it had never been there in the first place.

"Giselle? Why Giselle?" Fleur started speaking much faster than she's ever spoken before, "She's...she's just a nerd. She bit her tongue saying her name when I first met her. And she's clumsy. And she breaks shit. And starts fires. And accidentally eats moldy bread because she's not paying attention and doesn't see the mold. You could get a Giselle anywhere."

"I could?"

"She's just a human."

"For realsies? Why could she banish Belephegor then? I don't think she's human, Fleur. I think she can command my army of darkness. I think we can layer the Earth in nothing but darkness. Think about it, Fleur! No sun, no happiness, no joy, no growth! Desolate. Barren! Just darkness! That is nice! I neeeeeeed this, Fleur! I've been waiting for this!"

Fleur turned away from her grandfather and gazed at the surroundings. The portraits loomed larger than ever before.

"Why her?" Fleur snapped. "The only army Giselle has led is in Call of Duty. You have literal war criminals down here and you want some eighteen-year-old dork. Why?"

Satan merrily bounced up and down on his seat.

"Just a feeling I have. Will you bring her to me? I'll send yoooouuu baaaacccck to your Poppy."

It was a good thing Fleur was facing away from Satan. For if he saw her frown, the frown that made her feel like she would never smile again, he would be wroth.

"I'll get her for you, grandpa. No problem."

***

"The King?" Giselle asked, sagging her head. "Thee King?"

"King Fenrisson Elvrina. Darling, we simply had to tell him," Anika replied.

"What did he say?"

"Well, the king is a man of few words and these words might be fewer than usual. He simply said you'll be useful in a fight. Then he left. Princess Constantina tried to speculate on what type of supernatural you were. But you being able to hold Phoebus confuses matters. She pondered you being a half-elf for quite some time, and yikes that can girl can ponder. But the problem with you being a half-elf is that there is simply no such thing as a half-elf. An elf, pure or corrupt, that mates with any other being will produce an elf."

Giselle had to feel her ears. Just in case.

"Prince Trygyrr, as chancellor, announced he will watch over you," Anika stated, nodding to Trygyrr who was having a conversation with Dawn.

"I will not go home when my daughter is in this state," Dawn barked at the prince.

"You will return to California by royal command," Prince Trygyrr replied calmly. "My duties as Giselle's protector cannot shield her heart from breaking when your stubbornness inevitably leads to your death."

"Moms are tough," Dawn snapped, puffing herself up.

"Though far from tough enough," Prince Trygyrr retorted.

Anika went on, "Prince Krisdane wasn't happy, but the poor thing is stuck in Golden Land now with Princess Maggie, who I believe is on house arrest at Lady Chevalthorn University now. No one was happy that Princess Tristabelle chased down Gorick either. But she did save the students. Back to you, however, my supernatural darling."

"What does it matter? If I was supernatural I could have saved Fleur! She wouldn't have had her heart ripped out! She'd be in the kitchen eating pizza and saying something like 'Giselle, supernatural? That dork? You losers are out of your fucking mind.' That's what she would say and she can't!"

Giselle felt a gold leaf brush across the back of her neck. It was just a leaf, but there was a heavy coldness behind it. Yet it was a comforting coldness. Like a layer of ice that was somehow laid upon her with love.

"Giselle, turn around," Anika muttered, her grey eyes wider than they had ever been.

Giselle did as she was told. She nearly fell into the arms of the woman who spoke these words:

"This dork ain't supernatural. You guys have to be morons. All you elf and witch losers are out of your fucking mind. She eats moldy bread on accident!"

"Fleur, how?" Giselle asked through tears.

"How? Because I'm the baddest bitch you've ever met, that's how."

Giselle fell into Fleur for the tightest hug she'd ever given anyone. She guessed Fleur would be showing off her big happy smile.

But Fleur was out of smiles.

About The Author

Dacy Alex is an author that has also taken home several screenwriting awards under a different name. Dacy loves the possibilities of the supernatural but also the inherent weirdness of the everyday world and likes to combine the two whenever possible. Dacy likes to focus his stories on new adults, which might explain why he can subsist on a steady diet of CW shows. The 100 and The Originals are the best ones don't @ me, bro. Dacy's an avid video gamer; Dacy's favorite games are Final Fantasy X-2 and Persona 4: Golden. You can contact Dacy at dacyalexandria@gmail.com or at dacyalex.com or at roxy_kitten on IG

Stay tuned for Splendificent 3! If you liked Splendficent 2 please leave a review. I'll give you my firstborn if you do. Seriously.